Blue Wolf

Carlos Durm

Contents

One • Reckless is My Middle Name

Chapter One———

Ylva

"Blue?" Nathaniel gasped, staring at my wolf in awe.

I glanced down at myself, admiring the fluffy blue fur that has recently sprouted. I was dark blue with streaks of purple and white in my fur. My black claws dug into the ground as I stared at my uncle through my violent orbs. I nodded, my tongue hanging out my mouth in excitement.

"H-How? Its the most rarest kind of wolf..." My uncle touched gently my fur. I sat beside him, enjoying his touch, it reminded me so much of my Dad. Nathaniel was Dad's brother. Both as daft as each other, but when it came down to family, nothing would stand in their way of protecting us. I missed his strong hugs, the way he would train me. He made sure that I was the best I could be.

Today is around two months until my birthday. People call us werewolves, though I prefer the term shifter. And I finally got my wolf. Misty. She has always been with me, but this is the first time she's been in wolf form. I learnt to shift when I was five but a lot of the time it was too painful and took up a lot of energy - most of the time I ended up passing out. It is unusual for pups to shift and my parents warned me if I did it too often, it could've called for unwanted attention.

When your born with two parents as wolves, you grow up with your wolf. They are always there with you, they can speak to you, make you feel different things, help you smell and see better in the dark. But you would only find your mate when you turned near enough seventeen - even then, there's not really a certain time when you find them.

"You must be very careful, Ylva" my aunt, Sunbrooke, said, walking out the house. "Hybrids have powers that other rouges and bad wolves would want." She laid against my uncle who wrapped his arms around her. Mates, I scoffed.

I looked out onto the lake that surrounded the house. It was always silent and beautiful at night. The full moon shone out over the lake, making it look like mini crystals and the sky would almost always be clear so you could look up and see every star in the sky. It was always a good place to come and think.

I lived with my uncle and aunt after my parents died. I remember my mum hugging me, securely, tightly and crying. She left. Only a few hours later, she returned. She was screaming at me, telling me to run, hide, leave. I didn't understand what she meant, until four other people came in a grabbed me. Their faces were pure evil, filled with so much hate and envy when they glanced towards me. My Mom was thrown away from me and a heavy object came crashing down on my head.

All I remember was pain. I remember my Dad coming, both my parents trying to force the rouge and his 'pack' back to prevent harm from coming to me. But it only resulted them in... death. Their blood was covering the floor in seconds. Their eyes so lifeless, so blank, so scared.

I was only eight at this time. The men left and I stayed with my parents, curled up against their lifeless forms. We lived in the forest, so no one was nearby. All I remember was laying with my mother's arms wrapped around me and my Dad's arm around her. I think, if Nathaniel didn't come over a week after, I would have died.

He found me wrapped up, no longer crying because my eyes were dried out from doing that for so long. He took me from my home and took me to his. Nathaniel stayed in my room for five days, trying to calm my nerves, my wolf and my nightmares. Yes, I did have nightmares. They were horrible. Every night, these men would come and kill my parents again. Then Nathaniel would take me with him, and the men would find out and kill my aunt, uncle and cousins, just to leave me crying. It's like they wanted me to feel pain and sadness- break me down and make me an easy target.

I would wake screaming, crying. Sometimes, I would even find blood and cuts on myself. I had obviously been fighting myself during the nightmare. Sometimes, my older cousin, Faith, would come and lay with me. I guess she wasn't my proper cousin though, she was adopted. Sunbrooke found her alone in the woods, bleeding and crying. She invited her to stay, and she stayed. Now she's twenty.

I sometimes still have nightmares. But Faith comes in a talks to me, because she knows how it feels. Something similar happened to her. It horrible thinking about it, shivers always crawling up my body.

I thought life would maybe be better after that, but... I stopped believing in that once my childhood memories were chased away. The only thing I can remember before the age of eight are my parents and ability to shift early.

If I wasn't a shifter at the time, I would have died or had been critically injured by that beast.

I didn't realise I was whining until Faith's ginger wolf came up and laid down beside me. I snuffled into her fur and sighed heavily. All memories that were once hidden floated through my mind.

'It will be okay' she whispered though my mind. Oh, I forgot about the mind-link!

'Thank you for being with me through all these years. I couldn't have done it without you' I whispered, resting my head on my paws.

'Its fine, you went through something similar to me, I know how it feels' I could feel her shiver.

'What happens now? I mean, I've shifted for the first time...Now what?' I asked.

Faith would be the first person I go to if I had a problem. If it was my wolf, my mate, anything, I know that she would always be there for me. Only her and Nathaniel really knew about my true form; Nathaniel more than ever. Even I hardly knew about it and it was inside me.

'Well, now you should sometime, find your mate..then you would normal go live with him' I could see Faith smirk. She made Elliot, her mate, come and live here with the rest. He didn't like it much, but he would do anything for her. Any male would jump off a bridge for their mate, even if they rejected them, the bond would always be there.

'What about, running and stuff?' I asked.

'You can go for a run anytime, but be aware all the time, your father and uncle have trained you well in case of an attack.' she looked at me, giving me a knowing look.

'Yeah...any places I should avoid?' I scratched my ear and shook my fur, before laying down again, on my side. My wolf was purring softly, enjoying the feeling of being free.

'Yes, there are two main ones. Don't go anywhere near the Blood Thirst pack, they are rouges. And dont get too close to Golden Raven pack. Their Alpha will kill any outsiders, rouge or not' Faith shivered again.

'Anyone?' I echoed.

'Well, he does it within reason. If your considered a threat, probably, but if not, he'll either keep you and not let you leave or let you be on your way. ' she told me, 'Once you get used to running, all the places will be mapped in your head and you'll know where to avoid.'

'Who are the Alpha's of those packs?'

'Alpha Soar is the Blood Thirst's Alpha, I think. But I am not sure what the Golden Raven's Alpha is called, I think its something along the lines of Raiden or Rage. I have no idea!' She laughed slightly, 'They like to keep to themselves.'

We watched the moon rise in the sky. I mentally thanked the Moon Goddess for giving me such a beautiful wolf and an amazing family.

'The Golden Raven pack is strong. Its the biggest pack in the country. The Alpha, Beta and third in command are the strongest out of all the packs higher ranking people.' Faith continued.

Higher. Ranking.

I was only an Omega. I was technically a slave or maid or whatever to an Alpha, or a Beta. Even though I felt weak thinking of them like that, like anyone under them would, I frowned. What's the difference between them and us? All they have is a title thrown in front of their name. I knew I was a tall wolf and faster because of my hybrid stamina, but that doesn't change the fact of an Alpha is much bigger and stronger - possibly faster.

'Faith, are Alpha's faster than hybrids?' I asked, turning to face her. Faith's body tensed and she looked at me.

'Not normally. If you push yourself, you could probably get away from them. But dont go doing anything reckless!' She warned.

I laughed at her. I usually picked fights with my eighteen year old cousin, Aden. He used to complain I was cheating, because of my hybrid strengths, even though he was older. But whenever we did have an actual argument, it turned in World War III! There would be hits, punches, kicks. It was basically wrestling, sometimes even Nathaniel or Sunbrooke couldn't break us up and needed to call in some pack warriors. The amount of times I've been on the first floor of the pack prison, a place for troublemakers like me, is unaccounted for. We weren't punished, only in the cell for a week or so, though it was easy to escape.

I remember one time I got so angry at him, I smashed his head into a wall and knocked him out. I made a hole in the wall and, if it weren't for our ability to heal quicker, Aden would've been in hospital for a while. I thought he would hate me, but Aden said he deserved it. I guess, but I still felt bad.

When I was in school, I was always in fights. It's not my fault. Most of the time it would be with boys because I could usually knock out the girls with a few punches, but some of the guys hated the fact I was faster and stronger than most of them! They'd like to try and test their luck but they all failed miserably, a few broken bones, lots of bloody wounds- you get the picture.

'Don't worry, I won't' I shook my head at her but secretly crossing my paws behind me- reckless is my middle name!

My wolf was howling loudly. She was so happy to be herself now. I shared in her excitement, by jumping into the lake. The water was cool and refreshing in wolf form. I drenched my fur, relaxing under the setting sun before getting out and shaking off.

'I love this!' My wolf howled, delightedly.

'I know, so do I Misty. Thank you for being so patient.' I smiled. She had been waiting a long time for this moment. And now that is as finally here, she wasn't going to let it go for a while.

'Thats only task one!' She frowned.

'What do you mean?' I asked, turning me head to the side.

'Well, now that we've shifted for the first time, we are almost complete!' She howled, slightly painfully.

'You aren't making much sense,' I said, 'What does almost complete mean?'

Misty sighed at me, 'For a werewolf, being a human, 25%, being able to talk to each other, 50%, now that we've shifted, 75%, there's one missing...'

Misty gasped while I groaned slightly. We knew the answer for it, but were we ready? Hell, was I ready for it , was more the question.

'Mate' Misty mumbled.

I rolled my eyes, 'Who knew you were so mathematic.'

Two • David Guetta is My God

C hapter Two------

Ylva

I woke up from and amazing sleep. After yesterday, I am really happy. It felt like everything that had once been bolted up had suddenly sprung free from my wolf finally making her official appearance. I stretched before rolling out my warm bed. Rushing into the bathroom, I undressed, turned the shower on and stepped in allowing the cool water to relax my muscles. The water trickled down on me like raindrops.

That was a good thing about this house, it was big enough for every room to have an ensuite. My shower was perfect for me because I loved being outside in the rain. Aden and I had a bet going that if he ate a whole double chocolate sponge cake, without throwing up, he'd get the shower. But he failed and I got the cool shower! The whole top of the shower area ran like rain would.

I washed the shampoo into my hair, massaging my head in the process.

'So, this mate thing...what actually happens?' I ask my wolf, closing my eyes. I still didn't feel any different about this. Even though werewolves are brought up learning about your pack position and the mating process, no one knew better than your own wolf. Sometimes it can be different for everyone.

'Well, usually, we have to look into their eyes. The world seems to stop. You suddenly feel attracted to them, you can't live without them. You don't feel empty anymore.' Misty sighed. I knew that her being a werewolf, without your mate, there was no point in life. You were nothing without the one the Moon Goddess chose you to be with.

I quickly scrubbed off and got out, wrapping a towel around me. I hate it when it gets too hot and you can hardly breathe. I stumble in my room, the heat immediately leaving. Shivering slightly at the cool air, I went to my drawers to fetch some clothes.

I got dressed into some sports leggings and vest top before running down-stairs. I'm not a girly girl. Dresses and skirts are a no-go, but scorts are okay, I guess. I slipped on some Nike's before moving to the kitchen.

Everyone was still in bed, I decided to make them breakfast. They've always been there for me, it's the least I can do! I plugged in my iPod and switched on the music before starting to cook. Let's see, Faith likes pancakes. Nathaniel likes French toast. Sunbrooke likes a healthy breakfast so fruit and yogurt. Aden likes chocolate chip pancakes with whipped cream, Toast Me's and a bowl of Sunbrooke's infamous homemade yogurt! I laughed and shook my head. Aden's a fat pig and he knows it!

I pour the pancake mixes into a sauce pan and leave it on low heat, adding chocolate chips to one. I cut up some apples, pears and put them in a bowl with grapes and strawberries. I scrunch up my nose at the pear before chucking them in the bowl.

I'm a sort of picky eater I guess. I don't eat meat except chicken, sausages and bacon. I don't like mushrooms, nuts, sprouts or too much onion. I hate oranges, pears and bananas. I don't know, I guess I just don't like them or just not a big fan of them.

A shot in the dark... a past... lost in space.Where do I start, the past and the chase.

You hunted me down... like a wolf, a predator.I felt like a deer, in love lights...

You love me... and I froze in time.Hungry, for that flesh of mine..

But I can't compete..with the she-wolf that has brought me to my knees. .What do you see in those yellow eyes?Cause I'm falling to pieces..

I'm falling to pieces,I'm falling to pieces,I'm falling to pieces,I'm falling to pieces...

Falling to pieces...

I started singing to the lyrics of one of my favourite songs. It never gets old. David Guetta is the king of music collaborations, no doubt. I prance around at the music before continuing with my song and making the pancakes. I placed them on a plate, smothering one with whipped cream.

Did she lie in wait?Was I bait to pull you in?

The thrill of the kill...You feel, is a sin.

I lay with the wolves, alone, it seems.I thought I was part of you.

You love me... and I froze in timeHungry, for that flesh of mine.

But I can't compete, with the she-wolf that has brought me to my knees. .What do you see in those yellow eyes?Cause I'm falling to pieces.

I'm falling to pieces,I'm falling to pieces,I'm falling to pieces,I'm falling to piece,

Falling to pieces...

I dance around, humming the beat whilst gathering the knives, forks, and placemats, before creating Nathaniel's French toast. I poured yogurt on Sunbrooke's fruit before putting everything on the table. Quickly, I posted the Toast-Me's in the toaster.

I'm falling to pieces,Falling to pieces,I'm falling to pieces,Falling to pieces...

I jump in surprise when I hear clapping and cheering. I looked towards the door and saw Faith, Nathaniel, Sunbrooke and Aden standing there, my face immediately flushing red. I hate it when people clap for me or tell me something good about myself.

"That. Was. Amazing!" Faith smiled, wrapping me in a hug.

"No, it wasn't." I laughed, standing awkwardly - I'm not a big fan of hugs.

"Dude, that was great!" Aden smirked before stuffing some of his pancake.

"My singing or the food?" I asked, smirking back and punching his arm.

"Both." we all laughed while me and Aden fist bumped, "David Guetta is the best!"

"Nah, Calvin Harris is better." Faith grinned, sending a smirk to Aden.

The brunet scrunched his nose and shook his head, "Nope, David Guetta is the king!"

"Calvin Harris is the God."

"David Guetta is my God." Aden declared, stuffing his face with pancakes. Nathaniel sent Aden a weird look, shaking his head.

"But seriously though," Sunbrooke said, taking a seat at the table by her meal and facing me, "You have an amazing voice!"

"Ha! No, don't be ridiculous!". I protest, taking a bite out of an apple from the fridge and placing the last plate of food on the table.

"Okay, whatever floats your boat!" She smiled, taking some fruit out of her bowl.

"What's all this for?" Nathaniel asked, taking a large chunk out of his toast.

"Well, I just wanted to say thanks for everything you've all done for me, your all always been there for me." I thanked, taking my normal seat next to Faith.

"Well, that's what we're here for, so anytime" Sunbrooke answered, ruffling my hair.

After breakfast I decided on going for a run. It would be a great time to get used to my wolf and become stronger in wolf form as well as human. "Just going out!" I called.

"You want me to come?" Faith asked.

"You don't have to if you don't wanna?" It came out more like a question than an answer.

"Well, Elliot does want me to see him. And I still have to prove to Aden that Calvin Harris is the best." She grinned.

"You should stay, it seems like you've got a lot on your plate today." I laughed. Even though I've never had a mate, I know that the males are very protective over what's theirs - especially after marking.

"Okay, you have your phone, more importantly, your iPod?" She smirked. I frowned.

"I love my music." I said, hugging my small iPod.

"Yea, noticed!" She play nudged me. "I'll always have my mind-link open, if you need me, I'll be here. Stay in our territory. You will shift back into your clothes, like you found out yesterday, be sensible, be safe-"

"Yeah okay, Mum!" I laughed as she gave me a whole speech.

"I'm not acting like a mother!" she waved and walked off before yelling, "Be back before tea!" I chuckled lightly, shaking my head.

I took a deep breath and stepped outside. The cool air brushed against my skin, goose bumps appearing from my anxiousness. Walking deeper into the woods, the tall trees and mucky ground created my path. I came to an opening where the sun shone brightly through the trees and rested on the morning dew.

'Ready?' I asked Misty.

'Ready!'

We took another deep breath before the shift took place. Purple eyes, blue fur. Hands to paws, skin to fur. Nose to snout, butt to tail! A few places ached but I continued with the transformation. I rested on the ground, tall and proud in my wolf from, digging up dirt with my claws.

Panting lightly, I let out a growl before howling out. I pricked up my ear. I faintly heard the howls of my family, telling me they heard me. My wolf wandered through the trees, inhaling the scents around her.

'So, this territory thing - how will we know if we crossed it or come close to it?' I asked as I listened to the rustles of trees and tweeting of birds.

'Well, I'm not exactly sure. I think, something inside snaps. If it's on accident, I don't think we notice as much, but if we cross another packs territory, we feel on edge, I guess.' Misty answered, keeping high alert in case of anything.

We wandered around for a bit, the calmness of the forest was settling and unsettling at the same time, but it gave me a sense of who I was. I was a werewolf. I could transform. Misty and I, together as one. I was different but isolated from the outside world, no human other than hunters knew of us, but even the hunters got laughed at because of their belief. Sometimes, I do feel sorry for them but then I remind myself that they destroy families and kill us because they don't know the truth about us. They kill because they're afraid.

Not to tell Misty, but I didn't really care about finding a mate. Why do we need someone holding us back too much, protecting us? I can look after myself. Why be attracted to someone we just met? I know, it's a werewolf thing, but its... I don't know, weird? I wouldn't be free anymore because every male werewolf is protective of their mate. It would be, 'Where you going?' or 'Where are you now?' or 'Be home soon!' Get what I mean? No freedom!

If I was with a mate, I would always have someone on my tail. Him. It wouldn't be just me anymore. It would be us. There wouldn't be one side of me. It would be half of me without him. I would feel lonely without him if I accepted him, and that's something I don't fantasize about, as people do.

Misty said a werewolf was nothing without their mate. I guess that is true. So much has happened in my small lifetime. Would I be able to trust him? Would he like me, an omega? Would he accept my true self? What if he was an ALPHA?!

God, that would be awful. I'd have loads of guards around me, he'd be possessive and, fuck... I'd be a damn Luna. I am not Luna material. I will not and will never be, I am not 'strong' enough. An Alpha would turn me down for sure. I was weak to him. I was a coward compared to him. I was nothing compared to him. An Omega is and always be a maid to them, they serve them.

I was too busy wandering about my thoughts to notice where we were. 'Where are we Mist?' It seemed darker, even though night time was upon us. Everything seemed quiet... Too quiet for my liking.

'I-I dont know!' She gulped. My wolf form started shivering violently at the thought of being lost.

'How far have we gone?!' I yelled.

She flinched at my yells, looking around nervously, 'I've been running all the time, you were talking to yourself.'

I looked around. I tried to contact Faith but I was too far away from her. I started feeling worried about everything. Rouges, other packs. What would I do if I came across rouges or another pack? I was new and I haven't been training in my wolf form yet. I know myself, I should be natural at it because of my wolf hybrid but you never know.

Misty stopped at a lake, looking around while judging the area. I felt uneasy. Something just didn't feel right. I kept looking around me to check for anything. The slightest snap or rustle would have my heart racing and me on high alert.

We were lost...

Three • The Chance of Getting Struck By Lightning

C hapter Three------

Ylva

It was now completely dark. Even with my wolf night vision, it was almost impossible for a first timer out in the open. We were lost. Misty was fretting about what could happen and all the possible negative thoughts that ran through her mind, went through mine and it was pissing me off. She was whining, seeing if anyone could hear her - sure. Middle of nowhere, let's let out a distress signal.

I hope we are in neutral territory; no one came out here.

We wandered around, silence deafened us as we tried to communicate with someone. Anyone. The only thing that could be heard was my heart racing through my ears and my paws that snapped twigs and leaves. My paws trudged on the grass, leaving paws prints and scents.

I flinched under the sudden sound of thunder. It poured down with rain, soaking our coat. I didn't really care about the rain or thunder but the thought of being lost in this weather was a little bit different.

'What if we get hit with lightening, or- or, what of rouges find us, or another pack harms us... What about if-'

'SHUT UP!' I yelled. Misty kept going on about the negative possibilities. It was worst that I was hungry - I'm always in a shitty mood when I need food, I guess is a wolf thing, 'The chance of being hit by lightning is one to nine million.'

'Not helping!' she snapped, shivering, 'I'm just scared. I'm sorry, it's my fault. I ran and didn't think about were I was going.'

I wonder what Nathaniel's doing right now. Is he worrying? Is he trying to contact me, I'm just too far away? Nathaniel was my main guardian after my parents' death, he should trying to be doing something. I don't doubt that he's not because he's always been amazing to me and our little family.

I had no sense of were I was going. I took another turn and walked either deeper or closer to the edge of the woods. I didn't know whether I was walking away or closer to home. Maybe I was walking right into a trap of rouges? Maybe there were stronger wolves surrounding me, I just haven't smelt them yet? I shivered at the thoughts.

Maybe no one cares that I'm gone- that's what I've always been told by my pack. I'm sure Faith is trying to do something. Maybe she's out searching for me right now? In the rain, getting soaked and mucky. I regret telling her she didn't need to come. Truth be it, Faith did need to come. I had no sense of what it could be like. No idea about territories, no idea about scents and other packs because they don't teach you that until you turn wolf.

I pricked my ears up, listening out for anything. I sniffed, trying to find a scent of home but... Nothing. My stomach grumbled and my throat was dry. Needing water and food, my skills and running would be sloppy and slower than normal. I froze as Misty suddenly broke through and took of running.

'What the hell are you doing?' I yelled as she ran faster through the forest.

'I can smell someone... Ylva, I'm scared!' She whimpered.

'Okay, okay. Calm down a bit. We would have smelt them if there was someone.' I calmly told her.

She slowed her pace but didn't walk. The rain seemed to pick up even more. What, are we in a storm or something?

I suddenly let out a loud whine of pain as we tripped over something. I rolled over and down a steep hill. Leaves and dirt coated my fur as I tumbled over. When it stopped, pain coursed through my back leg and my body began to ache. Mud covered my blue fur and my nose felt as though it was bruised.

I reluctantly stood up, wincing in pain as I applied pressure to my back leg. I clambered up the top on the hill, and wandered back through the forest. Misty was whimpering softly, begging for anyone to help her. We carried on, stumbling over rocks, trunks and roots. Fresh cuts were wounded into our flesh as we feel.

With my back leg seemingly turning numb and my stomach growling in protest, it was becoming hard to concentrate. Man, I would never survive on my own, I thought. I felt on edge. Nothing seemed right. The smell was different, the forest was partly lighter. My wolf was anxious too, worrying what's to come.

'Where are we?' I asked Misty, turning this was and that.

I wish I didn't leave. I wish I didn't shift yesterday. I wish I never left home. I wish I never left our territory! My mind was blank and I couldn't think. Nothing felt like home or even close to it. Like I was in a different place. What if I was in the Blood Thirst's or the Golden Raven's land? Crap. I would be kill straight away. I didn't want to be challenged for power or control with any of these Alpha's. But just because I'm an Omega, doesn't mean I wouldn't try to kick their asses a little - if they attacked me that is.

After studying the area a bit, Misty finally answered. 'I-I think...I think we're-'

She couldn't form a sentence. She didn't get the chance. We were harshly tackled to the ground, a large brown wolf standing over us, preventing movement. His claws dug into my shoulder, blood oozing from the small, yet painful, wounds. The wolf had a large and strong stamina, some sort of low power radiated off him.

Misty growled before knocking him off. She pushed up with her hind legs, he was forced stumble back under the pressure.

'How did you do that?' I asked as we got up and growled at the other wolf, getting into fighting stance.

'Hybrid strength.' was all she answered before the wolf attacked again.

We were stood on our hind legs, hitting, biting and growling at the wolf as he did the same. He growled angrily before clamping down on our front leg. Misty whined in pain before grabbing his skin in our teeth. The sound of ripping flesh echoed through our ears as Misty tore away a small patch of skin on his shoulder.

The brown wolf whimpered in pain before backing up slightly. He jumped suddenly in the air landed on us again, his teeth nipping at our ear. His large body crushed mine under him. We tackled him over and snapped at his snout, grazing his nose.

Our back and front leg hurt a lot. But Misty didn't seem to notice as she attacked the wolf who threatened her. Even with our hunger and weakness, our power was at a high as we attempted to make him back off. Some sort of power radiated off him. He wasn't an Alpha though. If he was, I'd be dead already.

Blood, rain and mud filled my nose. Ripping, growling and snapping was heard through my ears. Misty was terrified. I was terrified. We were a new she-wolf. The energy that we had right now was good, even if we were a hybrid.

I don't think the brown wolf liked me a lot. He snapped and growled louder than before. I was suddenly flung into the air, crashing down into a tree trunk. The base of the tree shook and crumbled on impact as I crashed into the floor.

My back was pained and my head felt dizzy. I looked into the eyes of the brown wolf. Black. Pitch black. No sign of emotion except anger and hatred. Fear rose in me as he growled angrily - and fear is something I rarely have. He leapt forward, he teeth sink into the flesh of my neck. Not to kill me, only weaken me and put me to sleep for a bit.

Each wolf has a place in their neck for killing, and a place for putting to sleep. If done correctly, you can put wolves to sleep by biting down on the lower part of the neck. Like a pressure point but it's difficult to find for many. Obviously this wolf knew exactly what he was doing. It still hurt like a bitch though.

The pressured on my neck, my wolf howling, begging him to stop. He growled lowly. Misty was mentally begging him to stop, telling him that we didn't mean a threat. The authority in his growl was obviously heard. He wasn't an Alpha. He was a Beta. I was fighting a Beta! Holy shit!

Misty wouldn't stop wriggling so he placed his foot over her and rest down so we couldn't move, especially since we were already injured. His wolf weight was too heavy for us, and our weakness was already sensed. We were becoming drowsy and unconscious. The world around me seemed to spin. Misty let out one final whine of pain before falling unconscious.

The world went dark and all I could feel was the pain. What a great start to shifting...

Four • Enough With the Compliments, Mister

C hapter Four-------

Ylva

I jumped up from the nightmare, pain pulsing through me. The room was pitch black, an eerie smell filled my nose. My heart raced as I peered around - in the emptiness. I can't see a thing. I guessed was in a holding cell. A place were the Alpha would decide whether to kill me here, put me in an actual cell or let me go. The latter sounded the best to me.

I went to get up, only to fall back down. Soaring pain ran through my body, so much so that tears welled in my eyes. I glanced down and saw the thick chains on my wrists. What? My legs were locked around chains as well. I didn't realise they trapped you. Misty was on edge. Her whimpers echoed around the room. I looked at my wrist and ankle again. There was a tight bandage wrapped around them - that's when everything came back to me. Me in the woods, falling over, fighting a wolf I believe was a Beta. He could have killed me. Then I remember tearing some of his skin off. If he was a Beta, his Alpha would have my head. Shit. I wasn't planning on dying today.

I looked down at myself. My clothes were torn and dirty. My skin was covered in mud and dirt and my hair was wildly messed around my face and matted on my skin. I must have shifted when I was asleep.

I rested my head back, wincing at the ache that ran through. What were they going to do to me? Would they kill me? Was I going to die? My heart raced and I tensed as I thought of never seeing my family again. This was all my fault.

Tears clouded my vision as the iron door creaked open. I growled lowly before cowering back into the corner as a tall man walked in, his dark brown hair, rippling muscles. Something about him made me just want to run over and hug him. Why did he make me feel this was? He just walked in.

'Oh. My. God' I could feel Misty with wide eyes as she stared at this man with me. She pranced around like crazy, making my heart beat differently.

He growled lowly, causing me to flinch. His stamina was great, and power radiated off him. Shit, he was an Alpha.

I bowed my head in respect but thought of a scarcy comment, "Before you kill me, can I ask you something?" I smirked to myself, but didn't look at him- it was considered a threat if you weren't in their pack.

"Yes?" his deep voice responded. Something about that voice made me feel safe. Why?

"What's the point of chains if you have a huge metal door that can't be opened from the inside?"

I felt his presence closer. My heart rate picked up dramatically as he squatted down beside me. Did I go to far? "Look at me" his whispered.

His voice was deep, calming. Even though anger radiated from him, his voice was soft; it made me feel safe. My wolf was going crazy, I didn't understand why. I shook my head quickly, tightly shutting my eyes. He growled.

"Look. At. Me" The warning in his voice caused me to snarl lowly.

"But I'm not a threat, and I don't want to be considered one!" I told him. I slowly raised my head at his command though and looked at him, staring into his orbs.

Those eyes. Green eyes. I tilted my head, with a hint of brown? I suddenly felt very different. His tense body seemed to relax, a confused but happy emotion came to his eyes. I stared at him, he stared at me. The world seemed to slow and stop, no one except us existed. I felt his hand reach out and touch my cheek. Sparks flew from where he touched but I hissed and the moment was over. I am not ready for this.

He cautiously retracted his hand, looking at me with worry. "My mate?" He questioned.

Mate? Mate? He's...he's my mate!? My eyes widened as I stared at him again. I got lost in those green eyes. My eyes seemed to shift. His face went to shock before turning back to normal. "Uh...?" Was my brilliant response.

"You have beautiful blue eyes, you know" he smirked.

"Blue?" I questioned.

"Yes, they changed. You're a hybrid?"

"Uh, yeah?"

'Why did our eyes turn blue?' I quickly asked Misty.

"Because we found our mate. If we like something he does, they will go blue. It's because we are a hybrid. I thought you knew that?' She explains, eyeing up the man in front of us who claims to be out mate. Good God!

I looked at him. He reached down and unlocked the cuffs. He stood up, as did I, but with not much luck. I fell down over my weak legs and toppled to the ground. Before I hit the rough concrete, I landed in strong arms. I looked to my mate who had caught me. He gently smiled. Awkward!

"Thanks." I awkwardly spoke, pushing away slightly. Hurt crossed his face so I stopped.

I was so anxious and nervous, I didn't know what was wrong. I have never felt like this. I now felt weak, fluttery almost. Every place he touch created sparks and butterflies in the pit of my stomach. Ugh, I think I'm going to throw up.

"Your welcome, my little mate. What's your name?" He asks, pulling me to my feet and helping me stand.

I gradually got my balance before moving away and looking into those mesmerising eyes again. "I'm not little!" I frowned, tilting my head. "My name's Ylva."

"Beautiful name for a beautiful person" he smirks. I growl, hating compliments.

"Okay, enough with the compliments, Mister. I'm far from beautiful." I confidently say, crossing my arms. All I want to know is where I am so I can leave. And I am currently in ratty, dirty clothing with limpy black hair.

"I assure you, you are more beautiful than you give yourself credit for, Ylva" my mate whispered, his face leaning closer. His eyes scanned my face, finally resting on my lips. He leaned closer, closer...closer...

A loud slap suddenly echoed through the air and it took me a moment to realize I had slapped the man in front of me. No, no - I slapped the Alpha in front of me. I flinched back, body tensed and eyes wide. I know I wasn't ready. I had never kissed anyone before. But I did not mean to do that, "Oh my God... I am so sorry! I just-"

"You weren't ready." he interrupted, rubbing his cheek where a red mark was beginning to appear.

"Yeah? But you can't just kiss people out of nowhere!" I answered. I put my hands in my jeans bum pockets and looked around, anywhere to avoid his gaze.

"You say that like I just do that all the time." He answered before smirking, "But you've got a mean swing, I'll give you that."

"Who are you?" I asked. I looked around again, we were still in the dungeon. Hm, very interesting four walls with no windows...

"I am Ryker Dawson. Alpha of the Golden Raven pack." he announced proudly, edging us towards the door.

Wait, WHAT?!

Alpha RykerALPHA?Golden Raven...oh no.

"Fuck. " I whispered to myself.

Faith told me to stay away from this pack. The Alpha kills any outsiders, or never let's them leave. If I was his mate, he would never let me leave. I would never see my family again... Faith, Aden, Nathaniel, Sunbrooke.

I stopped walking, tears filling my eyes. Ralph looked at me with concern. "What's wrong?"

"Is it true you never let people leave?" I stumble.

"Yes, most likely, why? You will sure as hell not be leaving. You are my mate."

"But... my family."

"Did you not leave them?" He raised an eyebrow.

"So, you assume that just because I ended up on your territory I ran from home?" I snapped. His face grew shocked before a small glare crossed his face. "I did not leave my family! I went for a run, got lost and ended up in this shit hole! So don't assume things, Alpha."

He growled lowly, "Don't yell at me."

I took a step back, twitching my nose, "Will I be able to see them again?" I asked, hopeful.

"Who's your Alpha?"

"Alpha Greyson."

"No."

What? What the hell!

"What do you mean 'no'?" I frowned, growling angrily.

"You will not be going back." He confirmed, walking up to the stairs, out of the cell.

"Yes I will. They are my family!" I yelled angrily. How dare he say I cannot see my family again!

"If you go back, I will not see you again. Your Alpha and I do not get on well."

I huffed. "What, just because you Alpha's can't share a stick means I can't see my family ever again? Is this a joke?"

"I didn't say ever". Ralph answered, ignoring my last comment.

I stared at him. He is so confusing. I only just met him and he was already annoying me, "So I can see them again?"

"Yes but you have to be patient."

Dickhead. Growling, I took that answer for the minute. "Fine!"

We had come to the top of the stairs and had entered a large room, like a dining room. The oak table sat in the middle with loads of handmade chairs around it and a thick velvety cloth covering the top. Teenagers sat in front of a large TV, playing some sort of race game, yelling at each other. I mentally laughed and continued to look around. That reminded me of when I used to play with Aden and Faith.

The kitchen was covered with a black tile flooring. There was three islands in the middle. Two elderly ladies stood by the stove, cooking something that smelled delicious. The white cupboards and black marble artwork on the top.

I was filled with anxiousness and worry. I have no idea why. Everything here was different. My wolf had been quiet since we've been here. We were walking up some stairs when I saw a group of girls. One of them turned around. Oh look, Miss Fabulous! I could tell by looking at her that she had most males around here wrapped around her pinky finger. Her face plastered in makeup, short skirt and thin top, so thin you could see her bra. She fluttered her eyebrows at Ryker. Such a Barbie.

"This is the pack house, darling, not Love Island." I spoke aloud.

Misty growled lowly. Oh, make an appearance now? I watched as the girl glared at me. I studied her, taking a mental note to avoid people like her here.

"Who's the mutt you've brought with you?"

Ah, ha, ha... Well, she wants a death wish.

Five • I'm Going Deaf With Your Smelly Breath

C hapter Five------

Ylva

I scoffed at the brown-haired, makeup plastered, bimbo in front of me. Crossing my arms, I watched her, "Excuse me?" I raised an eyebrow.

Miss Precious strutted towards me, "You heard me, tramp" she snarled a bit, obviously trying to scare me, but she had the wrong girl.

"No, I'm sorry, you know...I'm going deaf with your smelly breath, blocking up my ears" I smirked.

She angrily gasped as a crowd started surrounding us. It was mostly the younger ones, always eager to see a fight. I glanced at Ryker, who happened to be grinning. He looked into my eyes. The tingles arrived as I stared back at his dark orbs. I snapped my glance away at the sound of a cough.

"Sorry, what was that?" I surrounded my ears with my hands. I heard what she said but I wanted the ass to repeat it.

"Whore." she said loudly, receiving a growl from Ryker. I put my hand up to him, showing him I had it covered. It's funny. People like her think that it insults me, but to be honest, I mentally laugh at them - sometimes aloud.

"Sorry, I'm not a mirror." I smirked, listening to the gasps of her friends and the chuckles of the crowd.

"Your such a bitch!" she exclaimed.

"Well, I am a female dog so... Yeah, I guess I am." I smiled sarcastically, putting my thumbs up.

Her face hardened, "Stop being sarcastic, you fucking Omega!"

"Omega-d, like I haven't heard that one already." I grinned at the princess.

"At least I don't go round looking like a dead rat. I actually have standards." She growled.

"Well, at least my body isn't pumped with plastic. I have realistic standards." I directed down myself. She flinched at my words, glaring harder. Damn, I got her. Some of the crowd (mostly boys), laughed at my meir comment. I smirked at them before a growl cut me off. I stared at the heaving bitch in my face.

"Just know one thing," she snarled, "Mate or not, he belongs to me." she pointed to Ryker. Wow, they have a relationship? Misty growled loudly, I know everyone could hear it because they took a step back.

"Bitch, you wish." I smirked. She growled loudly, her face turning red and her eyes blackening. Wow, her wolf must be jealous. "If you want him, you'll have to go through my wolf - and I don't think she plays fair."

My wolf laughed maniacly at this pathetic Miss Perfect in my face, wasting our time. 'She touches Ryker, she's dead' she hissed. Possessive much?

'Oh relax, he fucked her millions of times' I answered, glaring at Ryker, who was smirking widely now. Ass.

'Don't say that!' She whined.

'It's true though, you can tell.' I swallowed thickly, think of Ralph and her while I'm still here all innocent. Yes, I am a virgin. Go ahead, gasp, laugh, whatever. Jees, I'm seventeen, ain't getting laid now, far too young!

"Stay the hell away from Ryker." the brunette hissed at me.

I looked up, pretending to think. "Hmm," I stated, like it was a really hard question, "As much as I want to, I don't think my wolf would be all too happy with that." I smirked at her, just to piss her off I blew a kiss to Ryker who smirked as if he knew what I was trying to do.

Do you think she hates me? Haha, I'm so funny.

Her face hardened again. "You will or I'll make you" she growled lowly. Ryker growled louder than before, warning her. "But baby, don't you hear this mutt?" She pouted, battering her eyelashes.

She walked over to him, placing her hand on his shoulder and trailing her finger down his abs. My wolf was on an all time jealously mode. 'Let me snap her fucking neck!' She hissed.

I rolled my eyes, "Jees, someone pass me the sick bucket." I got a few laughs and chuckles from the crowd.

"I like her already." someone yelled.

"Thank you, I like you too." I answered to whoever gave me that compliment.

"Ugh, listen mutt," Bimbo came storming over to me, "You don't belong here, Ryker is mine so just piss off!" The bitch in my face yelled. I stare at her emotionlessly - a thing I've been doing so well at lately.

"Yeah, I've been told many times, don't belong, I'm a mutt - Omega's don't get much appreciation, do they? But you wouldn't know because you're a perfect princess. Oh well, guess you'll have to live with it, won't you Barbie?" I patted her shoulder.

She flinched away. "Don't fucking touch me, slut."

I faked a tear, "Look who's talking."

She growled extra loud, and her fist came hurtling towards me. She was aiming for my face. She was getting closer, closer. Ok, that's close enough. See, as a hybrid, I was able to see vision slower than normal wolves when someone tries to attack me and could sense what most were about to do - but that all still came with training.

I swiftly positioned my hand so her fist flung into it. I gripped her knuckles so she couldn't pull away. I stared at her hand while smirking at the gasps from the crowd. Some of the boys wolf whistled, in which they received a growl from their Alpha. Possessive much?

I looked to the makeup plastered face, still smirking. "Well! That wasn't a very nice thing to do to a guest."

She growled again, trying to remove her hand from my clamp. Straining and tugging, her face began to redden. I've had enough of her petty games. I yanked her forward, a yelp escaping her mouth. I whispered into her ear.

"Ryker, is mine, go near him again, your pretty, fake locks won't be on your head anymore. Got it?" I warned, my wolf at bay.

She stared at me in shock before slowly nodding her head. I smirked before pushing her away and walking to Ryker.

"Come on now, baby." I smirked, copying Precious' words, "Where were we originally going?"

Ryker growled lowly and walked away from the crowd. I slowly followed.

'Oh shit.' my wolf gasped.

'What?'

'What did you just do?' She asked.

'Got really angry and my- oh fuck' I growled in annoyance.

'Exactly.'

Anger - love it. When my angry side comes out, all I see is red. I want to kill, I want to taste blood, anything violent. My violet eyes changed to an angry red, I knew it because I could feel it, "R-Ryker." I gasped, leaning against the wall, my fists balling.

He spun around, looking at me. His face dropped and his smirk disappeared. He stared at me in anger and dread. I'm a hybrid. I have anger issues. Every hybrid does. When our eyes go red, we need to either hunt, kill or fight something. We can't control it until the anger has faded. Misty was hurtling around like crazy, wanting to be let out and go insane.

The Alpha grabbed my arm and pulled me through corridors. I hissed out lowly, my fists balling up tighter. We reached a metal door, before Ryker barged in, "Everyone out now! We need this area!" He yelled. Everyone quickly scuttled away at their Alpha's orders.

Before anything else, my eyes flashed and my supernatural power took over. I growled loudly before sprinting to the nearest punch bag, whacking it so hard, it flew off the hinges and smashed into a wall. I smirked darkly and stared at the weapons on a desk. Stalking over, I picked up the metal blade. After admiring its strange markings and carvings, I growled again and smashed it into the middle of the target.

I looked at Ryker. His broad body facing me while his eyes watched my every move, staring at me. I saw his eyes turn colour. From those dreamy green, they switch to an envious, stormy grey. I stared into those eyes. His wolf's eyes. My body relaxed as if this side of him was calming Misty and I.

She whined slightly, our tense body shutting down. I continued to stare into those orbs, while my eyes turned azure. My claws retracted and my muscles relaxed. Those stormy eyes stared deeply into my own. Ryker's hands jerked, as if he wanted to hold me... and I complied. Walking over to him, my hands trailed over his chest as if we were in a trance. His tense body relaxed. His stormy, grey eyes turned back into those forest green eyes, hypnotising me. Full of memories, hope, love and satisfaction.

Ryker grabbed my hips, pulling me closer to his welcoming body. My wolf was partly in control, forcing me to stay put. I wanted to pull away, leave, go home; but Misty was having none of it. She purred lightly receiving a low growl from our mate. I rested against his chest, and he pulled me into a bridal carry, kissing my head. I sighed deeply.

Was this meant to be? Was I really Alpha Ryker, of the Golden Raven Pack's mate. His Luna? This can't be right. The Moon Goddess has made a mistake somewhere along the line. Misty was in a world of bliss being around her mate. I'll give it a few days. She deserves this, she's waited so long. But, I just don't know how I feel yet.

I never wanted a mate in the first place. Misty has always been so good to me. She's always there for me, always happy to be around me. What that brunette said was partly true. Some people did call me a whore at school, only because I hung around with boys. Personally, I think they were jealous. And being told I didn't belong, yeah, people said that too. That's why I never went I to the pack house, only my house with my family.

My body, well Misty, relaxed deeper into our mate, my mate. My Alpha mate. Still I wonder how... Why would the Moon Goddess choose me of anyone to be an Alpha's mate? I was an Omega, a slave, a maid, nothing. The sadness I had been through in my short life made it hard for me to trust anyone.

I never wanted to go out with my little amount of friends at Alpha Grayson's pack house. I always stayed in, on my iPod, training or walked around by myself. At night, I always used to walk out into the woods and over to a lake. It was beautiful, especially at night, the Luna's prize possession, but she didn't mind me going there. I was the only one though.

I would stare up into the stars and wish my life was better. Don't get me wrong, I love Nathaniel and everyone, but nothing could take away the horror of that day. Nothing could leave and take the pain away. That's why I was so afraid of getting a mate. Afraid of getting rejected, afraid of love, afraid of trusting them in case it's a mistake.

"Now, Kitten," his husky voice interrupted my thoughts, "Tell me who exactly left the marks and bruises on you." he growled deeply, gripping my petite figure.

Six • Now Would Be a Good Time to Be Anyone But Me

Chapter Six------

Ylva

I swallowed thickly. Should I tell him? He might kill his beta! I don't really want his beta to hate me either. And what was that nickname? Kitten. I am not a cat, if anything I'm a dog, 'Well, it's not like he can call you Puppy, is it?' Misty butted in.

I rolled my eyes, 'Stop being so snarky and help me get out of this.'

"No one." I answered, hoping he'll believe that.

"I know someone did. You couldn't knock yourself out like that." he glared at me, demanding a honest answer.

Well damn. Of course an Alpha wouldn't believe 'no one' especially if you were his mate. He would hurt anyone who hurt me. That scared me. I didn't want people hating me for the Alpha always beating up people who hurt me. It was kind of pathetic really. If I was really angry with that Beta, I could just beat him up myself.

"Ryker, it was no one!" I repeated. I stared down to my wrist and leg; the bandage still tightly wrapped around my almost healed joints. They didn't hurt anymore, it was nothing more than a dull ache.

"Ylva, anyone who hurts what's mine will be punished." He growled.

I glared at him now. I was not an object. I did not belong to him. I belonged to myself. I didn't need him bossing me around all day or locking me somewhere. I got up from his hold and stared down at him, my arms crossed, "I do not belong to you or anyone." I stated firmly.

Ryker snarled, his fists balled tightly as he stood up. His tall figure almost intimidating, but not enough for me, "You are mine, whether you like it or not. Anyone who hurts you will be hurt by me." he snapped, gripping the top of my arms, staring deeply into my eyes, "Now. Who hurt you?"

"I said no one! I tripped and fell down a hill!" I pulled away from his grip, only to be tugged back by his strong hands.

Ryker pulled me closer and leaned down, down to my neck. "Wait, what are you - no!" He inhaled deeply, smelling the different scents on me. His body stiffened and he shot back up.

"That fucking-" he threw his fist against the wall, a large dent notifying where it had landed. I swallowed, fear surrounding my body, "I'm going to kill him." he barged through the doors and walked down the hall.

"No!"

I groaned internally, now would be a good time to be anyone but me.

Following his scent to the next room, I quickly pushed the cream door open and froze at what I saw. Ryker already had his hand wrapped around his Beta's neck, a girl not to far away, shouting at him to stop. I needed to stop this. I sprinted toward Ralph.

I tugged at his arm and yelled, "Ryker, stop!" I tried yanking him away with no avail.

"No!" He roared, his wolf in full control, "He hurt you!" His jaw clenched and his dark eyes could've burned holes through his Beta.

"No, Ryker! I was fighting him! It was the only way he would stop me!" I shouted, trying to pull his arm away. I knew that I was in the wrong when I entered the Golden Raven's territory, but clearly Ryker didn't see it that way. He only saw me as his hurt mate.

He growled and shoved me away, hard enough that I ran into a wall - I grunted on impact, slightly hurt. He was going to kill him. His Beta gasped and struggled to get air into his lungs and I gritted my teeth, "Ryker, please stop!" I growled, not wanting hatred from anyone.

Ryker continued to glare at his Beta, not stopping. There was only one way I could think of stopping him. Misty yelled in happiness about it but I didn't. This wasn't for us or Ralph, it was for the Beta to save his life.

I ran over to Ralph, pouncing on his chest. I wrapped my legs around his torso, pressing my lips firmly against his. I tried to ignore the sensation of our touch, the pleasurable burn that his lips caused but it was no easy task. Ryker's hand let go of his Beta, causing him to gasp for air and fall to the floor. His mate, I presume, ran over and hugged him tightly, leaving small kisses all over his face.

I felt arms wrap around my back and a strong hand go through my hair. I closed my eyes and leaned deeper into his touch. It was everything I needed. Ralph groaned slightly against my mouth, licking and nipping at my bottom lip, asking for entrance. I denied.

He growled and slid his hand down my back, a shiver leaving me. This wasn't for me, or Ryker, it was for the Beta and his mate. I pulled away from his grasp, pushing my mate. Turning to face the Beta, he was still breathing heavily, whispering into the girl's ear.

"Are you okay?" I asked, concerned about the dark bruises beginning to form on his neck.

The Beta looked at me. When he realised who I was, his eyes blackened, muscles tensed and he growled lowly, shielding his mate, "That doesn't matter to you, mutt." he snapped. I jumped back, my heart racing from his cold tone as I clenched my fists and growled back. I was pulled back into a chest, the strong grip of my mate resting on my hips. I squirmed uncomfortably, trying to release myself from his grip.

Ryker growled lowly, "That 'mutt' is my mate, Reece." he hissed at his Beta.

The guy, who I'm guessing is name Reece, glanced back to me, eyes widening, "Forgive me Luna, Alpha." he spoke, bowing his head.

I huffed in annoyance, "I am no Luna. Let me go, Ryker!" I whined, straining against his hold.

He growled as one of my flying elbows connected with his already bruised jaw. I froze and looked at his, his eyes blackened as he looked at me. That's twice.

"It's fine, Beta." I smiled back still trying to escape from my mate's hold.

"Thank yo- how did you know I was a Beta?" He asked, his head tilting in confusion.

"I'm a hybrid, I could smell it." I smiled, holding my hand out for him to shake, "Plus, you are strong in your fighting."

His eyebrows raised, "Is that why you have a blue wolf?"

"Yep."

"It's very nice." He complimented, wrapping an arm around his mate.

Ralph growled at him. I sighed angrily and glared at him. "Fucking hell, all he did was compliment me!"

"Only I am allowed to do that, especially since you are not marked." He hissed.

"Well, your going to be waiting a long time. And your Beta did not mean it in that way! He has a mate, and I'm sure he is loyal enough to not go to someone else and fuck them!" I growled, referring to the princess from earlier.

He flinched at my words, "It wasn't like that."

"Really? Cause it sure as hell seemed like it!" I yelled, pulling myself out of his grip. I said a quick goodbye to his beta and ran out the room.

'Why'd you yell at him?' Misty whined.

'Cause he's pissing me off!' I hiss, making my way to the back door. Before I reached the handle, an arm wrapped around my waist and pushed me against it. No tingles were felt, and that made me gulp.

"Hello there, Missy! Where are you going this fine afternoon?" A small grin appeared on his face.

He had blond hair and light blue eyes. Classic heartthrob. I shoved him away and glared at him, "Leave me alone."

He smirked, "Na, ah!" And he pushed closer towards me. I growled angrily, "Ooh, feisty, just the way I like it." he grinned.

My wolf hated hands of people other than her mate touching her. His touch didn't feel right, it felt wrong - terribly wrong. I shoved him harder so he stumbled back, then I balled up my fist and flung it towards him. My hand collided with his head and he tripped over a chair that was behind him. If it wasn't a bad situation, I would have laughed, but I held it in.

His eyes scanned me as they turned black. He snarled out before using his wolf speed and smashed me into a wall. Misty whined gently in pain, but I kneed him in the nuts. A growl echoed through the room.

I froze and spun around. Just as I did an arm wrapped around my waist, roughly pulling me into a hard but warm chest. My wolf relaxed but I stayed frozen, ignoring the tingles that erupted through us.

"Mine." he hissed lowly, growling at the blond in front. He stared at me wide eyed before nodding his head.

"I am very sorry Alpha, please forgive me, I did not know." He said, in a pleading manner.

Ryker nodded his head as he ran away, "Yeah, run, your horny prick." I muttered angrily. I felt Ryker's intense glare piercing my skull.

"You shouldn't let another man touch you." he roughly grabbed my hand and dragged me who knows where.

I glared at him, "What the fuck do you think I did, go up to him and say, 'hey stranger, come grab my ass if you like?' No I didn't so don't act like I did!"

Ryker's grip tightened as he growled and pulled me up some stairs. Wai t...where are we g- oh no. I flinched away from his grip and backed away. He stared at me confused. I crossed my arms and glared even more at him, "I'm not sleeping with you"

His stare hardened, "You think I'm going to let my new found mate sleep on her own?"

"Yes." he raised an eyebrow.

"Well, sorry to disappoint you, but you are staying with me, like it or not." He shrugged.

"Fine!" I growled. I'm doing a lot of growling today!

I barged into his room and froze. Did he know she was in here? This must just be a regular thing around here. I turned and glared at Ryker. He stared at the female, face blank and eyes blackened in anger. I stared at Miss Fabulous, half naked on his bed. I growled lowly. Again.

Seven • Ed Sheeran Wouldn't Treat Me Like This

C hapter Seven------

Ylva

I stared at her. How many times do I have to put her in her place? Her head snapped towards me and fear flashed across her face before it was quickly replaced with a smirk. She purred at Ryker. Purred. I squinted my eyes before glaring at him, letting out a growl.

Miss Princess walked over to us and ran her fake nails along Ryker's arm, "He's mine, mutt." she hissed lowly, placing a small kiss on his shoulder. Misty growled lowly and our eyes turned a pitch black. How many times does she need to be told? Does she not give up?

'How dare she!' She hissed, begging to be free so she could rip her throat out. I don't think that would be the best. Ryker just stared at her, growling warningly.

"But baby, you love me. I mean look at her. She probably couldn't even hunt a rabbit!" She smirked at me. Before she could do anything, my hands had wrapped around her neck. I slammed her against the wall, a satisfying crack echoing around the room.

Misty was in control of my actions and I couldn't take her back. Not that I wanted to. This dog deserved to be put down. She muttered something under her breath. With my hybrid hearing, I could just hear it.

"Did you just call me weak?" I hissed.

"So what?" She challenged.

"Katie." Ryker growled. I glared at him as his eyes filled with worry. Great! He's worried about a bitch?

"Are you worried about her!?" Misty snarled. Katie was struggling against my grip, her claws digging at my hand. I knew that my wolf's grip got tighter because blood began to dribble from small wounds.

"No."

"LIAR!" Misty screamed. We could hear his heartbeat accelerate when he answered. Either he was worried for his packmate, or he really liked Katie.

"Ylva, stop." he commanded. Why the hell is he talking to me? I wasn't in control.

'It's not me, you dickhead!' I snapped at him through the mind link, 'Can't keep is in your pants, huh, Alpha?'

'Your wolf?' He inquired, ignoring my snarky comment.

'Misty. And she won't stop, Katie touched what was hers. We are not some toy, you player!' I growled at him.

"Misty. Down!" He shouted, trying to stop her from killing a pack member.

She growled angrily at him, "Do not treat me like a fucking pup!" She snarled, her voice filling the empty halls.

"Now, Misty! Put her down!" Ryker yelled, using his Alpha tone. As much as she didn't want to, she had to obey an Alpha. Rules were rules. Misty dropped the princess on the floor and she coughed harshly. Katie stared up at us in fear but a small smirk still appeared on her face.

"You're a bitch. Go near him again, mutt, you're dead." Misty whispered in her ear. She squinted her eyes as her smirk grew. Misty growled lowly before shoving past Ryker. She sprinted down the stairs and ran towards the door, shifting before we even got outside.

'Are you okay?' I asked as she let me take control again.

'No. And I meant what I said. If that bitch goes near my mate again, she's dead.' she growled loudly, the birds shooting off at the thunderous roar.

'Where the hell are you?' Ryker asked through the link.

'Why does it matter to you? Go fuck your girlfriend' I hissed back.

This short experience just proved to me that everything I heard about Alpha mates was true - there's always competition. I was an Omega and he was an Alpha. I should have known he was too good to be true. He has his little friend, he can fuck her to his heart's content. I'm not going to be the one to let him get to me and do what he wants with me. I am not some toy.

If Ryker wanted me as his mate, he is going to have to change. I know I don't belong here, it's not my home. I don't really care what people say about me, it's not my fault I'm their Alpha's mate. But I'm not being a Luna for a long time - maybe even never. Ryker will have to be patient.

'Your my mate, get your ass back here.' he growled.

'No. Leave me alone. Ed Sheeran wouldn't treat me like this.' I snickered, 'Better get your act together, Alpha.'

'Come back now or I come get you. My wolf won't be contained.' He answered roughly.

I laughed, 'My wolf is a hybrid.'

'So?'

'Faster, stronger. You wouldn't want me to use powers would you?' I smirked slightly.

'Yeah, okay, you have powers. I'm coming to get you.' he growled, cutting off the link.

'Do we have any powers?' I asked Misty.

'Uh, maybe, why?'

'Ralph's coming.' I sniffed and located his scent.

'Hey, dickhead. I can smell you. Come out from behind the tree.' I remarked, growling lowly.

'Come home or I do it the hard way.' he hissed, his large figure appearing from the trees.

I may or may not have underestimated Ryker's wolf. Instead of the big black ones Alpha's usually have, his wolf was a dark silver. His shiny fur glowed under the moonlight and his startling grey orbs flickered black.

Ryker's wolf was at least twice the size of his Beta's wolf. It towered above me.

Misty whined, 'Man, I would kill for some super soldier serum right about now.'

His height and stamina could only mean one thing...

Alaric...

'Y-Your an Alaric Wolf?' I gulped. His tall stance walked towards me.

Alaric's are the strongest of all wolves. They are basically a hybrid, but both their parents come from a wealthy and powerful family. Hybrids are slightly faster, but only if you push for it. Can we push it? When Alaric's are in wolf form, like hybrids, their fur lightens and their blood is a darker red than any other wolf.

'Yes.' he growled.

'I'm not backing down for this Jerk.' Misty snapped. I knew she was scared but not enough to obey him. Which was a shocker. Usually she would be the first to cower under an Alpha's orders.

'Let's go.' Ryker turned and started to walk back.

'No!' My wolf howled at me and we took off sprinting in the opposite direction.

'Ylva!' His voice roared.

Misty growled in return and pushed herself faster. The thud of paws echoed around me, pumping my adrenaline to go faster. My claws dug into the dirt as we shot past the trees. Everything was a blur and my world seemed perfect. Well, almost. If Ryker wasn't here chasing me, yeah.

'I can get you Ylva.' he taunted. It was an evil but playful voice.

'You can try!' I hissed back.

'Don't worry I will.' he snapped.

Before I knew it, paws struck my hind legs causing me to go flying. I crashed against a tree, howling from the new surge of pain. Sharp teeth gripped the scruff of my neck, pulling me off the ground.

'Put me down!' I yelled. I cried from the injury that travelled through my body.

'No. Stop wriggling.' he muttered, clearly in no mood for games now.

'Never!' I snapped, stretching out my legs and pounding them against his chest.

He snarled and clamped down on my neck, hitting the sleep point. I screamed out in pain, tears poured from my yellow eyes.

'Why did you do this to me?' I whimper before my body went limp and darkness took over. That's twice!

Eight • Genetics Suck

C hapter Eight-------

Ylva

"Mummy?" I asked, hearing the door unlock.

"Ylva! Ylva!" I hear my Mum shout, panic laced in her voice.

"Mummy? What's wrong? Where's Daddy?" I asked as she embraced me in a tight hug. She cupped my face, looking at me through tearful eyes.

"Please honey. Go! You must run and get away from here and never come back!" She whispered, smoothing her thumb over my cheek as tears began to form in my orbs.

"Wha-what?" I asked, my stomach tightening as I smelled danger.

"Baby girl, please run! Go to the pack house." She kissed my cheek.

"But, why?"

"I love you so much, please just-" The front door came flying through the hall, smashing against the wall.

"WHERE'S THAT MUTT?" I heard a rough voice full of venom hiss.

"No! Leave her alone! She's only a child!" I heard my father shout.

"Daddy!" Me and my stupid mouth. The people barged in and threw my mum against the wall.

"Mum!" I screamed, the tears spilling from my orbs.

"Ylva!"

"Honey, run!" My mum yelled but it was abruptly cut off as someone snapped her neck. I screamed. Two large hands clamped around my arms and a fist crashed into my face. My tears streamed out as I tried to scramble away from their strong grip.

"Leave my daughter alone!" My father yelled. He grabbed the man's head and smashed it into a wall. His heartbeat decreased as my dad slaughtered him.

"Oh, honey." my dad whispered, cradling my shivering form.

"Daddy, look out!" I screamed as another man came behind him and slit his throat, "No!"

"Ylva!"

"Your parents are useless. Weak. But you are very valuable." The man grumbled. He came over and hit me over and over. Blood poured from my wounds and I struggled to breathe.

"See, you do not die." He slapped my face before tossing me away, "You will see me later in life! I will be waiting." He hissed and he ran away.

I screamed again.

"Ylva!" I looked fearfully into Ryker's worried orbs. They looked generally concerned, "What's wrong?"

With wide eyes, I look around the room, panting heavily. I could feel sweat coat my face and body and even though I was hot, my body shivered violently. Where am I? Blue walls, blackout curtains, bedside table near me.

"Yes, we are in my room, Ylva." Ryker's voice echoed in my ears. I stared at him. His voice was calming Misty, which is who I was mostly worried about. She was there when all this happened, but she blamed herself because she couldn't help me, or help our parents.

I look down to see his arm tightly wrapped around my waist. Smacking it away, I jumped out of his bed, "I told you I didn't want to sleep with you." I muttered, barely able to even put up a fight with him right now.

'You will see me later in life.' That voice echoed through my mind.

I gasped suddenly and fell towards the wall as a sudden pain shot through me. It raced through my bones, causing my mind to become dizzy and faint, "Ylva?" I heard Ryker's voice say. I stared up at him through glassy eyes until I felt something building up inside me. I jumped up and sprinted to the bathroom, emptying my insides into the toilet.

'I'll see you soon, flower.' I heard a voice say, a shiver running through me.

I slumped heavily on the floor as Ryker came in, "What happened?" He asked, squatting down next to me.

"Nothing." I say sternly, not wanting to talk about it.

How could I tell Ralph? I didn't even know if it was real or not. Who was I going to see? All I knew was that dream was real. Everything that happened in the dream, the nightmare, happened. It played out like a memory, like I was only there to watch.

I felt a sudden change in my eyes and looked at Ryker. He stared at me, his eyebrows furrowing in confusion, "Ylva... your eyes" he whispered.

I got up and looked in the mirror, letting in a sharp intake of breath. I heard Misty gasp. Looking at the girl in the mirror, her eyes were a dark, piercing hazel. I saw my orbs changing from brown, to black, then back to my original violet.

"What's happening, Ylva?"

"It doesn't matter to you!" I answered and walked out.

I knew exactly what was happening. Nathaniel had told me of this. I know I said I was a werewolf and a hybrid, but there's a secret I never tell anyone. The reason why I'm a hybrid.

The truth be it, I was actually a Lycus. I know, that sounds like Lycan but they are two very different things. Lycan's are wolves who are generally stronger than the average wolf. They are a full wolf. I was part werewolf, part human, part vampire - I hate my genetics so much. I looked at the date on my phone: 19th October, a week before my birthday.

I sighed and walked to the door. Before I could get there, I was pinned against the wall.

"You are my mate and it's my job to make sure you are okay." He growled lowly, "What's wrong?"

I glared at him. His eyes were stormy grey... I guess his wolf didn't like what I was ignoring him. I couldn't get away, he had my arms pinned beside my head, "Nothing is wrong. Just another day in my fucked up life. Leave me alone, go fuck your girlfriend. I hope she doesn't find out I was sleeping with you!" Misty growled lowly in my mind.

Using my hybrid (and vampire) strength, I shoved him away. He tripped back and growled at me, "Don't push me away, I know you love me." he hissed. Damn it, his wolf was in control.

"Oh really, what if I don't love you?" I replied with a smirk. Ryker's eyes blacked.

'What the fuck are you saying! Don't make Raiden angry.' Misty yelled.

'Who's Raiden?'

'Ryker's wolf.' she answered.

"Then we'll have to change that then, won't we?" Raiden snarled.

"Well, Raiden," I hissed his name, "You have a brunette mutt whose outside your door!" I ran over and opened the door. Katie fell in and toppled over, growling out.

"Here Raiden, here's your little friend to have fun with again!" I smirked. As I walked down and into the kitchen, an annoying arm wrapped around my waist.

"What part of 'leave me alone' don't you not get?" I huffed.

"I just wanted to tell you, the only person I will be having fun with, is you. And when I do, you'll never want to leave my room." I felt a kiss on the marking spot of my neck.

"Don't you dare." I warned, trying to pull away. But he uses his Alaric strength and kept me in my place.

"In due time." I felt him smirk against my skin before my back became cold. Raiden had gone. I blew out a shaky breath before making breakfast. I took my iPod out my pocket - it still happened to be in their through everything! I switched on a song and listened.

I was half through making my breakfast when one of my favourite songs came on. I tried not to want to sing, but failed. Besides, who can't resist singing along to a good jam?

This is not a Game, now,Nobody can save you.Spent up all your change and,Now your turn is done.

OhWe won't be afraid, Cause we're the ones who make you.Knock you out the frame,We won't stop until your gone.

Game on!

I pranced around the kitchen like a crazy lady, making up my pancakes. I sit down to eat them, humming to the rest, "Luna?" Someone asked.

I choked on my food and looked down at the little girl who was standing beside me, "Uh, yeah?" I asked, not being a fan of younger children. What if she starts crying... what do I do?

"You have a pretty voice." she smiled.

"I-uh. Thanks... but I am not your Luna." I knelt down to her level.

"But your Alpha Ryker's mate, aren't you?" She questioned, tilting her head.

"Yes but, I am not your Luna."

"Why?"

"Because your Alpha likes someone else." I muttered with a small sneer.

"What was that, Luna?" I fought the urge to growl when she called me Luna. I am not a Luna.

"Nothing, you should head back to your Mum, she might be worried about you" I sighed.

"I don't have a Mummy" she whimpered. Oh, good going, Ylva!

"Why?"

"She was killed in a rouge attack. I have my Daddy though." she smiled a bit.

"Oh, well you should get back to him." I suggested.

"Okay... bye Luna." She wandered off.

This time, I did growl out...loudly.

Nine • The Good, The Bad and the Okay I Guess

Chapter Nine———

Ylva

I was quick to run out the back door. Sprinting towards the trees, I allowed Misty control before shifting into my wolf. I had to shift, my wolf was roaring to be let out. She raced off into the mists of the early morning, listening to the birds tweet at the crack of dawn.

I've been here a week. A whole damn week. I've made a few friends, and one that is most important.

I wandered through the halls of the empty house. Everyone either was out training, patrolling or hunting. I entered door after door, just trying to find a flipping bathroom! I ended up walking into some couple's room and trust me - I did not need to see that!

I was suddenly knocked down, my head hitting the wall beside me.

"Oh my gosh! I'm so sorry, I didn't mean to!" A soft female voice whimpered.

I looked up and saw a ginger haired coloured girl, tears pouring from her forest green eyes.

"It's okay... Are you okay?" I asked, jumping up and pulling her up with me.

"Y-Yes, I am." she tried to firmly say, but her voice was wobbly and delicate.

"No, you're not."

She looked at me, "Luna?" She asked.

"No, I am not a Luna. Please, call me Ylva." I said, pulling her towards the stairs and into the kitchen.

"But your Alpha Ryker's mate, right?" The redhead asked.

"Yes, but-"

"No it's okay, I understand - you do not trust him yet." she smiled.

"Very observant." I gawked at her. "How did you...?"

"My mum went through the same thing as you."

"Oh." I answered. Misty was yelling 'Amista, Amista'... each wolf has a person whose their best friend. Its a bit like their mate but you don't love them like that. They can feel some of your pain and you can always trust them with anything. They can either be your greatest ally or your worst enemy.

"Amista?" She asked.

"Yeah, seems like it." I smiled. Her green eyes lit up and I chuckled, there are so many weird worded things for werewolves.

"What's your name?"

"Maisy." she brought me into a hug.

She never told me why she was crying, but I'll find it out soon. Yeah, she was my Amista. Maisy was a small Dania wolf. A Dania is a werewolf whose position in the pack is just above an Omega.

'Hello!' I froze, looking around wearily at the voice that cracked through my head.

'Misty?' I called, freaking out slightly.

'Hey! We have a new friend!' She smirked.

'What?' I am beyond confused.

'Well, because your vampire side has come out, the vampire in you has too!' She answers excitedly.

'Hello!' The voice yells happily.

'Uhh. Hey?'

'Hi, I'm Lucine. It means moon. I am the vmpire in you. Like Misty, I am always with you and can always talk to you!'

Great, another annoying voice in my head. Isn't one enough?

'Cool, but why am I a werewolf then?" I asked, intrigued.

'Because the werewolf part of you is stronger, idiot' Misty remarks. 'And now that your talking to both of us, we can have full on discussions about how Ryker is so handsome.'

'Yeah, that's not happening.' I told her.

'So, Lucine, how do you feel about Ryker?' Misty snickered as I groaned.

Lucine smiled, 'I think he's great! Like werewolves, vampires need mates as well. Ryker is made for all of us, because he's a Alaric.' Her eyes went droopy and she smiled longingly.

'Oh, brother. Someone save me. Am I the only one who sees Ryker as annoying, extremely irritating and that he fucks another girl?' I questioned, rolling my eyes.

'Yes!' They both yelled. I just sighed and shut them out. They can discuss him to their heart's content now.

I reached a lake and sat down, gulping up some of the water. I groaned. Was Ryker really ours, mine? I knew his wolf could be deadly, what if he hurt me? I needed to see my family. They were probably worried sick.

I wonder if they were scared about were I was? I needed a phone. A phone... I ran back to the house, Misty and Lucine going crazy at the smell of their mate. I growled and made a detour, running over to the Beta.

"Hey!" I smiled, slumping down on the sofa next to him and his mate, Gracie.

"What's up?" He asked.

"The sky. Can I borrow your phone?" I asked quickly, looking at him with puppy eyes.

Gracie growled playfully. We were good friends, she knew I would never try anything with Reece. He was more like a brother to me.

He curiously raised an eyebrow, "Why?"

"Just please, can I borrow your phone!" I whined.

"Oh for peets sake, give her the phone, baby." Gracie smirked before digging in his pocket and pulling out his phone.

"Hey!" He mumbled. Gracie just smirked, kissed him and typed in his password before passing it to me.

"Thanks." I smirked before going to the phone book. I typed in a number and drew a deep breath. Twiddling with the hem of my borrowed shirt, I waited for the phone to be picked up.

"Hello?" I heard Faith's voice echo down the phone line.

"David Guetta is Aden's God." I stated, tears building up in me from happiness. Gracie and Reece sent we a weird look but I simply shrugged them off.

"Ylva?" She whispered.

"Yeah."

"Oh my God! Where have you been? We thought something happened to you! Ylva, where are you? Are you okay? Are you safe? Where did you go?" She rambled on, but I could hear the happiness laced in her voice.

"I found him." I interrupted and she stopped.

"Y-You found your mate?" Faith asked.

"Yep."

"Well, who is he? Is he nice? Good looking? Have you marked yet, mated yet?"

"What! Eww, no!" I growled.

"Well then, who is he?" Faith asked. This is the time I could basically see her jumping up and down, begging for an answer.

"He's... He's..." I couldn't say his name. What would she say? She told me to stay away from this territory and now here I was, about to tell her who my mate is.

"Yes..." Faith said impatiently.

"He's Alpha Ryker."

"Okay, first, wow an Alpha!" She squeal before continuing, "And secondly, what pack?" Faith asked confused obviously.

"Golden Raven." I whispered.

"WHAT!" her voice roared through the phone, "I told you to stay away from there!"

"Look, I'm sorry, I got lost and I don't know but I had a fight with his Beta when he thought me a rouge and then I found him when I came to his pack house." I rambled quickly.

The end of the phone line was silent, Faith taking in all this information, "Well, I'm happy for you!" she answered eventually.

"And Faith..." I called uneasily.

"Yeah?"

"That side came through." I gulped. Only my family and I knew about it. It was the one thing I refused to talk about with anyone.

"Oh." was all she answered before a shuffling sound echoed through.

"Ylva?" Nathaniel's voice came through.

"Hello, uncle." I smiled slightly.

"Oh my God. I'm so glad you are okay! Sunbrooke and I have been worried sick! Faith told me you found your mate and who he was. Don't worry, he'll protect you. And...you came through?" He sighed.

"Yes."

"Well, I'm going to call Ryker in a minute, asking him if I can come over. I need to tell you a lot!"

"Wait, what... no, don't please just don't!" I shout out, not wanting him to see my mate and what an ass he really was. The couple beside me jumped at my sudden outburst, now watching as I talked on the phone.

"Nonsense! I am coming to see you Ylva, whether Mr Big Bad Alpha likes it or not!" And the line went dead.

I sighed, "Thanks." I passed the phone back to Reece and walked up to bed.

As soon as my face fell on the pillow I slipped off to sleep. But just before I did, the bed dipped and a strong arm wrapped protectively around my waist. I was too tired to knock him off, so I just left it for now.

Ten • The Game of Trust

C hapter Ten———

Ryker

I laid next to my mate, the steady sound of her breathing calmed me and my wolf, 'I love her so much.' he whispered, staring down admirly at our mate. Leave it to the wolf to fall too fast.

Her dark, blonde hair flowed down her back, naturally curled at the ends; slightly knotted from having turning around a lot during the night. I could get lost into her violet eyes that had seen so much pain and hurt. They were like none I'd ever seen before - then again, she was the first hybrid I'd seen for a while.

And that personality - wow. Her sarcastic attitude and strong will, that was something I wasn't expecting. When the prison guard told me that a rouge had been brought into my territory, they are often weak and damaged. Sure, Ylva was both of those things, but she was quick to show me that she could take care of herself.

I knew something had gone on in her past. All of that anger she held and those nights where she had awakened screaming had to be because of something. But something about Ylva was blocking me from the past of her mind. I could only smell scents on her, whereas on someone else, I could read them, maybe find out a little of their life. Ylva was hiding something from Raiden and I. It bugged us, knowing that she'd probably never tell us.

I stiffened when she made a small whimper, thinking that she was having another nightmare. But she snuggled deeper into me. I smiled slightly.

'I love her too.' I answered Raiden.

'So...when are we gonna do it?' God dammit. It's been just over a week and Raiden has been going crazy about making Ylva ours. Marking her.

'Not yet... she would hate us. You know she doesn't trust us yet.'

Raiden whimpered slightly then growled, 'Yeah cause that bitch messes it up.'

I could tell by the sound if his voice it was Katie he was talking about. There is nothing going on between that she-wolf and I. Yeah, okay, I admit we may have done things a few times but I didn't enjoy it because she wasn't mine.

I had found Katie as a rouge, battered and bruised. She was hurt, so I took her in. She told me she had come from a pack that had been taken over by rouges and they abused the girls and continuously trained the males for war, so she ran. She begged me to stay. Even though it was hard to bring a rouge into the pack, my sister's best friend loved her.

Because they were all great friends, my sister had whined at me to let her stay. I gave in, but Katie took over and pushed my sister around. Now she is always quiet, they did something to her. She would never tell me and I never forced her too. I told her I could kick the rouge out, but she simply shook her head, saying that she didn't want to be a bother. I hated Katie after that and ignored her.

'Yeah, I hate her too.' Raiden growled again but then purred slightly, 'Our mate has some skills.' He smirked happily.

Damn right she did. So much possessiveness was travelling through her and her wolf earlier. And the way she fought against that blonde haired boy was great. It showed me she didn't want anyone touching her. And she hit me in the face - twice. Now, usually, that would result in me attacking them, but what shocked me most was that it was my mate. She really did have a mean right hook.

Ylva was playing a game with me. The game of trust. I knew she didn't fully trust me, but sometimes she was okay around me. Like now.

Her singing this morning was beautiful. Her voice was delicate and in tune, even without the actual song in the background. I heard her talking to my Beta's, Reece, younger sister. She growled lowly when Laura said the word Luna.

I sighed. She was my mate, the packs Luna. We need her, I need her.

I was interrupted from my thought by a phone call. I sat up, gently pushing Ylva onto her pillow and answered the phone, "Hello?"

"Hello, is this Alpha Ralph of the Golden Raven pack?" A male voice answers.

"Yes, who is speaking?"

"This is Nathaniel Endrin from the Blue Ice pack."

I growled slightly before firmly stating, "I don't want to speak with anyone from that pack."

"Wait, wait, please, just can I talk to you? Its really important!" Nathaniel begged.

I sighed, "Okay, you have ten minutes."

"Thank you." He sounded very relieved. Why?

"What would you talk to me about?"

"Well, you see, your mate, is my niece. Ylva. We are very worried about her back here and-"

"How did you know she was here?" I growled.

"Ylva called me. Please, don't be angry at her. I was just wondering if we could possibly see her?"

I sighed again. Ylva would want to see her family, right? "And why would you like to do that? You know that your Alpha and I do not get along well."

"Alpha Ryker, we understand how protective you are of her, but I asure you, we are not going to harm her or take her back. We would like to because Ylva is family, and we miss her. I also need to speak to her about her hybrid." his voice decreased at the last part.

"What about her hybrid? It seems perfectly fine." I answered.

"Yes, well, there are, um, other parts of it that Y-Ylva needs to know about." he stuttered slightly, informing me he is either lying to me or worried about telling me the truth.

"What other parts?" I growl slightly.

"Please, Alpha Ryker, I really do need to see her. I will get her to tell you. Please, I'm begging you." he pleas.

I can hear the concern and worry behind his voice. I immediately tense up for some unknown reason. The thought of our mate hiding something from us, lying to us maybe.

"Very well." I answer.

'What the fuck! We need to know what's wrong with our mate!' Raiden yells.

'Just shut up and listen!' I growl back ignoring him

"Really Alpha?" Nathaniel answers, shocked.

"Yes, only if I can speak to you as soon as you get here!"

The other end of the line is quiet, like he is debating whether or not to tell me. It must be a big secret if he has to hesitate, "Yes Alpha, as long as you are understanding." he replies with a sigh.

"Fine. You can come on the 21st. You may stay as long as you like. How many if you are coming?"

"Only four Alpha. Thank you so much." Nathaniel thanked.

"No problem, I will tell my border to let you through." I answer.

"Thank you again Alpha Ryker, see you in a few days." He ends the call.

I stare back at my beloved mate. She rested against me, her light body, not even taking up a quarter of the bed. She was so small and adorable. I would love her forever, even if she didn't love me.

I got up and undressed, slipping under the covers in my boxers and pulled Ylva close.

"What secrets are you hiding?" I whispered, more to myself than her. I inhaled the scent I came to love before drifting off with Ylva in my arms. The way it should be.

Eleven • Who Puts Ketchup in the Fridge?

Chapter Eleven———

Ylva

I woke up, wrapped in arms. Of course, Misty and Lucine were far from unhappy. Huffing, I shoved them, much to their dismay. I'm hungry. Yeah, that's what I think. I just woke up, wrapped in arms, had a conversation yesterday with my family and I think about food!

I chuckled slightly before changing into some shorts and a t-shirt. I also picked out one of Ralph's jumpers because I was cold. I was cold! As quietly as possible, I snuck out the room and padded downstairs, raiding the kitchen cupboards.

'Maybe we should make the pack something?' Misty said.

'What? No!' I answered.

'Yes! You are their Luna after all!' Lucine decided to join the conversation. I sighed. I am NOT their Luna.

'Are you two ganging up against me or something?'

'No, just making the flipping food!' Misty hissed.

'Fine. I will for you two!' I growled before plugging in my iPod to a speaker, allowing it to play on its own accord.

Searching through the fridge, I looked for anything to make a fry up with. Butter, ketchup - do you put ketchup in the fridge? Bingo. I have found the bacon. I tore the packet open and fished a saucepan out the cupboard, placing it on the heat and putting the bacon in to sizzle.

I cracked some eggs into another pan before looking for some hashbrowns. I found them under everything in the freezer. Tipping them on a tray I stuck them in the oven and switched it on.

One of my favourite songs came on. Don't sing. I mentally yelled to myself.

'Sing!' Lucine eagerly encourage.

No. Don't song. Don't sing. Don't sing.

'Flipping sing, wussy!' Misty shouted and I sung. She happened to make me sing as well. Wolves always make you do things you don't want to do.

"All hands on the trigger.All eyes on the gun.They don't believe that we're..Strong enough to hold on. "

"Cause I'm the only one to get you," I flinched as Maisy came up beside me, singing as well. Her voice was amazing! She grinned when she saw me watching.

"The only one to figure you out," I sung along with her as she helped me make breakfast.

"Your a place that I can go to.A face I couldn't live without.And nobody sees what we do.We don't need anybody else around.

No matter what they told us.Gravity won't hold us down."

Maisy sung the instrumental while I carried on making breakfast. The smell of bacon filled my nose making my stomach growl in anticipation. Maisy laughed.

"Even gravity can't hold us.Even gravity can't hold us down.Even gravity can't hold us.Not even gravity can't hold us down.

Cause I'm the only one to get you.The only one to figure you out.Your a place that I can go to.Your a face I couldn't live without.

And nobody sees what we do.Don't need anybody else around.Cause no matter what they told us.Gravity can't hold us down.

Can't understand the logic.Of how we came to be.Or what we're gaining from it.But we should be able to dream.

Cause I'm the only one to get you.The only one to figure you out.And there's nothing left to go throughJust look at where we are right now.

They'll never see it in the way we do.Cause they'd never have what we have found.It don't matter what they told us.Gravity won't hold us down!"

Maisy and I continued to sing to the words, rotating and dancing around the kitchen - which probably isn't the safest thing to do considering all the food. I noticed a small crowd of the pack come out to the kitchen. They probably smelt the food. But they were bopping up and down, dancing to the rhythm of the song.

I dished up the bacon into a bowl and placed some eggs on a plate. The hashbrowns were cooling so I put a load of beans on to cook before searching for some more sauce. Aha! Brown, red, BBQ - all still in the fridge. Who puts sauce in the fridge? But still - perfect. I set them down on the table and placed the bacon and eggs in the middle. Maisy set out some plates and cups, soon followed by a jug of juice.

I toasted some bread and bagels and buttered them. Stacking them up on top of each other, I placed them on the table as well. I turned off the beans, pouring them into a bowl and finding a place for them.

"Even gravity can't hold us down.Can't hold us down.Can't hold us down. Oh.Now..."

When the song finished there was a huge roar of cheering. Maisy and I flinched, our faces turning bright red. Turning, I saw more than a little group of people. Almost like half the pack were standing behind the table watching us. Some of them where eyeing up the food, looking hungry.

'I hate being centre of attention.' Maisy whispered through our link.

'Same. I hate people hearing my voice.' I blushed deeper.

'Same.' - best friend conversations people.

"I, er...bon appetite?" I tried to smile, putting on my best French accent and pointing to the food on the table.

They all eagerly sat down and began digging in. A few said 'thank you Luna' I which they received a small growl from me. I am NOT their Luna.

'The time is coming, my dear.' a voice filled my head, breaking me from the heart warming sight. Who the hell said that? It was no one I knew of. Who was-

I was knocked from thoughts when arms wrapped tightly around my waist. I jumped in surprise and tingles erupted through me. A small chuckle erupted from my mate behind, causing Lucine and Misty to go lovey eyed. I rolled my eyes at them.

"You have a beautiful voice, Ylva." he kissed my neck, causing my breathing to hitch.

"I, er, um thanks?" It came out more like a question than an answer.

"Maybe you could sing for me some time?" he smirked against my skin.

What does he- HELL NO! He is so rude! Ew... how can he even, ugh, idiot.

'Our idiot.' Misty spoke.

Then Lucine added, 'Our hot, sexy-'

'No!' I shouted at them, "Haha, no... very funny, just, just no." I gently tapped him and pushed away.

"Oh, I need to speak to you." He growled slightly, making me curious as to what he wanted to speak to me with.

"Really? About...?"

"Nathaniel." I tensed and stared up at him with wide eyes.

"But, how-how do you know my uncle's name?" I crossed my arms, demanding an answer.

"He called. Your family are coming in two days." Ryker replied.

My heart was thudding against my chest... he could probably hear it.

"How did you call him?" Ryker asked, raising an eyebrow.

"I, uh, used Reece's phone..." I mumbled, looking down. I didn't really want to get his Beta in trouble but Ryker would've found out anyway.

A finger lifted up my chin and I made eye contact with my mate and his dreamy - Misty - green eyes, "Why didn't you ask me?"

I looked around, noticing we were still in the kitchen and everyone was staring at us. I grabbed Ryker's hand, ignoring the sparks that flied and dragged him into the hall. Staring at the floor, I answered, "I-I didn't think you would let me." Damn, why did I stutter?

"Why wouldnt I?" He placed his hands either side of me against the wall, moving closer to me. I do not need to be caged.

'I am not an anima- oh wait, yes I am.' Misty snickered.

'Shut up, Misty.'

"Because you don't like my Alpha." I answer trying to compose my tense posture from his closeness.

"So? It's your family, not your Alpha." He sighed.

"Well, I just... I don't know" I sighed too and looked back at the ground.

"Please give me a chance." he asked. What did he mean by that? "Please give us a chance." Ryker looked me in the eyes.

"I-" Should I? I've seen so much pain in my small life. I have three sides of me, me, my wolf and my vampire. I haven't even told Ryker about my vampire side yet!

I thought for a bit more. 'Please!' Lucine and Misty begged.

I let out a sigh and looked into those forest eyes, "I promise you, there is nothing going on between Katie and I." Ryker continued.

"Okay." I answered. His tense body relaxed and he smiled at me, "As long as you promise me you'll always be mine." I growled.

"I'm all yours baby, all yours." He smirked, obviously liking the possessive side of me.

And with that, he gripped my hips, pressing me closer to the wall and moved his body closer to mine. Ryker's hot breath fanned against my lips before sparks flied as our lips collided. I closed my eyes, moving my lips with his. My hands made their way instinctively to his hair, messing it up. He pushed me even closer to the wall, gently nipping at my lip with his teeth. I allowed entrance and his tongue slipped in.

Perfect match. Lucine and Misty howled and hissed in delight. Our bodies perfect together.

"By the way," I pulled back and frowned, "Who puts ketchup in the fridge?"

Ryker chuckled, whispering, "God, you're so perfect." And he kissed me again.

Twelve • Y is for Ylva is Not What She Appears to Be

C hapter Twelve———

Ylva

Today was the day Nathaniel, Sunbrooke, Faith and Aden were coming to visit. It was just gone 10 o'clock and I had over heard Ryker notifying his patrollers to let them through the boarder, so they should be here in about thirty minutes. And I... was still in bed!

"Hey, baby." I heard Ryker whisper, laying over me. "Come on, wake up."

I peeked open an eye to see Ryker's green orbs staring down at me. I quickly shut my eye tightly before a grin spread across my face, "I saw that." I could feel him smirk. "Come on, your family are gonna be here in a minute."

I sighed out, trying to pretend I was asleep. A squeal suddenly left my lips and I burst out in fits of laughter as two hands clamped down on my sides and tickled me, "So, you are awake!" he smirked and raised an eyebrow playfully, "And ticklish!" He continued to tickle me.

"S-stop! R-Ryker! Please." I begged.

"Fine. Only cause you begged." He laughed and stopped my next comment by stealing a kiss of my lips.

Pulling him in closer, I grabbed his hair, a groan to leaving him. Our lips moved in sync and moulded together perfectly. I pushed him away breathlessly and smirked up at him. Ryker pouted, "Payback, huh?"

"Paybacks a bitch." I grinned.

"Come on, get ready. Otherwise I'll make sure you stay in that bed." he winked before leaving me with wide eyes. Misty and Lucine purred at the thoughts. Gross.

But the warmth of his body leaving soon made Lucine and Misty whine. What a shame! I mentally laughed and wandered to the walk-in walldrope. I wandered over to the girls side, that happened to be filled by Gracie and Maisy, and pulled out a t-shirt and some shorts, nicking one of Ryker's jumper that I loved. Mainly so I was always surrounded by his scent and it made me feel safe.

I was combing my hair when I smelt my family nearby. Tears welled and a rush happiness came over me. I raced down the stairs, following their scent until I saw them.

"Ylva!" I heard Faith call, crushing me into a hug.

"Faith!" I exclaimed, hugging her back. We stayed like this for a few more seconds before we pulled away.

"I was so worried about you!" She looked into my eyes, her own had tears in them.

"I know. I'm sorry." I wrapped her in another hug before going to my aunt.

"Sunbrooke!" I smiled. She clasped me close. Her hug was almost like my mothers, but my mum's was softer and her scent made me feel more safe. But that doesn't matter now, this is my family. Sunbrooke has always made me feel protected in the house and around the pack.

"Oh, Ylva! Where have you been? I was terrified something had happened to you." she mumbled, kissing my forehead.

"What's up, man?" Aden interrupted.

I grinned, "The sky?"

"I think you mean David Guetta!" He responded with a laugh.

I gave him an 'are you serious' look and he just shrugged. Fist bumping him, we pulled each other into a bear hug. There was a slight growl behind me and I jumped to see Ryker standing there, his fists balled.

I rolled my eyes at him, "Oh relax, he's my cousin!" I touched his arm, immediately calming him.

"Someone's got possessive issues." I heard Aden mutter, causing me to snicker.

"Alpha." my family greeted, bowing their heads in respect.

Ryker nodded back and his eyes locked on my uncle. "May I speak with you, Nathaniel?" Ryker asked, more like ordered, him. Nathaniel hesitantly nodded before walking over to me.

"I'm happy you're safe and in good hands." He whispered before wandering to Ryker's office.

I raised an eyebrow at my family when my mate left.

"They're just sorting some stuff out." Sunbrooke gave a weak smile, but I knew there was something more to it than that. However, I just shrugged it off... for the minute anyway.

"So... how have you been?" Asked Faith as we walked into the kitchen to get a couple of drinks.

"Fine, I guess." I shrugged opening the fridge.

"And how is he?" Faith nudged me with her arm, wiggling her eyebrows.

I rolled my eyes at her and sighed, "I don't know... okay for the minute." I sat on one of the islands and stared into space.

"What happened?" Faith asked, leaning next to me.

"Well, he has this bitch that follows him, Katie. I can say they have done it in the past because of the way she looks at him. But, I've decided to give him a chance."

"Wow. Don't let her get in the way of your mate. You belong together and there's nothing she can do about it." Faith shrugged.

"You really have a way with words. The other day, I thought me and Ryker didn't belong together." I sighed, taking a gulp of my water.

"Yeah, I know." She laughed. "And how's - you know... the other side?" She gave me a knowing look.

"She's okay. I have another voice in my head with her now."

Faith's eyes widened, "What's her name?"

"Lucine."

"Can I see her?" Faith pleaded.

"Okay, quickly though because Ryker doesn't know." Faith nodded her head and I closed my eyes.

'Lucine. Faith wants to see you.'

'Hell yeah! New people!' I mentally laughed at her.

My eyes changed to their glowing brown and I looked at Faith.

"Hey, Lucine!" Faith smiled.

"Hey, Faith!"

"So... how do you like Ryker?" She asked.

"I love him! He's so handsome and cute." She squealed and I rolled my eyes at her.

"Wow, your completely different to Ylva. I feel like you and Misty will get along though!" Faith laughed.

'Come back now Lucine.' I told her.

"Well, Ylva wants to come back now. So, see ya later!" She did a peace sign before switching with me.

My eyes cleared back to their original violet colour, "You two will fit together perfectly!" We shared a laugh.

Ryker

"So? What was so important that you needed to come here for?" Nathaniel flinched under my tone, clearly not wanting to say it.

"Well... it's something about Ylva. She's...not all she appears to be." he replied, looking down to the floor.

Not all she appears to be? What the hell does that mean?

"She's a hybrid she-wolf... Correct?" I spoke.

"Yes..." He paused, fiddling with his thumbs, debating on whether to tell me or not.

"Yes?" I needed to know. When things like this happen, I am not good with patience.

"Ylva is part of something else. Her mother, my sister-in-law, was part of this too, because her grandmother was one." Nathaniel said, finally looking up at me with worry.

"Why do I not like the fact that worry has crossed your face?" I crossed my arms, staring at him, trying to read him. Nothing.

"Because you probably won't like it." He sighed, rubbing the back if his neck nervously. I could hear his heart rate pick dramatically.

"Please, do tell what I will not like." I answered, annoyed with his slow talking.

"Okay but please be open minded that it was not Ylva's fault.... she hardly knows what she is either, but I do." Nathaniel looked at me again.

"Okay. Tell me." I demanded. Raiden was on edge, desperate to know what Ylva was hiding.

I saw Nathaniel take an uneasy breath before he spoke. "Ylva's a Lycus."

Thirteen • Vampire History is Better Than Werewolf History

C hapter Thirteen———

Ryker

"SHE'S A WHAT!?" I yelled, anger clearly laced in my voice.

"A Lycus." Nathaniel answered more confidently.

"Holy shit." I breathed, running my hands through my hair. This does explain a lot more...

"That's why it was so improtant for me to come today. It's her birthday in under a week, she needs to know the history of her family." Nathaniel swallowed down his fear, now answering everything easily.

'Damn...why-how is Ylva a Lycus?' My wolf growled. 'Why the fuck didn't she tell us!'

'She was probably afraid.' I told him. Raiden was still on edge but calmed slightly.

"Why wouldn't she tell me this?" I asked her uncle who was standing there, watching me for any sudden reactions. But no, it wasn't her fault.

"She was probably afraid you would reject her, Alpha Ryker." Nathaniel admitted, "She doesn't know much about it herself. Ylva's never been one to trust easily."

"I wouldn't ever reject! She's all I need!" I growled at him.

He took a step back, "I understand that Alpha, but Ylva doesn't know that. Put yourself in her shoes. She doesn't know anyone else except her Mother who is dead that was a Lycus!" Nathaniel told me.

'I wouldn't ever reject her. Maybe she didn't trust us because of that BITCH!' My wolf shouted, authority in his voice, 'I was never the one who wanted to sleep with her in the first place.'

'Don't blame me for all of this. I don't want to hear any more about Katie. I want nothing to do with her.' I grumbled.

"May I speak with my niece now?" Nathaniel asked, clearly desperate to get away from the tension of the room.

"Yes, but I will be listening in." I growled. I knew he really didn't want me to listen, but there was nothing he could say against an Alpha.

"Very well, Alpha." Nathaniel answered and took off out of the office to find Ylva.

Ylva

I was talking to Sunbrooke when Nathaniel walked into the lounge, "Ylva, may I speak to you, privately." He asked.

"Uh, sure." I signaled for him to follow me out the back, facing towards the training field.

We sat down, watching some of the younger ones train. Nathaniel's posture seemed tense and his eyes flickered between black and brown. This usually only happened when he was either worried, or his wolf was on edge.

"So... what's up?" I asked. He finally looked at me but he still seemed a bit hesitant.

"Ylva, you have become a full Lycus now, you should know about some of the history." He rubbed the back of his neck nervously.

"Uh... Okay?" I raised an eyebrow. Lucine and Misty were listening in carefully to our conversation when Nathaniel started to begin.

"Your mother, " He started and my body was already tense. The mention of her always did, "She was a very independent lady, never wanted anyone to hurt you. If you were older back then, you would have seen how many people she killed to protect you." Nathaniel looked at me.

"What do you mean?" I asked.

"At the age of eight, you began to smell a mix of both vampire and werewolf together. As you grew into a teenager it went away. You smell like werewolf now because it was uncertain if your were going to be more werewolf or more vampire."

Misty and Lucine were now glued to the conversation.

"As you know, your grandmother was a vampire and your grandfather was a wolf. The council didn't know it was possible to have a child with both vampire and werewolf genes at that time but your mother was born."

"When your mother and father met, your father didn't know whether to accept your mother or not. But when she became pregnant with you, he marked her and accepted her as his own. When you were born, you had blue hair and your eyes were more purple than violet."

Nathaniel brought a photo with a tear along the left side. On the image was a picture of a baby on it. That was me? My hair was multiple shades of blue and my eyes were a dark purple. How?

"It was because of your vampire and wolf side. But your dad was a Beta." My head shot up to look at Nathaniel with shock.

My Dad was a Beta?

"Yes Ylva, he was a Beta. So it made the wolf gene stronger. But both your parents knew they had to protect you more than themselves. Your mother had a gift; she had visions. I don't know whether you do or not but your mother did. So on that night that your parents left you for a while, she came to me, where she had a vision. She told me someone was after you, they wanted your power. Then she screamed and shifted into her wolf. Your father followed." Nathaniel explained.

"Your father mind linked me, telling me someone was surrounding your house. While your mother went inside, your dad fought some of the men. But it wasn't enough. When your mother was killed, half of him died inside. The last thing he said to me was to protect you." Nathaniel looked at me. Sorrow, guilt and uncertainty was covering his eyes.

"Why didn't you tell me this before?" I asked.

"You weren't of age. Your parents came to me in a dream. They told me they would never rest until you knew and the guy that hurt you was killed. When your birthday comes, you should be able to talk to your mother."

I was lost for words.

'Hell yeah! Vampire history! Better than werewolf history all the time!' Lucine yelled happily.

'Nope! Werewolf history is always better!' Misty hissed.

'Is not!'

'Is too!'

I blocked them out. All they were doing was arguing.

"That's why your voice when you sing is so angelic. It's a power. It can't really stop anything, it's just beautiful." He smiled at me.

'Do you know of any other powers we have?' I asked Misty.

'Uhh... no, ask Nathaniel.'

"Nathaniel, do I have any other powers?"

He thought for a moment, "Well, you should be able to speak to your mum, your fighting skills will always be stronger, but other than than, I have no idea. You must find your powers within yourself."

I stared at the ground. I had powers. I was an Alpha's mate, and that Alpha was an Alaric wolf. Would I be even stronger? I looked around the training area. A few pack members were out here. Some of them smiled and nodded my way, I nodded back politely.

I am not their Luna, no matter what Ryker says. I am not good enough - the first day I came here I was in a fight with another pack member! What kind of example is that? I sighed slightly before talking again, "Would I be stronger if I had an Alaric for a mate?" I asked staring Nathaniel dead into his eyes. His eyes widened and I silently nodded.

"Well, I don't know. Maybe, I guess. I'm not really sure."

I sighed again. What would Ryker think if this? I was so afraid to tell him, I didn't want to be rejected with nowhere to go, "Do you want a drink?" I asked Nathaniel.

"No I'm okay but we can go back inside if you like?" I nodded and walked back inside.

Entering the kitchen, I froze, 'I'm sorry. I told him. He's an Alpha, I can't refuse to him.' was all I got from Nathaniel. Ryker stared at me, his arms crossed. His expression was blank and I couldn't tell whether he was glaring at me or if he was happy. His eyes were flickering different colours. My body trembled in fear. I swallowed thickly, sprinted outside and shifted.

Fourteen • Don't Touch the Butt

C hapter Fourteen———

Ylva

I kept running, my paws thudding along the muddy ground, dirt splashing up against my clean fur. It didn't take long for me to recognise the strong pounding of Ryker following behind, quickly gaining on me.

I quickly shot my head around to see an Alpha on my tail. Was he angry? I really couldn't tell but I didn't want to stop to find out. I've heard being rejected is one of the worst pains you could possibly imagine and I don't think I'm ready for that yet. I pushed myself faster, with the help of Misty and Lucine.

'Why are you helping?' I gasped for air, racing forward.

'Because we are just as scared as you.' Lucine replied sharply.

'I don't know how he'll react. I'm afraid he'll reject us!' Misty whimpered.

Continuing forwards, the trees were just a blur past me and the other pack members looked at me confused and worried.

It had already been a while since I started running, the ache in my feet hurt but I continued, not wanting to hear what Ryker had to say. I was either fast enough as a hybrid to outrun an Alpha, or he was toying with me, waiting until I was tired before he pounced.

'Ylva, please stop!' He growled through my mind.

'No! I don't want to get hurt!' I whimpered speeding on.

'I'm not going to hurt you, Ylva.' he whispered back.

I quickly came to a halt at the boarder line. How fast was I running? It usually took ages to reach here, and now in under half an hour, there I was. I wasn't crossing it. I didn't want to. I didn't want to be a rouge again, get hurt again, or get attacked again.

I froze when sharp teeth picked me up by my scruff. I whimpered slightly, wriggling to get free, 'Please don't make me sleep again. It hurts.' I whimpered, frightfully.

Ryker paused and set me down, 'Do I scare you?' He titled his head.

I shook my head but my body was against me and shivered in fear.

'Please don't be afraid of me. I would never hurt you.' his calm voice echoed through, slowly walking closer.

My figure was still hunched, on the verge of submitting, my tail between my legs. I still wouldn't submit though, no matter what.

'I thought you would reject me.' I whispered.

He came to a halt and looked at me as sternly as possible in wolf form.

'Lycus or not, I don't care. You are mine and no one else's. I don't care if you are different. All I care is that you don't belong to anyone but me. You are mine!' His voice was full of love, trust and promise.

'Really?' I asked, a bit to hopefully.

'Really!' He nudged his head against my fur, sparks flying from the contact. Misty purred in satisfaction, 'Come on. Let's get back' he nudged my butt for me to move.

'Hey, hands off the butt!' I stood up and walked towards the back home.

'I'll touch what I want, mate.'

'Okay, that was Raiden.' Misty purred happily, Lucine not far behind. I felt myself suddenly being lifted up again at the scruff.

'No... put me down, you big bully!' I whined, scratching lightly against his chest. He growled lowly.

'No. It makes me feel better when I know you are with me and are safe.' He whispered, his hot breath fanning against my head.

'I'm walking right beside you!' I let my body go limp, knowing he wouldn't put me down even if I begged.

'At least set me down when we get nearer the pack house?' I asked.

'Fine.' and he took off running.

After a few minutes, the pack house came in sight and he set me down. He licked my snout and pushed me forward again, by my butt, leaving me to send him a warning glance. Some of the pack were still out here. A few women and children were having a picnic, them all laughing and having a great time. Some boys were having pretend battles with each other in wolf form, I smiled at their cute little growls.

A small girl came running up to me. She had two tiny plaits and bright brown eyes. She wore a blue flowery dress and she smiled up at me, "Hello, Luna. Please may I put this flower in your fur?" She asked polietly. Her voice was soft and gentle.

I twitched slightly at the Luna part but reluctantly nodded my head and laid on the ground. I felt her tiny little hands run through my wolf fur before a small flower was place just above my ear, "You have very pretty fur" she admired my blue and white streaked fur as she reached out to touch my chest. Her hands felt relaxing and calming.

I gently licked her nose as her mum called her. "Goodbye, Luna. I hope to see you soon!" she waved and run away. I looked to Ryker, who almost looked proud.

'She is so adorable! Who is she?' I asked, watching her play with her brother, I think.

'Shes my cousin's daughter, her name is Nora. The boy next to her is Nora's twin brother, Lee.' Ralph watched with me as the pack had fun in the sun.

"That flower suits you eyes, you know." Ryker smiled as we shifted , gripping my waist and pulling me into him. I blush slightly, resting my hands on his chest, as sparks flied.

"Thanks. But I don't really like compliments." I told him as we walked back to my family.

"Well, get used to it because your going to be getting alot from me!" He smirked, kissing my head.

We came to the living room. Nathaniel and the Beta, Reece, seemed to be having a great time talking because they were laughing like crazy. I smiled at that. Faith and Gracie seemed to get along well, Sunbrooke was laughing at them. Aden looked lost, deep in thought. And that was strange for my older cousin.

"Aden, are you okay?" I asked, walking over to him, ruffling up his neat hair.

"I, uh... yeah, yeah." he said, but there was still a distant loom in his eyes. Okay, something was definitely wrong - he never lets me mess up his hair.

I sat on the couch opposite him and Ryker sat beside me, pulling me closer to him, "I think Maisy should come down. She seems left out a lot." I sighed. She was always in her room.

"Why'd you think of her?" Ralph asked, slightly growling.

"She's my Amista." I told him.

His eyes suddenly softened in realisation, "Oh - she's my sister." he spoke proudly. I smiled at how loving he really was.

'Maisy, come down and meet my auntie, uncle and cousins.' I said through the link.

'Nah, I don't think I should... I mean - I'm not good with people and interactions so... uh, yeah.' she answered.

'No, come please! Please, Amista!' I pout, even though she couldn't see me.

'Okay, I'm coming.'

I heard footsteps along the stairs and then Maisy's scent appeared around me. Looking over, I saw her with wide eyes and fear across her face. But she wasn't looking at me. I followed her eyeline and saw them lead directly to Aden. He shot up and stood there, staring at her in admiration.

Wait a second...

I couldn't think before Aden used his wolf speed to get over to her. She was pinned up against the wall as she stared into the eyes of my cousin. Then Aden roared one word I never thought I'd hear so passionately from him, "MINE!"

Fifteen • Error: Is This a Rejection?

C hapter Fifteen ———

Ylva

Maisy and Aden?

My Amista and my cousin?

Holy... SHIT!

I looked up at them. They were perfect for each other. Aden was a strong warrior, who would protect Maisy, and Maisy was an independent girl, who had so much to offer, she just didn't know it yet.

I looked into Maisy's eyes. I was expecting to see hope, love and lust. But they were covered in fear, horror and terror. Before anyone could say anything else, she pushed Aden away with force and used her wolf speed to sprint off.

I stood up and walked over to Aden. He glared up the stairs but sadness covered his orbs. I saw him stiffen when I touched his arm. I knew what he was about to do. Aden was going to follow her.

"Aden, wait!" I shouted, just as he went to run.

Ryker grabbed his arm and held him back, growling softly but in a warning tone, "Why would she run away from me?" He looked back at me with dismay and his fists balled up.

"She has a lot going on right now." Ryker answered.

I told them I would find out what was wrong before wandering up the stairs and into the hall. I followed her scent before coming to a halt outside Maisy's door. I knocked softly, "Maisy?"

"Come in." I heard her faint voice mumble.

I walked into my room to see her pacing around, tears streaming down her face. Naturally, I walked over and pulled her into a hug. Maisy was just taller than me but her slim body was easy to hug.

"What's wrong? Why did you run?" I asked and she let's out some loud sobs.

"I thought I'd never get a mate." she whimpers, shivering, "I don't deserve him."

Maisy pulled away and sat on her bed, "Why wouldn't you deserve him? You two are made for each other." I sighed, sitting down next to her.

Maisy

I felt Ylva come sit next to me. It was nice having her around. She was always fun, always there for me; she was my Amista and our wolves got along really well. I could already see the improvement to the pack with her being around and the improvement on my brother.

And I had found my mate, Ylva's cousin. His muscly figure was glorious and mouthwatering but he was too good for me. His deep growl when I ran from him made me more scared, even my wolf was whimpering. Hetty, my wolf, was just like me. Felt as if we were nothing and didn't belong, thought that we didn't deserve a mate and we were terrified to meet him after what that she-wolf did to us.

I stared at Ylva, she was giving me a knowing look that only Amista's could give. I ran a hand through my hair nervously, tears still spilling.

"B-Before you came, there was this girl, she's still here. Ryker found her as a rouge and brought her back. She told him that she had been part of a group of girls that had been abused when her pack got taken over by rouges. My old best friend adored her. They got along almost instantly and soon I was in the mix. Since we were all good friends, I begged Ryker to let her stay. Her name was-"

"Katie." My Amista finishes. I saw Ylva stiffen and growl out lowly.

I raised an eyebrow, curiously, "You know her?"

"Yeah, she's the bitch Ryker had an intimate relationship with and the one I, well Misty, threatened." Ylva snarled.

"You have to tell me about it sometime." I laughed.

"It was a great day," she smirked a bit before turning her attention quickly back to me, "Sorry, please continue."

She'll make a great Luna. Hetty howled in agreement.

"Well, when Katie was fit and well, she joined the pack and our little friendship group. But it was obvious the rouges had given her a bad side.

Katie started to pick on me a lot, calling me weak and pathetic for an Alpha's sister. It was then I realised she was only swarming around me to get my brother." I sighed.

"One evening, we all went out for a night. I didn't really want to go but my best friend begged me to and I reluctantly went along. When we came back from a club, we were all a bit tipsy. S-She gripped my arm and roughly dragged me towards someone's van. She yelled, 'here's the one you want!' And threw me over to them. I landed in a heap, while they all grinned at me. They roughly grabbed me and shoved me in the back of their van, saying awful and disgusting thing I will never forget. I was so terrified that I did everything they told me. I-I was so weak and defenseless." I started to shake and fresh tears trickling down my face and landing in my lap.

Ylva pulled me into another hug, tighter than last time.

"They abused a-a-and-"

I felt Ylva swallow and she shook her head, "You don't have to finish that sentence." She whispered.

I mentally thanked her before continuing, "W-When I came back the next day, they told me to never tell anyone or they would killed everyone I loved. A-Apparently, Katie told Ryker I have fallen asleep on the bar and stayed there. I have never told Ryker what had happened." I whimpered, "I never told anyone."

"How long ago was this?" Ylva asked.

"Three years." I gulped, sighed heavily. It felt as if a ton of bricks had been lifted off my shoulders in telling my Amista. I thought she would hate me and reject me as her Amista if I told her. But now I knew I could trust her with anything.

Something about Ylva grabbed my attention towards her. Something had happened in her past that changed her, I can tell. And something has recently happened to her too. Her eyes are a darker shade of violet, more purple and blue.

"Well, if you don't mind. I'm going go tell Ryker and Aden about this?" She whispered hugging me.

I slowly nodded, but my heart rate picked up dramatically. I didn't want my mate to hate it reject me and I didn't want Ryker to be mad at me for not telling them.

"Please tell them not to be mad at me. I didn't mean to, I-I-" Ylva cut me off with another hug.

"It will be alright Maisy, Aden won't reject you. He is kind and loving and he loves you more than anything now. And I'll make sure Ryker doesn't get pissy either!" I winked and we shared a laugh.

"Thank you, Ylva." I smiled.

"No problem. You calm down a bit and I'll speak to them. Aden will probably come up later, okay?"

I nodded and she walked out. I laid back against my pillows, thinking of my mate. Aden. It sounded like a strong name, someone you could trust.

'I'm still afraid.' Hetty sobbed.

'Hey, it's okay. I promise you nothing will happen. We'll get through it.' Even if I didn't know whether it was true or not, I reassured myself as well. I sighed and closed my eyes, thinking of him.

Sixteen • Honey, I'm Your Worst Nightmare

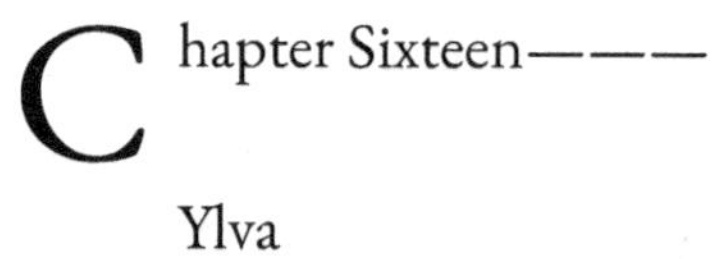

C hapter Sixteen———

Ylva

I stared at Ryker and Aden. I had just told them exactly what Maisy had told me. Who the fuck would do that go such an innocent girl? Maisy is so pure and kind hearted; that bitch was going to pay the price of hurting my Amista. No one deserves to be treated that way.

Aden's face was full of sorrow and anger, I could tell he wanted to rip Katie to shreds. His fists were clenched on the table and his eyes were a menacing black. But he couldn't harm Katie because he wasn't part of the pack, but I could, I was Ryker's mate.

I glanced to Ryker to see him glaring into space. The distant look on his face was telling me he was trying to control his wolf. If Raiden was loose right now, I doubt there would be any Katie left.

Aden got up, "I am going to see my mate." he looked to Ryker who just nodded. Aden gently smiled at me before following her scent to her room.

I heard Ryker's angry growls fill the quiet room. How could Katie do that? What did Maisy do to have something that bad done to her? She begged her brother for Katie to stay and all she did in return was hurt her!

Misty and Lucine were hissing at the thought of Katie hurting our Amista, 'She should die in the pits of hell.' Lucine hissed.

My eyes grew darker.

'How fucking dare she hurt our friend. I'm gonna kill her.' Misty yelled, causing my nails to grow, sharp and long. They were drawing lines in the table, a clear sign to anyone close to back away.

My body was shaking in anger, and my nails dug deeply into my palms of my balled hands as I clenched them. I felt Ryker's presence near me and he touched my arm. It didn't work. I was a full on Lycus, nothing would stop me when I was like this so quickly.

'We should rip her hair out, watch her bleed.' Misty growled. The thought of her blood being spilled flooded my mind.

'That would be very satisfying.' Lucine snarled.

I felt my body tense then all I saw was red. My eyes completely blackened as I let out a low, menacing growl and shot from the table. I could hear Ryker's footsteps behind me, chasing after me. But nothing could stop the fact that I wanted to kill, and see blood and pain from that bitch.

I stormed through the house, various pack members looking very scared of me. But right now, I didn't give a fuck. All I wanted was that she-wolf's head. Just the thought of my claws digging through her flesh had me hungry for revenge.

I inhaled her ghastly scent before barging through her doors. A shriek of surprise filled my ears as my eyes landed on the bitch that hurt my friend.

Her orbs widened when she saw my fuming figure, probably afraid of the full black eyes I withheld.

I leapt through the air over to her, pinning her to the ground. A strangled scream came from her as I gripped her hair and hauled her up. I growled darkly before shoving Ryker out my way and headed through the halls.

"You're a bitch! How dare you hurt such an innocent girl!" I hissed, dragging her down the stairs. I knew exactly were I was going. The cellar. Exactly were she belonged.

"W-What are y-you talking about!" Her idiotic figure shook violently.

"You know exactly what I'm talking about. What you did to Maisy!" Lucine managed to take control as she pulled the bitch along. My claws were gripping her hair so tightly, if she pulled away she would definitely have a bald patch. I inhaled the scents of rouges and followed that. The only time I would actually follow their smell. It lead me straight to the cells.

I crashed through the doors and threw her into a cell, clamping a steal chain around her wrists.

"You deserve to be here! Your a heartless bitch.You're lucky these chains aren't silver!" Lucine growled.

She stared frightfully at my red orbs, "W-What are you?" She gulped, probably fearing the answer.

"Honey, I'm your worst nightmare." I smirked before storming out.

"She does not leave this area, let alone that cell!" I growled at the guard.

He silently nodded, raising his hand go his head, "Yes, Luna." he replied confidently.

I ran out, shooting straight past Ryker who had a shocked expression on his face. I smirked a bit in satisfaction before shifting. I couldn't kill that snob right now, I needed answers. But first, I had to get this anger out.

I dug up the dirt in my claws before charging straight into a tree. It wobbled weakly against the impact, a few branches fell down. Growling angrily, I snapped them to pieces. So much hate was flowing through me right now, I had to get away from everyone. I had to hunt. I closed my eyes, inhaling deeply. I listened out. I heard the whistles of birds, leaping of frogs, the sound of a deer.

Deer!

I crept slowly around, hiding behind a tree. I saw the tall brown deer, his black eyes closed and his ears pricked up. I slowly stalked towards him, my eyes locked on his back leg. I heard a branch snapped. Looking down, my paw had snapped a twig. I growled lowly, shooting my head back up at the deer who was running.

Hell no! That's my dinner.

Misty growled loudly before helping me sprint towards the helpless creature. His back hooves clipped me a few times as I grew closer. I gritted my teeth before leaping, landing on him. I snarled as he tried to shuffle away and sunk my sharp incisors into his neck.

I harshly bit down and soon his body became limp into my grasp. I wondered to his back leg, hauling it up in my mouth before dragging him back to the clearing. I flung him on the floor before ripping the flesh of his stomach.

I laid down, enjoying the taste and smell of blood. A familiar scent filled my nose and Misty and Lucine instantly relaxed. His silver fur appeared from behind a tree, and Ryker walked towards me, his paw instantly stopping mid air when he saw the dead deer in my grasp.

I growled and snuck my leg around it, pulling it closer to me, showing him it was mine. He shook his head a me before walking over to me, laying down in front of me. I growled again, this time more harshly.

'Don't worry, I'm not going go take it away from you.' He huffed.

I felt a little bad about keeping this chunk of meat to myself. Standing up, I gripped one of it's back legs, before ripping it off and slumping it in front of Ryker.

'Have it before I take it.' I sighed. He shuffled closer, brushing his head against me, saying thanks before he dug in.

A few minutes passed and the deer leg was gone. I had been eating the stomach of the lifeless creature, my anger leaving soon after, 'Wow, you were really pissed at Katie.' I could hear Ryker smirk, almost as if he was happy.

'She hurt my Bestie, she will pay.' I snarled, ripping another chunk of its flesh.

'I know, you handled it better than I would.'

'Really?' My head shot up to him.

'Yeah, she would be dead by now.' He growled slightly before sighing in anger, 'What are you going to do with her?'

'Maybe make a few rips in her flesh, demand her to tell me why she did it, then she's being a rouge. I don't want her here.' I let out a howl, declaring that what I was going to do was final.

'Sounds good. Let me watch?'

'You have a sick sense of humour.' I told him.

'That was hot, by the way.' He chuckled deeply, looking at me.

I smirked internally and answered, 'I know.'

We sat there for what seemed like hours, getting to know each other better before walking back to the pack house. I shifted back into my clothes and walked through the door.

"Hello?" I called out. Ryker's arms wrapped around my waist as be kissed my neck.

"I really need to mark you soon. Raiden wants to claim you." he smirked against my skin, "After today's performance, I don't know how much longer I can hold him back."

"No, not yet" I smiled gently. He sucked on my neck, forcing a small groan to leave my lips.

I spun around, crashing my lips into his own. Sparks flied and everything seemed perfect. Well - almost. We stopped at the sound of someone moaning. I instantly cringed before walking into the lounge. There on the sofa was Aden and Maisy - kissing very passionately. My eyes widened as I slammed the doors shut. Did they even notice?

I stared at Ryker who just laughed at me, "It's what mates do." he wrapped me close again, pulling me against he hard abs.

'Oh how I would love to see them without his shirt on.' Misty whispered.

'Me too.' Lucine smiled.

'What! Ew, no!' I yelled at them before blocking them.

"Hey Ylva, we've been invited to a party tomorrow night. Maisy will take you shopping in the morning to get you a dress." Wow, do I get much of a choice? Guess not.

"Okay" I smiled, kissing his chin.

He smirked down at me before picking me up in a bridal hold and taking us up to bed.

"Good night, baby."

"Good night, Ryker."

Seventeen • No One Wants to See You Lip Lock

C hapter Seventeen------

Ylva

I was scaling through the clothes rack at Next, searching for a dress to wear this evening. I hated clothes shopping. Wait, scratch that, I hate any kind if shopping! Misty and Lucine were whining in my mind, giving me a terrible headache. You cannot take them anywhere.

'Oh I'm bored! Can we go?' Misty yawned, clearly annoyed at looking for a dress for the past three hours!

'I'm hungry!' Lucine complained before pausing, 'Wait, do I smell KFC?'

"Ugh, there's nothing here!" I snarled, flipping at one of the dresses as my stomach growled - and Lucine was not helping by naming all the closest restaurants.

"But there is! Look at all these gorgeous things!" Maisy pointed at some dark blue dresses.

"It smells weird in here." I muttered.

Maisy chuckled, "That's just the natural aroma of perfumes." I shot her an annoyed look, "Okay, I will find you a dress! Go get some Burger King or something!" She snickered, now flicking through a rack of black and white dresses.

"Yes! Don't pick anything too flashy though!" I warned, hastily walking out before she could change her mind.

I walked over to a KFC that was in the mall. God, I love KFC, it was my number one favourite. I ordered two chicken popcorns, two Big Daddy meals and two Krushems before gathering it all and walking out. Man, Maisy better hurry up before I eat all of this! I slipped onto a chair and took a chunk of the burger, digging in.

I was popping the last few popcorns into my mouth when Maisy came running over, excitement crossing her face, "Should I be worried that you look so happy?" I pointed as she sat down in front of me.

"Nope!" She beamed, "I have the perfect dress for you!"

"Can I see it?" I pondered, looking towards the bag.

"No!" She snatched the bag and placed it away from me.

"Why?!" I whined, pouting my lower lip.

"Because you'll ruin the surprise!" She smiled, before digging into the popcorn.

"Fine! As long as it's not flashy!"

"Well... it's not too flashy." she smirked. When I asked why she blatantly ignored me. God, dammit. Now I kind of wish I didn't leave her to pick the dress. Who knows was dress she picked up from that weird smelling store.

'I'm worried that she picked something really flashy and Ryker won't like it!' Lucine whined, wanting to peer into the black Next bag that was so close.

'You're the one who was complaining.' I mumbled. It was so tempting to snatch the bag and see what was inside; but when I tried again, Maisy smacked my hand away and put the bag on her lap. I huffed at her.

'Don't worry, Hetty told me it would look great on us.' Misty told us, even though her voice sounded uncertain and weary too.

'Who's Hetty?' I asked, confused at all the new names.

'Maisy's wolf.' Misty said in a 'duh' tone.

'Okay, Sarcy.' I replied smugly.

'Sarcy?' Lucine asked.

'Sarcastic, Luc, sarcastic.' I muttered before closing the link.

We finally arrived back to the pack house. Ah, home sweet - kind of - home! Everyone was still weary around me, especially after those who saw me yesterday. I tried to smile warmly, but who could blame them after that performance? Katie deserved it, so I could care less.

"Right! You get yourself ready. I'll be up in two hours to give you your dress and to do your hair and makeup as well!" Maisy smiled widely.

I spun around to look at her, my eyes wide, "Whoa, hang on. Who said anything about makeup?"

"You have never wore makeup, have you?" Maisy raised an eyebrow. Her smile turned into a smirk at my uncomfortable manner.

"No. I hate i.t" I rolled my eyes, sighing at her.

"Well," she shrugged, raising her arms, "Time to change that!"

"I hate you." I growled lowly before walking away and up to my room. On the way I ran into Ryker. I smiled up at him as he pulled me into him and placed a kiss on my forehead. I leaned against his touch before pulling his collar down and catching his lips. His hand came behind my neck, pulling me closer.

"Ugh, guys, get a room." said Aden.

I blushed and pulled away, "We have a room."

"Then use it." my cousin gave me a pointed look, "No one wants to see you lip lock."

Aden and Faith were staying for a few days since Aden found Maisy and Ryker decided he wouldn't allow mates to part from each other. It was a rule his parents had that kind of stuck. I raised and eyebrow, resting my hand on my hip, "I could say the same to you." He playfully glared at me when I smirked.

"Pft, whatever." he waved me off before walking into him room - actually, Maisy's room!

I shook my head and laughed, looking back up to Ryker, "I'll see you later." he winked before leaving to his office.

I opened our bedroom door and saw a box full of; body lotions, shampoos and conditioners, a hairbrush and comb, a toothbrush and some toothpaste, clips and hairbands, some necklaces and bracelets and some other luxuries. I read the note that came with it:

'Can't wait to see you tonight. I brought you some stuff. I didn't know what you liked so I asked your cousin Faith to help. Have fun with my sister when she comes to do your hair and makeup - I bet you'll love that!

Ryker xx'

I felt a blush rise from my neck up to my cheeks and a smile form on my face, 'Aww!' Both Misty and Lucine cooed as I walked into the bathroom with my box of goodies and turned on the warm water. Undressing and stepping in, my hair and body became soaked. Rubbing the shampoo and conditioner through my hair, massaging my scalp as I went, I thought of the evening ahead.

'Who else is going to be there?' I asked Misty and Lucine.

'I don't know. I'll ask Raiden. Hold on a sec.' Misty replied, cutting off.

I rinsed out the hair cleaner before laverishing my body with the body lotion. It smelt like strawberry marshmallows, 'Apparently some of the other Alpha's will be there and his parents. Everyone is coming to see us.' Misty told me.

'Oh great, spotlight!' Lucien's sarcastic voice came into hearing. I laughed at her. Yeah, no one likes a spotlight.

I stepped out the shower, wrapping a clean towel tightly around me and another one bunched around my hair. Walking into the room, I slipped on some lounge clothes, knowing that Maisy still had my dress. I growled not knowing what it looked like. What if it was really flimsy? Or showed too much skin? Or-

'Would you stop?' Lucine rolled her eyes, 'Gosh, and you complain that we're annoying.'

'Rude.' I muttered.

Sighing, I looked through the nail varnishes in the box. I only picked out a clear one with sparkles in it because I don't know what the outfit looks like. I quickly painted my nails and toenails, blowing on them to dry. Going back into the bathroom, I brushed my teeth, rinsing out with mouthwash. I slapped on some skin softener just as I heard a knock on my door.

"Hello?"

"It's Maisy! Can I come in?" Her excited voice answered through the wood.

"Uh, sure." I responded and went to open the door.

She walked in and placed the Next bag on my bed, "Ready to see it?"

I shrugged, "Ready as I'll ever be!"

She took that and pulled the dress out the bag. It was white. As she spun it around I could see one of my legs would hang out and I would have a bare back. I wasn't meant to wear a bra with this and there was a split in the middle to the centre of my breast. I gaped at it, "I cannot wear that! "

"Why not? It's perfect!" Maisy answered, eyeing up the dress.

"Don't you think it shows a bit... much?"

"Nope! Ryker's eyes will pop out his head when he sees you in this!" She smirked, pushing me towards the bathroom.

"Yeah and something else." I muttered.

"Change." Maisy ordered.

"Fine!" I huffed, slamming the door in her face and locking it.

Looking in the mirror, I drew a deep breath. I can do this. I took off the lounge wear and slipped on the dress. It fitted perfectly. I stared back to the mirror; I had never worn a dress before. My curves stood out, my shiny moisturised skin was mostly exposed.

'Wouldn't Ryker think I was showing too much?' I questioned.

'No, he would think about how perfect his mate is and how no one else but him could have us!' Lucine smirked, looking at us.

'Yeah, okay, sure.' I sighed. My nerves were on edge. 'What if it doesn't look right?'

'It does.' Misty calmly said.

'I don't know, maybe I should take it off-'

'NO!' Lucine roared.

'Chill out girl, you gotta loosen up a bit! Walk out the bathroom!' Misty yelled, 'Strut your stuff!'

'You have never said that in your life, have you?' Lucine snickered.

'Never.'

Rolling my eyes at them, I took a shivery breath before touching the handle. I slowly turned it before pushing it open. Maisy was sat on my bed looking through a new load of makeup she had bought that day, "Oh Ylva, I was thinking may be pure black would suit the-" she stopped when she looked at me.

Her eyes widened as her face lit up. I felt myself burn and I became suddenly awkward. "I know. It looks stupid, I'm gonna take it off-"

"What! No! It looks gorgeous! You can see all your natural curves and beauty! You are wearing that dress!" Maisy squealed.

I felt my blush go darker, "I've never worn a dress before" I whispered.

Maisy's eyes widened again before she smirked, "That's probably why you look so scared!"

"I'm not scared!" I protested as she dragged me over to a chair, "I'm just nervous."

"Okay, so I was thinking black eyeliner for your eyes and your lips are fine. Your hair doesn't need much done to it because it curls beautifully naturally anyway." she smiled.

I closed my eyes as she began her art. I wondered what this party would be like. Would their parents like me? Would they know that I threw a pack member in a cell and understand why I did it?

'Oh, stop worrying!' Misty whined.

'Yeah, we'll be fine, we have Ryker and he won't give us up for anyone!' Lucine insisted.

'Aren't you guys just a little nervous?' I asked.

'Well, duh. We have to make a good impression on his family and friends though. Other Alpha's are going to be there, so best behaviour!' Lucine replied with a snicker.

'Yes, but if anyone touches or flirts with what's mine, I will, I mean WILL, growl.' Misty snarled.

'Bipolar much?' I answered and Lucine laughed.

'No, it's called protecting what's mine and mine only!' She replied and blocked us out.

"There! All done!" Maisy squealed.

I stared into the mirror at the girl reflecting. Her violet eyes had a smoky effect because of the dark black point that came off the edges. Her hair was natural; neatly curled and bounced along her shoulders, coming to mid back length. Her face seemed to glow with happiness and her eyes turned blue. Actual blue! That girl - was me.

"Oh my God! Wow. Thanks Maisy!" I breathed, turning to wrap her in a hug.

"No! No ruining my masterpiece!" She cried, but hugged me all the same. Maisy walked over to the Next bag and pulled out a pair of studded diamond heels. I gawked at them, "Don't tell me. You haven't worn heels before?" She laughed when I shook my head. "There only small, you should be fine."

She place them on the floor and I slipped them on. I stood up, the same height as Maisy. I smiled at her, "Thank you. You are the best Amista ever!"

I saw her eyes water, "Thanks. Your the best Amista ever as well." She hugged me again before continuing, "Let's go show your mate!"

Eighteen • None of the Formal Language

C hapter Eighteen-------

Ryker

I was silently waiting for my glorious mate, leaning against my red metallic Alfa Romeo. I couldn't stop thinking about her. Every hour, every minute, every second, Ylva was on my mind.

I was still surprised that she actually took Katie down to the cell. After what she did to my sister, she would have been dead if I got to her. And the way Misty and Ylva, and whomever her Vampire is called, caught that deer was so graceful, and hot. It was rare to find a deer coming into the winter season. I thought she wasn't going to share it with me.

'Mark her! Please dammit, mark her!' Raiden barked in my mind.

'I will, soon.' I responded and blocked him at the sweet scent of strawberries, nature and oak wood. A smell that would make my wolf go crazy. I saw Ylva standing by the door and my eyes widened when I looked at what she wore.

A long white dress, one on her legs hanging out. A split down the front revealing some of her chest that Raiden and I craved to touch. The dress was backless and her heels gave her that extra bit of height, easier for me to kiss those pink lips.

Her eyes were smoky and her orbs were a mix between violet and blue, her happy colour. I smirked at her as she wobbled her way over to me, obviously not liking heels. All in all, she looked absolutely sexy... and she was all mine!

"God, these heel are killing already." she growled, slipping one off and rubbing her red heel. She looked back up to me with those beautiful eyes.

Ylva

Ryker looked very handsome. And I was not saying that lightly. He was dressed in a tux that fitted him perfectly. His muscles were rippling through the white shirt he had on. He had shaved his face and his hair was gelled so he could flick it across his forehead. Ryker had put on some spray, which made him smell more mouthwatering than he already was.

"You look beautiful." he complimented, stealing my lips.

"Uh, thanks..." I answered awkwardly. I hate compliments! "You don't look so bad yourself. You clean up real nice."

He smiled and opened the passenger door of his Alfa Romeo for me, what a gentleman! I was in love with this car! The black fitted chairs allowed me to get comfy as soon as I sat in them. The all-black inside was perfect with the red, metallic paint job.

"Sweet ride." I said, stroking the side of the door.

"Thanks. I have other sweets rides if you want to try them sometime." he winked.

I opened my mouth in shock and stared at him in horror, "I really hope you were talking about cars!" I raised my voice.

"Maybe, maybe not." he smirked, pulling off. The sound of the tires stretching as we left calmed me, it sounded as amazing as I hoped! My heart was racing in my chest, nervous about how the party will go. Ralph placed his hand on my thigh, in a comforting manner, "Relax." he spoke, keeping his eyes on the road.

I took deep breaths, trying to calm myself from having a heart attack. I've never been this scared in my life! What if they don't like me? What if they tell Ralph to reject me?

"Ylva, relax." he repeated, "My parents have been dying to meet you. I've told them everything that's happened, they don't care. They just want to meet you!" He smiled and looked at me. Sparks flied where his hand touched, making me feel warm and fuzzy inside. Misty and Lucine were in sheer bliss. Their mate touching them was calming and supporting.

We finally arrived, metal gates opening as Ryker spoke to the guard. We drove up the path to this huge house! It was made of stone, possibly built in the Victorian times. The windows were tall and wide, as was the front door. Each window had its own pot full of sprouting bright flowers. I gasped as it glowed from the light inside.

"This is my parents house." Ryker spoke as he came around and opened the door, helping me to balance.

"It's amazing!" I smiled, looking up. Ryker's arm slinked around my waist, pulling me in closer to him. Tingles erupted from were our bodies met, I don't think I will ever get used to that.

We walked over to the door, Ralph knocking loudly three times. A slim lady, around her forties I would say, answered the door. She bowed down as she let us through, "Alpha Ryker, Luna Ylva, your looking well this evening." she spoke.

"Thank you, Kathrin. Please call my mother and tell her we are here." Ryker nodded his head to her.

"Of course, Alpha." She smiled at me and walked off.

"Who is she?" I asked as we wandered through the halls and into a sitting area.

"She's one of the Omega's that help my mother and father." He replied, sitting down and pulling me into his lap.

"Oh." was all I could respond before the door flew open and another lady came in. She had green eyes, just like Ryker. Her light ginger hair flowed straight down her back and she smiled brightly when she saw me.

"Hello!" She greeted cheerfully. She looked at me and pulled me into a hug. I was shocked and tensed, "I'm Ryker's mother, Gwen Dawson."

I smiled at her, "Hi, Mrs Dawson. I'm Ylva, Ryker's mate"

"I know, I've heard so much about you." she grinned when Ryker growled in annoyance, "Hush, Ryker. We all know it to be true." I laughed when he sighed and looked away. Gwen turned back to me, "And none of that formal language - please, call me Gwen."

I smiled and nodded. Gwen suddenly linked my arm and pulled me from my mate, "We have so many people to meet!" she grinned before turning to her son, "Ryker, your father wants to discuss something with you in his office."

Ryker nodded and placed a kiss on my forehead before leaving me with his mother. Gwen tugged at my arm, dragging me to the ballroom, I believe. It was gigantic! There was a golden chandelier in the middle of the ceiling, a small bar to the side and a second floor where guests could look down at the dancefloor. White benches and seats were covering a whole corner while the rest was space to stand and talk. The room was buzzing with people who all stopped to look at me when Gwen yelled out to them from the stage.

"I would like to introduce you to Alpha Ryker's mate, Ylva!" she smiled. My cheeks burned at being centre of attention and everyone clapping and bowing down to me wasn't helping.

'Calm down Ylva...I can hear your heartbeat from two floors up!' Ryker spoke through the mindlink, calming my nerves a bit.

Gwen dragged me over to some people, "Ylva, I'd like you to meet our closest and most trusted pack leaders, Alpha Franklin and his mate, Luna Emerald. They are from the Moonlit Howlers pack." I smiled at them, nodding my head.

"I told you, I don't like my name getting in the way of my title." Emerald chuckled to Gwen, both of them giving each other a hug.

"Lovely to meet you." I said.

"The pleasure is all ours!" Emerald smiled, pulling me into a hug. I shook Alpha Franklin's hand before Gwen introduced me to their children.

"This is Yhanna and Ellis, who are twins and the soon to be Alpha of the Moonlit Howlers, Mason." I shook each of their hands, once again I was bombarded with hugs from the girls. Mason looked maybe one or two years younger than me while the girls looked maybe five years younger.

"Girls, please. Your overwhelming the Luna!" Franklin hushed them.

"No, it's fine. Really." I smiled a him, hugging the girls back.

A few hours had gone by and Gwen had introduced me to most packs. Still no Ryker, which made me concerned about him. Misty and Lucine were on edge about not having their mate around them in such an unknown place.

'Where are you?' I asked through the link.

"Right behind you." his husky voice whispered in my ear. I jumped in surprise as hands latched onto my hips.

"My wolf was worried about you." I sighed, kissing his lips, which I could now reach with heels on.

"Only your wolf?" He looked down at me giving me a knowing look.

"Yes, and her as well." I said, referring to my vampire side. "But I'll talk about that with you another time."

"Yes. You will. Come on, let's get a drink." Ryker answered, pulling me to the bar.

"I'm good with water." I told him. He looked at me weirdly before ordering our drinks. Ryker picked them up and I followed him to the seating area. My mate sat on a sideline and pulled me between his legs. Okay, this position is awkward. I tried to pull away, but the arm around my waist stopped me.

"Don't leave me." he whispered, grazing and kissing on my exposed neck.

"I won't. I'm here, Ryker." I smiled, running my hand through his stiff hair.

"Ylva?" He whispered, kissing my neck.

"Hmm?" Was all I could reply as he nipped at the marking spot. I tried not to moan, especially as there were others here too. And in his parent's house!

"Raiden wants to claim you." he gently pinched my neck with his incisors. I was caught off-guard with his response and my body froze.

'Say yes!' Misty and Lucine whimpered.

"Please let him claim you. I don't know how much longer I can hold him off for." His voice was husky again and closer to my ear.

Should I? What if I regret it?

Nineteen • Maybe We Can Nope Out of this Situation

C hapter Nineteen------

Ylva

His question rotated around my mind, over and over. Ryker had been closer to me, he was my mate. But was I ready to become officially his mate, his Luna? I knew that I still needed a Luna ceremony to officially the pack's Luna but this just made that process edge closer.

Misty and Lucine were begging for me to say yes. They wanted to be his, to belong to him, 'Please!' Lucine begged.

'We'll be complete with him!' Misty cried, trying to gain control.

'I don't know whether I'm ready! I want to be free!' I whined, 'Maybe I can nope out of this conversation.'

'No! You can't do this to us!' Lucine hissed.

I didn't know whether I loved Ryker yet. I mean, I did but... I sighed. I knew that I needed to have more trust in him, but I was never the one to trust easily. What if something happened? I looked into his pleading green orbs, "I know that it's hard for you to trust, and I know that you don't quite love me like I love you right now. But, I promise you will never get hurt again." Ryker whispered, moving slowly closer to the marking spot.

"I-" I sucked in a breath, "I don't know."

Ryker's hands clamped tightly on my hips, "Please, baby." he sucked on the marking area, a moaning threatening to leave my parted lips.

'Please!'

'Please!' Misty and Lucine were begging me to let him claim us. For us to belong to him was a big commitment. Like marriage, but if you reject them once your marked, you don't die, you just feel the pain for the rest of your life.

I looked at Ryker as he kissed softly and leaned back, his eyes tracing over my face. His arms wrapping around my waist made me feel safe and loved. His eyes connected with mine, "Please, Kitten?" His eyes looked lovingly and longingly at me. My heart was racing inside my chest at an insane rate. I didn't realise my fingers that clung to his tux blazer.

"I will always love and protect you." he whispered, standing up so he was a head taller than me.

'Please, Ylva! Please. I want to belong to him, he is my soulmate! The one I am supposed to belong to!' Misty whimpered, desperately trying to take control of me.

'But his do you know that he won't do something that hurts us?' I asked, feeling sparks as Ryker kissed my head.

'I don't but we, you, need to trust him!'

Not even a nope out. I looked at Ralph's promising eyes. I guess if I did get hurt, there's always back home. I sighed, nodding my head and looking up at him, "Mark me." was all I replied.

Ryker gripped my hand, a low growling sound erupting from his chest. He weaved us through the groups of laughing and talking people, before we were outside. The crisp evening air calmed me but I shivered at the coldness. My nerves were everywhere.

Ryker pulled me over to a fountain, it poured out clear blue icy water. We stood beside it, his arm wrapped around my waist securely. My breathing became rapid and my heart beat increased. I stared into those dreamy green eyes that held so much love and passion, "Relax, baby girl." Ryker whispered, "I will take care if you."

His lips connected with my own, my hands making their own way to his shoulders for support. Ryker's lips left mine and trailed down my jaw, to my chin, to my neck. I gasped loudly when he reached the specific area. His large hands held me in my place, wrapping around my body, making me, Misty and Lucine feel safe.

Ryker inhaled my scent and gripped my hair, pulling my head too the side. This is actually happening? Am I really letting him do this to me? What if he hurt me, or doesn't really love me?

I tensed as I felt a wisp of a tongue swipe across my empty neck. Ryker pulled back, looking at me, his incisors growing longer. His eyes turned pitch black, notifying me that Raiden was preparing to claim me. Swallowing, I slowly nodded my head, my breathing hitching.

"Calm down, baby girl," he whispered, leaning down to my neck again. I took a few deep breaths before a sharp pain rang in my neck. A painful pinch punctured my neck and my knees nearly gave way at the pain, but Ryker held me strong, his fingers digging into my waist.

I felt his teeth sink deeper, claiming me as his and his alone. Misty and Lucine winced but howled and hissed in pleasure. My hands were gripping his tux blazer, holes being ripped at my growing nails as I yelped in pain. I heard Raiden or Ryker growl lowly before he pulled his teeth out.

His dark green orbs stared at me lovingly, like I had just made his night. Well, I probably did. I felt my eyes flash yellow and blue. All the pain I felt in the past, my mother and father being killed, me feeling pain, everything faded away. At that present moment, it was just Ryker and I. No one in the world existed except us. I almost toppled over as pain cycled my neck again. I whimpered before Ryker's strong hands caught under my arms. I felt tears stinging my eyes as the pain increased.

"Hey, it's okay, baby girl. It's only the after venom." Ryker whispered, leaning down again and licking the burning bite of my neck. When he produced the mark, his venom went into me so I would always smell partly of him. It was to warn other unmated males, that I already belonged to someone.

He continued to lick the mark. All of a sudden, Misty howled in pleasure. Ryker sucked on the mark, making a small moaning like noise leave my parted lips. He growled lowly, pulling me closer. I buried my face into the crook of his neck, my moans quietening as he continued to work magic. Oh, wow... is that supposed to happen?

'Thank you!' Misty howled, her mate still giving her pleasure.

'Thank you for being so pa-' I gasped as Ryker's had rested on my hips, lifting me up and sitting down with my legs to the side of him. '-So patient' I finished.

Ryker's hand pulled my head closer to him, his lips devouring my own. I groaned slightly against his lips, wrapping my arms around his neck. His tongue wanted access. Hmm, not that easily! I smirked, shaking my head.

He looked at me and smirked back, his hand slipping past my waist, making me shiver. I yelped as he pinched my butt and his tongue slipped in. Lucine was hissing, her way of wanting more.

"What did I say about the butt?" I mumbled before Ryker's tongue explored my mouth as my hands trailed through his hair. He chuckled and I smiled, pulling away, resting my head against his chest.

"You don't know how delicious you look in that dress, baby girl." Ralph huskily whispered by my ear, "Thank you." he spoke, wrapping me closer to him, if that was possible.

Everything seemed right. My life seemed better, my friends were better, everything was better. I didn't need to worry about anything anymore. Ryker was there for me, through wind, rain, whatever.

"I love you." I smiled as his body tensed around me. I guess he thought he wouldn't hear that from me.

"I love you too, kitten." The way he used nicknames, it made me feel safe, and I knew nothing could happen to me as long as I held Ryker's claim. I rested into his arms, inhaling his addicting scent. Lucine and Misty relaxed, allowing sleep to take over.

Twenty • Raiden's Here

- -

C hapter Twenty------

Ylva

I woke up wrapped in arms. The pillow I was laying was comfy and warm and covered in Ryker's scent. I was back at the pack house, in his room, dressed in one of Ryker's t-shirts. I smiled as I remembered last night, allowing the feeling of sparks travel through me.

I did the right thing... didn't I? The arm tightened around my waist and pulled me in closer to a bare chest. I immediately blushed and awkwardly turned around in his arms, coming face to face with my mate. I reached out my hand and rested is against his pectorals, feeling the muscles he had. Misty and Lucine were in bliss, just looking at his body. I admit, it did look good.

'Finally, you see things our way.' Misty snickered.

Ryker stirred and one of his eyes peaked open. He smirked at me when he saw me looking at his chest, "It's nice to wake up to my mate checking me out." he leaned down and kissed my forehead as I blushed.

I rose my chin up to catch his lips. He groaned and pulled me to lay over him. Ryker sucked on my bottom lip, his hands slipped under the shirt, running over my bare back, "Thank you for letting me claim you, my wolf would've made you otherwise." Ryker smiled.

"Yeah, Misty and Lucine would have taken control and made me let you before I could say anything." I rested my head against his arm.

"Lucine?" Ryker repeated, confused. I froze and rethought about what I said. Shit! What did I say?

'Just tell him, he wants to know.' Misty said.

'Yeah but he may be really angry. I don't know... I-'

'He won't be angry. I've asked Raiden, he doesn't care. He wouldn't have marked you otherwise.' Misty told me.

I took a deep breath, swallowing my fear, "Lucine is my vampire side"

Ryker raised an eyebrow, "You have a vampire voice too?"

"Yeah, she's like Misty." I looked away from his eyes and added, "A pain in the ass."

'Hey!'

Ryker lifted up up my chin. My body was shivering in slight fear, "Why are you so afraid to tell me?"

I looked worriedly into his green orbs. I sighed again, letting out a shaky breath, "Because I was a afraid that you would reject me." I answered honestly, "It's not every day you see a half werewolf, half vampire hybrid."

"I would never reject you. You are unique." he whispered, kissing my head. "When did you find out about her?"

"Remember when my eyes went brown that morning?"

"Oh." he pulled me up for a long deep kiss again.

'Lemme meet him!' Lucine squealed.

I mentally laughed at her, "Lucine wants to speak to you" I whispered against his lips.

"Let her."

I nodded and closed my eyes, giving the control to Lucine. My eyes flashed brown, my incisors sharpened and my skin became slightly paler. I opened my orbs and stared at Ryker, his own eyes filled with curiosity.

"Hey, Rykey." Lucine smirked, winking.

Our mate growled lowly, "Don't call me Rykey."

Lucine placed her hands on his face and smiled at him, "Okay, I won't... Rykey."

Ryker shook his head, leaning down to kiss us. I took back control and nipped on his lower lip, a small growl rumbling from his chest, 'Hey Ylva. There's something I need to tell you.' Lucine spoke. Her voice seemed nervous and cautious.

'What?' I asked uncertainty.

'Well our grandmother is a vampire. She connected with me a few days ago. She wants to meet us.' She replied straight out.

'Okay... but why - how will we get there?'

'Our grandmother doesn't want to meet our mate yet. She wants to see you and you alone. She lives in the far corner behind the pack house. Almost fifty miles away.' She sighed.

'Okay. When shall we visit?' Ryker got up from the bed and stared at my bare legs.

"No staring!" I snarled.

"Why? I'll see more than that soon." he winked, smirking at me.

I gasped at him, my eyes widening and my jaw dropped. I growled lowly, "You can wait! You've only just marked me!"

"Okay. But I don't know how long I can hold Raiden down." He sighed, running his hand through his hair. His muscles flexed when he did this. I let out a long yawn, lifting my arms up and stretching. When I opened my eyes again, Ryker hadn't moved.

"What?" I asked as his eyes watched my every move.

"Just checking out my gorgeous mate." he winked again, "I'm going go take a shower, " Ryker paused, "Want to join me?"

I hissed, "No!"

He laughed at me before heading towards the closet. I sighed and got up, dressing in some loungewear, 'I connected with Grandmother, she said tomorrow' Lucine told me.

'TOMORROW!? Isn't that a bit soon?!' Misty cried.

'No! It's perfect! Then we can meet some of our elder family. Maybe learn more about our past.' I told them.

'Mm, okay. As long as you tell Ryker!' She snarled.

'What! No! He'll never let us go!' I replied.

'Do it, or I will tell Raiden!'

I swallowed. Raiden could be mean and aggressive if he wanted to be. He's an Alpha wolf, nothing would stop him. Except maybe....me, 'Either way, we can't go anywhere without a proper reason. He wouldn't even let us go alone.' I sighed, 'We have to tell him.'

I heard the bathroom door open and flinched slightly. I looked to see Ryker wearing nothing but a towel wrapped around his lower half. I couldn't take my eyes away from his chest; Misty and Lucine didn't help much either. Ryker coughed and I shot my eyes up to his face. He was smirking! My face reddened and I wandered my eyes away from him.

"I, uh, need to talk to you about something." I spoke, burying my head in my hands as he dropped the towel shamelessly.

"Talk then." I heard him shuffling around the room, opening drawers here and there.

"Well, Misty is my wolf side, she knows everything so far about her wolf life and family." My muffled voice spoke.

"Right." he answered. I looked up to find him in his boxers. My blush darkened even more.

"But, uh, Lucine doesn't. My grandmother is a vampire. She lives in the far back corner if this territory."

"You not planning on going, are you? Cause it's over fifty miles away and in one of the most dangerous places in the territory." His stern voice made me jump and look up to him.

Come on, Ylva! Don't let him make all the decisions! Your equal now, you deserve a but of freedom, "Yes actually, I was." I rose to my feet and stood my ground, his t-shirt falling below my butt.

"And you were planning on going this alone?" He snarled, his eyes slowly blackening. Fear slowly rose in my, my body slightly shaking.

"Yes! Because she's my grandmother!" I growled back. Lucine was slowly taking control, wanting to meet our grandmother, wanting to know our past.

Ryker stalked towards me, his wolf reaching full surface. Misty immediately regretted wanting to ask him and hid at the back of my mind, "You think that I'm going to let my mate who I have just recently claimed, go on her own, on a trip that would take over two days?" Raiden asked, towering over me.

"Yes."

He snarled and moved forward. I copied his movement but backwards until my back reached the wall. I stared into those black orbs of his. This wasn't the Ryker I knew. This was a completely different side if him. I lifted my head up, to show courage and bravery, but in fact, I was neither of these things.

"Well, you're not going."

Twenty One • I'll Take My Chances

C hapter Twenty One------

Ylva

I glared at him, my eyes flashing from a bottomless black to a dark, menacing brown. Lucine was in control. She raised our hand and slapped him across the face. So much force was penetrated that I was left shocked at her actions, my heart beat racing, "What?" Lucine hissed.

Ryker stared at me, Raiden in full control. He was clearly not amused with Lucine's actions. He gripped my arms and pinned them above my head, "I said your not going!" He yelled.

'Please don't make him angry.' Misty whimpered, frightened of what Ryker, well Raiden, would do.

'I don't give a fuck! I'm going to see my family!' Lucine yelled.

"How dare you! How fucking dare you say I cannot see my only vampire family. The only parent of my mother I have left!" Lucine screeched, trying to move from the hard grip Raiden had us in.

"Rouges go into that area. I will not have you hurt!" He hissed.

I stared into his ever growing black eyes. They squinted a few times, his mouth in one straight line. I knew that Raiden was very protective, but I also knew that Lucine needed to meet our grandmother. I haven't seen her in years, in fact, I hardly remember her, "I don't give a fuck about rouges! I want to see my grandmother and be at peace with my life! With this side of me!" Lucine screamed, our eyes become teary.

"YOU'RE NOT GOING!" Raiden yelled making us flinch.

His grip on my wrists tightened, his sharp claws piercing my skin. Lucine wasn't scared, not even a quick heartbeat flashed from her. She instinctively growled and kicked Ryker's broad body away with Misty and my's help.

"I AM GOING TO SEE MY FAMILY. NOT YOU, NOT ANYONE WILL STOP ME!" Lucine snapped, making her way to the door.

We were crushed against the wall, a loud growl rang in our ears. I groaned in agony as I tried to move, 'Get away from me, you ass munch. I deserve a break and to learn the history of my only thing of my Mum left!' I hissed at Ryker through our link.

'There are rogues that way! I will not have you hurt or taken away from me!' He snapped.

'So, you're going to keep me here forever! No freedom, just stuck in this fucking house for the rest of my days!' I yelled.

'No that's not what I-'

'I don't want to hear it! I AM going to see my Grandmother and I AM going to learn about my life!' I hissed.

With Misty and Lucine's help, we pushed him away using our Lycus strength. Ryker flew across the room as I barged out. I didn't stay long enough to see him slam into the far wall. I shifted into wolf form before I even got out the house. I ran down the stairs, people gasping and moving out my way as I shot past them.

I heard a growl when I reached the open front door. Turning my head, my orbs pierced holes into the silver animal at the top of the stairs, 'You go out that door, you will never leave when I get you.' he snapped.

'I'll take my chances.' I growled lowly and sprinted away. I ignored the stares and worried looking people when I heard a loud thud from the house. Raiden had obviously jumped the stairs.

'Ylva? What the fuck are you doing! Ryker's running after you!' I heard Aden's voice fill my mind.

'Yeah. He and I got pissy at each other.' I growled back.

'What did you do?'

'He wouldn't let me see my grandmother.'

'Is she in this territory?' I had told Aden that I was part vampire, so I could trust him with anything. He was almost a brother to me, I could probably mistake him as one.

'Yes. Behind the house at the far corner.' I answered, keeping hearing range on the thuds behind.

'Ylva, there are rouges over there!' He replied.

'How do you know that?' I snapped. I knew I shouldn't be angry at Aden, he had done nothing wrong. But the footsteps behind me were closing in. I pelted through the forest, sprinting past some patrollers.

'We came past them. Be safe, he's gaining on you.' I closed the link and concentrated on running away.

Misty was crying. We made our mate angry, he could do anything to us. She was afraid he would hurt us, like people had before. We knew we had to keep running, no matter how long it went on. If Ryker got to us, God knows what he would do.

'Ylva, get your fucking ass back!' He snapped through the link. Raiden's voice was covered with anger and Ryker couldn't take him back. I knew that. Once a wolf gains control when you are angry, you can't pull them back unless they come willingly.

'No! I AM going to see my family!' Lucine screamed before I could reject. Our paws pounded through the woods, the echo floating through the air.

'Come willingly or I make you. And you won't like it when I make you!' I heard him snarl behind me.

'No!'

'That's it! You asked for it!' Raiden suddenly growled louder than ever before. Paws smacked my back legs and I was flung into the air. I smashed into a tree and landed in a heap on the floor. Whimpering in pain, I looked up to see Raiden's tall figure. He snarled, towering over me with so much power and authority. He stalked towards me and I whined, edging back only to be greeted by pain. I howled.

Raiden didn't even bother to look at me with concern. Only anger was flowing through his veins and I was afraid of what he would do to me,

'Now look what you did! You fucking pissed him off!' Misty whined, terrified.

'I didn't mean to make him this mad, I-' a loud snap knocked Lucine out of her speech. I looked to see human Ryker standing there. Only, it wasn't Ryker. It was Raiden. He was fuming and his eyes flashed black and red.

He walked over to me, gripping my fur. I whimpered in pain, his grip tightening. Something snapped in me. Something bad. I didn't see red. I saw black. Nothing felt right. Inside me, Lucine's frightened face met my eyes.

'Ylva, calm down!'

'Ylva!'

Misty was trying to connect with Ryker, my anger on an all time high. I glared up at Raiden's figure. I rose in wolf form and growled lowly, snapping at the air. Raiden took a step back, fear laced in his eyes which was quickly replaced with more anger. He shifted back into wolf form. I stared at him, directly into his eyes. I was the same height as him at the moment. How?

I felt a rustle in me. I looked down to see my fur, black as night with blue streaks. I snapped my eyes back up to Raiden and slashed him with my paw. Ripping flesh filled my ear as I stared at him. Raiden's face, covered in blood, dripping to the floor. He snarled lowly before attacking me.

He smacked me to the floor, a loud cracking sound erupted from my leg. I whimpered before getting up and snapping at his own foot. Another snap filled my satisfaction and his paw went limp. One foot down, three to go.

'Ylva! Stop! The evil vampire side of you is coming out! And once it does it doesn't leave!' Lucine wailed, trying to gain control.

Whilst I was focusing on my vampire, Raiden whipped his claws across my side. I flinched, yelping in pain before retaliating. I shot towards him, listening to another crack fill the air. It wasn't until his whimper rang in my ears that black was removed from my vision. Raiden glared at me and I swallowed, 'Ralph! I'm so sorry!'

'Save it.'

'But that wasn't me! I swe-'

'Then who the fuck was it Ylva? Who!' He snapped. Raiden's teeth clamped down on my neck before puncturing the sleep. I whimpered a sorry.

'You need to see grandmother. This vampire side is coming in you and it's coming fast.' Misty whispered before darkness surrounded me.

Twenty Two • I am Running On Spite and Fury

C hapter Twenty Two------

Ylva

I woke up in the at same bed I woke up in yesterday. Only this time, I was alone. No one hugging me, nobody kissing me, no one with their arm wrapped around my waist. No one. I sat up, a throbbing sensation stung from my wrist. I looked down to see a bandage and cast locked onto my skin. Misty whimpered remembering yesterday's events.

'That fucking rat put us to sleep again!' I yelled.

I ran into the bathroom. I stared in the mirror at my awful face. My shaggy blonde hair was sprawled around my head and my violet eyes were now dull and dim, black bags under them from where I was attacking Raiden.

'We need to see our grandmother!' Lucine was wide awake, glaring at the mark on my neck. Was it a mistake?

'No!' Misty growled.

'What was with me yesterday? Why did I see black?' The girls went quiet when I asked that. Tension floated around the air as I sucked in a breath, 'Guys!'

Lucine sighed, 'The back part of your vampire side is coming out. If not controlled, you will lose both Misty and I, and you will lose you mate, you would have-' Lucine bit on her lip, her eyes going teary as she looked away and closed them.

'What Lucine?' I literally begged to know, even though I was sure I wouldn't want to know.

'You will kill him if you don't get the under control.' she burst into tears.

I stumbled backwards, balancing myself on the wall. I don't want to kill Ryker. Sure, I may not be on the best terms of him right now, but I still love him. I jumped into action, slipping off my clothes and changing into shorts and a t-shirt. I ran over to the door and pulled on the handle.

Wait, what!

I strained against it, tugging and pulling. The fucker locked me in! That fucking- 'Calm down!' I sucked in a deep breath. I needed to get to my Gran. She was the only one who could help me. I searched frantically around the room, looking for an escape.

Bingo!

I ran over to the window and pushed it open. I squeezed through the small gap and slipped out onto the roof, closing the window behind me. There's no going back now. I'm sorry, Ryker. I whispered before leaping and running into the woods.

Ryker

Why would she want to see her Grandmother? I get that she's the only one Ylva has left that's closest to her mother, but over the over side of the territory. Na, ah! No way!

'She was so angry yesterday.' Raiden mumbled to himself. He had to be hard on her yesterday. Lucine was a strong character, one who was wild and needed to be tamed but I knew that was easier said than done.

I ran my hand through my hair and sighed. What a mate I had. But those eyes yesterday. They were blood red with no return. She battled me, challenged me. If she wasn't mine, I would have killed her. She told me it wasn't her, then who the hell was it? She attacked me! I touched the scar on my cheek and winced. That really hurt. Pain throbbed from it as I hissed.

I needed to sort this out with Ylva. Something just wasn't right with her and I couldn't find out what, 'Maybe it's the vampire side of her that blocks us?' My wolf assumed.

'Maybe.'

Lucine was quite a character, almost like Ylva. No scared heart beat, no terrified look. Nothing! When Lucine was yelling at me yesterday, no sign of fear was laced in her words. I guess it was a vampire thing, they don't usually see werewolves as a threat. But not to be afraid of an Alpha? That needed to change, everyone should be slightly frightened of an Alpha, this is just ridiculous.

"Alpha!" Someone yelled outside my door.

"What?" I snarled back, clearly not in the mood for any shit.

"Rouges have been spotted inside the territory again." My Beta replied.

I hopped out my chair and ran to the door of my office. I spent the night in here. Ylva needed her own space, "What do they want?" I asked, walking down the stairs with Reece on my tail.

"They, uh, want to speak to you, Ryker." Out of anyone in this house, excluding Ylva, Reece was the only one who could call me by my name.

I froze. My father had seen this. I had taken the Alaric gene, but my father had a skill that I don't have - visions. My father sees various possibilities of the future and they almost always become reality. I growled in annoyance and shifted into my wolf, following Reece's chocolate brown wolf. We walked into the darkest part of our territory, the place I rarely go. I sniffed the air and growled at the stench of rouges.

We came to a clearing, three of my warriors guarding the four rouges. They were in human form, "Please, we are no threat." a woman said. I glared at her. Her mossy brown hair covered her pathetic face. I rolled my eyes. I have seen her before. She comes every month. I normally get annoyed and throw her out of the border line but this time she had come with three guys. To me, that is a threat.

I shifted back to human form, my clothes still on me.

"What do you want, Karen?" I sighed, crossing my arms. I saw Reece's head look at me in confusion beside before growling at Karen.

"You know what I want." she replied meekly.

I snarled at her, "Yes, I know what you want, but it's never happening."

"Well then, take me to the dungeon! Please! I'm begging you! I need to be with him, I am empty without him!" Tears flowed from her eyes the more she talked about her mate. His name was Andrew.

"No." I turned my back to leave before she spoke again.

"Please! Isn't it your parents who say to not keep mates away from each other?" She cried.

I shot over to her and gripped her by her neck, growling as she struggled against my hold. The people who came with her snarled at me but Reece and my warriors growled at them, making them shut up, "Do NOT blackmail me!" I snapped, making her freeze and shake in fear. I smirked and dropped her, wiping my hand clean.

"Take her to the dungeon and escort these other rouges to the end of the border." I growled.

Karen said her goodbyes before Reece shoved her away to the dungeon. I growled at the men before my warriors moved them away. I ran after Reece and Karen. We arrived at the dungeon and I opened the doors of Andrew's cell, his mate rushing in. She wept and kissed him over and over, saying how much she missed him.

'As Ylva says, 'pass me the sick bucket'.' Raiden laughed inside my head. I still remember that day. The day she didn't care, until her wolf came out. Until she told that bitch whose boss. She'll make a great Luna.

"Thank you so much, Alpha Ryker." Karen said before locking herself in the cell. I raised an eyebrow at her before walking over to another cell.

I stared at the brunette who slumped there. Her body was thin and her hair was shaggy. That person was Katie. And you know the best part? I didn't even care, "Hello, baby. Come to free me? Have you had enough of that snob?" She whispered, trying to sound sexy. Pshh, she wishes. The most sexy person I love is Ylva, the one no one can compare to.

I growled, "Your the only snob around here." I walked into her cell and glared at her.

"Oh, you don't mean that. I'm way better than her. I am Luna material." Katie smiled, sending me a wink.

"You, you little pup, could never be half the Luna she will be!" I growled in her face, making her whimper in fear.

Katie gasped as I lifted her up by her scrawny, pathetic neck, "I will always love you." she smiled.

I snarled. "You're lucky I haven't killed you."

"Then why haven't you!" She shouted.

"Ylva wants answers."

Katie scoffed, "Yeah, I'm not talking to that mutt!"

I tightened her grip on her neck, "You will otherwise I won't stop to hurt you!" I snapped, dropping her and storming out the dungeon. Bitch.

Twenty Three • Is it So Hard to Say?

C hapter Twenty Three------

Ylva

Two Days Later

I had been running forever!

'Oh my God! Are we almost there yet?' Misty whined, clearly tired from taking control for so long.

Lucine listened out, as if she was looking around for something, 'Wait, let me take control.' She spoke before they switched. She shifted back to human form before sniffing her way around.

I thought for a few minutes. Ryker has to be pissed right now. I have been gone for two days! He probably knew were I was going and was already near me. I'm dead when he finds me. I sighed and concentrated on Lucine. I touched the mark on my neck, it was almost healed.

We came to a halt and Lucine hissed out. Two men came out from the bushes and glared at me, "Who are you? Why are you here?"

"I am here to see Maylin Brown." Lucine responded.

"And why do you want to see our leader? She-Wolf."

"I am her granddaughter. Ylva Endrin."

Their eyes widened and they gawked, "The Lycus?"

"Yes."

They looked at each other for a minute before beckoning me over. We walked through a row of trees before coming towards a door. They knocked on if twice, then a further three. The door opened slightly and the men mumbled a few words to the lady that opened the door. Her eyes widened as the looked at me.

"Come, come." she said, opening it wider for me to go inside. I followed her through various corridors before we came to a large double door. She knocked once before entering, leaving me to stand outside. Looking around, I hobbled awkwardly from one foot to another.

'Time flies, doesn't it, Sweetie? You'll see me soon.' I shook my head and ignored the voice. That's been happening a lot lately. The same voice, similar words, everything.

'What if she's really mean and horrid, or really strict?' Misty worried.

'Don't worry! She's not. She just like Mother.' Lucine smiled.

'How do you know our Mum?' I asked.

'Because I was with you all along.' I was about to answer when the door burst open again. A lady, just smaller than me, with a plump body and violet eyes came out. Grandmother?

She looked at me, her face lightening as she pulled me into a massive hug, "Oh, Ylva!" She cried, instantly wrapping her arms around me, "You don't know how long I've been waiting to see you!"

"Grandmother?" I asked, looking at her. She had faded blonde hair and the same coloured eyes that were now blue.

She nodded, "Oh, I've missed you so much! The last time I saw you, you were this tall." she put her hand just under her waist to show me how small I was.

I sighed, "I'm sorry Gran, if I had known I would've-"

"No, no, no! It's fine!" She smiled, pulling me into the room. "We have so much to talk about, Ylva!"

Ryker

"Fucking hell!" I snapped. Raiden and I have been on an all time anger since Ylva left. I smashed my fist against the wall, letting it crack through, 'She's gone to her Grandmother! Go get her!' He snarled.

'No! She needs time!' I say. She'd probably hate me if I went and took her. I guess Ylva did need to see her family. She needed to learn more about her vampire side of her. She'd be back in a few days... right?

I slipped on a top and wandered out my office and towards my room, "Ryker!" I heard someone call my name. Maisy.

"What?" I sighed, leaning against the wall.

"Anything?" She asked, biting her lip nervously. I knew she missed Ylva. It's only been two days but I miss the hell out of her too.

I shook my head before growling, "No."

"She does need to know about her vampire side. It could help her and you!" Maisy told me with a small sigh.

"Yeah, I guess. I just hope her cousins don't kill me." I ran my hand through my hair, "That area is dangerous."

"Maybe Aden could help you."

"What do you mean?"

"Well, he's known her longer than you. He could maybe help her. Or Faith, Ylva used to always talk to her about anything."

Maisy and Faith had gotten on well the past few days. They decided to stay for a while until we know what's actually happening, "Yeah. You're right." I hated to admit that my sister was right. I was the Alpha, everything I said should be right, "Send Faith to my office, I'll be there in about ten minutes."

Maisy nodded and wandered to Faith's room to get her. I stormed into my room and growled lowly. I think everyone in the pack house could hear it because everything went quiet. Nothing was right without Ylva. I wanted to touch her, kiss her, breath her scent that I had become so addicted to. The dent where she I thrown me was still on the wall and I let out a deep breath - I guess that was our first fight.

I inhaled the air around me, catching a whiff of her scent, the only thing that kept me calm. I slumped on the bed and covered my face, 'Go to mate! Go to mate!' Raiden yelled.

'No!'

'Yes! I need her. She's mine!' He growled.

'Yeah, everyone knows it! She's ours, no one will take her from me.'

'Us!'

'Yeah okay, us!' I closed my eyes. I saw Ylva, her soft, blonde hair, unmistakable violet eyes that anyone could get lost in. Her small frame that I had grown to love and hold. I just wanted to touch her right now!

'Faith's waiting, Ryker.' Maisy spoke through the link. I got up and walked into my office, Faith immediately getting up from her chair and bowing. I nodded my head and sat behind the desk.

"Hello, Alpha! Anything I can help you with?" Faith asked, smiling.

"Yeah, uh... Ylva... What kind of things does she like?" I asked awkwardly.

"What do you mean by 'like'?" Faith smirked, trying to play with me. It was just like Ylva, playful, challenging, competitive. I smiled but looked at her seriously.

"Just like... in general?"

"By 'general' you mean dates, friends, colours, foods?"

I sighed, "The first one"

She laughed slightly, "Wow. Is it really difficult for you to say, 'What kind of dates does Ylva like to go on?'" She chuckled.

"For an Alpha... Pretty much" I raised an eyebrow.

"Well..." She rubbed the back if her neck, "I don't really know."

"What do you mean 'I don't know'? You've lived with her most your life!"

"Actually, no. Her aunt found me when I was hurt, took me in. I stayed, then Ylva came, and we just clicked, we kind of went through the same thing." Faith answered.

"What do you mean, 'the same thing'? What happened to her?" I asked, staring straight at Faith.

"She hasn't told you?"

"No."

"Well... she's not the one for trusting easily. But I can't say, it's against my nature and I don't break promises. You need to ask her yourself, Alpha." she replied, sighing.

"Fine."

"But you need to be careful. You can't just expect an answer from Ylva. It takes time and trust. You need to be gentle with Ylva, she's fragile,especially when it come to this particular topic." Faith finished.

I listened to every word. Her speech rotating in my mind. Trust, time and gentle. Three words I had to keep in mind. I rested my head back, 'Will she ever trust us?'

'Of course! It just takes time like Faith said.' I answered. I hope Ylva would trust me soon, my patience isn't good when it comes to answers.

"So!" Faith interrupted my thoughts, "You wanted date ideas?"

I nodded slowly.

"Well... I think Ylva wouldn't want a loud or expensive date. She doesn't like money spent on her."

"Well, she will have all my money spent on her. She's the one thing I care about most!" I tell her.

Faith laughed at me, "You are perfect for her." I smirked, "When Ylva lived at ours, she used to always look at the stars by the lake. She used to make wishes and dreams. So, under the stars would be ideal for a first date. Nothing too romantic. Just a walk along the beach or something." Faith smiled.

"Thank you, Faith. You have been a massive help!" I told her.

"It's my pleasure, Alpha. I am going to head back to home now, my mate is getting lost without me!" Faith laughed.

"Yeah, I know the feeling." I mumbled, nibbling at my thumb.

"Don't worry. Ylva needs this. Her vampire side is new to her. It can benefit both you and her."

Yeah but I can't help but worry! I sighed, "I will have two of my men escort you home. I wouldn't want your mate having my head!" I joked.

"Very well. Goodbye, Alpha Ryker, please take care of my cousin."

"I will. Goodbye, Faith" I notified Clyde, my best tracker and Jace, my best warrior, to take Faith home.

I know Faith said be gentle with Ylva, but I was still angry at her. Raiden was too. I know she's only finding out things about herself, but she disobeyed my orders and ran away with my knowing.

Raiden's anger came back and I couldn't stop it. He took over and gained control, grabbing the pen pot on my desk before throwing it, leaving it to shatter against the wall. Ylva had blocked out the link so I couldn't talk to her or smell her very well. Anything could happen to her and I wouldn't know. She needed to be back...now!

'Alpha! Rouges have been spotted entering the territory at the very far corner behind the pack house.'

I shot out my seat, and took of running. Ylva, your coming home, right now! Young, She-Wolf.

Twenty Four • Is That a Thing Now?

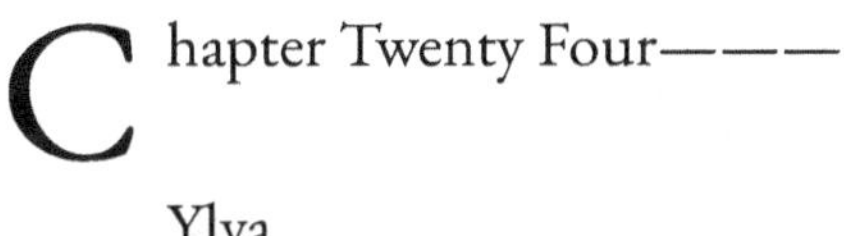

C hapter Twenty Four———

Ylva

I laughed at my Grandmother, "What did you do?" I asked, hiccuping my way through.

"I said no." she sighed.

"But why - what?" I stopped laughing altogether. Gran looked at me for a few seconds before she burst out laughing.

"Oh, darling! Your Grandfather asked the same thing!" She wiped a tear away from chuckling so much. "I then slapped him, kissed him and answered, 'you nut, of course I'll marry you!'"

"After all those mistakes during that one date and he thought you were going to say no because of it?" I giggled like a little kid, "Why on earth did you slap him?"

"Because he was really stupid to think that I would've said no!"

We had been talking all morning. I stayed over night, even though I knew Ryker wouldn't appreciate it. I stayed in a massive room across from her, so if I needed anything she'd be right outside.

'Ask her about the anger issues! You need to know!' Lucine begged. She had been on edge since we'd been here, so had Misty. Do they know something I don't? I expect Raiden was probably giving them shit, but this is important. We need to know about this so I can move forward with my life, not worry about things going wrong.

'Okay... I will.'

"Hey, Gran?" She took a sip of her tea before looking up.

"Yes, dear?"

"Do you know anything about anger issues?"

Her eyes widened and she set down her cup, "Have you been seeing red?"

"And black, yes."

She bit her lip with worry before getting up from her seat and moving over towards the bookshelf. She patted her chin, mumbling to herself, trailing her hand across each book, "Aha!" She pulled out a medium width book and wandered back over to me, "Vampires often have blackouts. When they get angry, all they want to do is kill. They can kill anything from animals to humans. If they see red, all they must do is attack something or being in the presence of their mate, but if black is visualised, they must be away from others, otherwise the vampire will kill the ones they love most." Gran spoke to me as if she had read it a million times.

"What does it mean by kills the ones I love most?"

"Like you could kill your parents, grandparents, closest friends or even... your mate." Gran explains.

I gasped.

"You would have no control over it. But it can be controlled." She says.

"How?"

"Well..." She rubbed the back of her neck nervously as if she didn't want to tell me.

'Or if she's kept something for us.' Misty snarled. She hates secrets kept from her.

"What, Gran? Just tell me!" I literally begged.

"The main way to help control the black is via sibling." She sighed.

"I don't have a brother or sister."

"Uh, yeah about that..." She coughed awkwardly.

"Do I have a sibling?" I questioned, angered rising from this having been kept a secret.

Gran nodded. I growled at her. Why would anyone keep a secret like that from someone? This is a fucking joke!

"Ylva! Stay calm!" My Gran hissed lightly. I took a few deep breaths, Misty and Lucine helping me, "It was for your own safety that you didn't know you had a twin brother." My Gran said.

"Wait... Twin?" I nearly screeched. That explains the ripped photograph that Nathaniel showed me.

"Yes. He looked just like you when you were a baby. Blue hair, purple eyes. But he had more vampire in him, so he had to live with me. Your parents were very upset but they had to do what was best. They visited him every month while I took care if you."

"Is he still alive?" I asked, eagerly.

"Yes. He lives here. But now that you have started to have anger issues, he must live with you in the pack house."

"Yeah... that will never happen. Bringing a vampire into a pack house isn't the easiest thing to do, even more so with Ryker's involvement."

"Well, if he doesn't want you to go to see black and keep the skin on his body, he'll have to!" Gran hissed.

"But he's a vampire. He doesn't go with wolves." I replied meekly.

"But he's a Lycus!"

My head shot up, "Just like me?"

Gran nodded. "He can shift into a wolf, he's just not very big. Whereas, you had the most wolf genes, you came out a proper hybrid. He's only half-hybrid."

Is that a thing now?

"Can I meet him?"

"Of course! He's been dying to see you. He's the older of the two of you though!" My Gran smiled before pressing a small button.

A small petite lady came through the door. "Yes, ma'am! How can I be of assistance?" She asked polietly.

"Please bring Clyde."

"How soon?"

"Immediately."

"Of course, ma'am, I'll be back in a few seconds."

She used her vampire speed and rushed out the door, "What's he like?" I asked, looking at my Gran.

"He's just like you - got into fights at school." my Gran smirked.

"How do you know that stuff?"

"Your parents and uncle told me about your fights in school and that you never did any work, but managed to get A's all the way!" She laughed.

"Oh-" and before I could say anything the door burst open. A man stood there, short blonde hair and his eyes were like mine - violet.

"Clyde, this is your sister...Ylva, this is your brother." My Gran spoke as we just stared at each other in shock.

This was my brother? The one I have been isolated from, the one I never knew about? I can see why they called it a twin.

"M-My sister?" His voice sounded just like Dad's. Tears filled my eyes before Clyde came over to me. I stood up, being at least a foot smaller than him! He was 6'3!

"My brother?" I asked, staring into violet eyes that made it look like a male reflection of myself.

He nodded before clamping me into a bear hug, "You don't know how long I've been waiting for this day!" He yelled.

I laughed at his stupidness. Gran was right, just like me. Our Gran laughed as well, we stared at her weirdly.l, "Oh, you two are so alike!" She brought us both into a hug. "Clyde, as you know, Ylva is a Lycus too. But she's having... anger issues." She sighed.

Clyde froze, "You need to control them, and fast." he spoke, looking directly at me.

"Yes, well she's recently been seeing black. You need to go with her to her pack house to help her." Gran told him, sternly.

"Who's your Alpha?"

"Ryker Dawson." Clyde suddenly burst into fits of laughter.

"Haha! Good joke, Gran. I'll never be there with her!"

"Exactly what I said!" I rolled my eyes.

"No, he will let you. I'm going go reason with him. He wouldn't want his mate to turn into a murderer."

Clyde froze again. "You're his mate?!"

"Yeah. How unfortunate!" I chuckled. My head was turned to the side, "Ouch, you fucker!"

"Language!" Gran warned, giving me a stern look.

"You've already been marked." Clyde sighed.

"Why? What's wrong?"

"It can make it more difficult to control." He ran a hand through his hair, "But it can still be done!" He hollered. Weirdo.

The door suddenly burst open again, flying off its hinges. I looked over and my breathing hitched. His black orbs burned holes in me; jaw clenched, fists balled, body tense. Even Misty and Lucine were frightened right now because we had never seen him this mad before. It was none other than-

"Ryker."

Twenty Five • I Lost My Temper... Again

C hapter Twenty Five———

Ylva

My heart beat picked up rapidly as he stalked closer, his pitch black eyes notifying me that Raiden was in control. No going back. I took steps backwards. He was growling lowly, anger building up even more. His glare moved from me to my Gran and brother, sending them warnings.

'Is he your mate?' I heard Clyde's voice fill my mind.

'Y-Yeah.' I swallowed as my back hit the wall behind. He towered infront of me.

"You disobeyed me." he snarled, slamming his hands on the wall beside me. I flinched under him, his tense body heaving with hatred and anger, "You came here without me knowing." he growled, leaning closer to me. I glanced at my Gran and Clyde, a few patrollers were behind them, holding them back as they struggled to get to me.

"R-Raiden, let them go." I gritted my teeth. I looked toward the door to find Reece. He stood there. I knew he wanted to help, but he couldn't. Alpha's orders.

Immediately, I grabbed hold of his hand as he went to grab my neck and let out a snarl - well, Lucine did. "Don't even think about trying to make me submit."

"You ran away and now you expect me to be nice?" He hissed. His other hand loosely wrapped around my neck and the other pinned my hand to the wall.

I stared angrily into his black, deadly orbs as I hissed, "Get. Off. Me."

'Reece. You're the only one who can help.' I told him.

'I'm sorry. I can't control an angry Alpha. You know that.'

"We are going home!" Raiden snapped, turning away.

"NO."

The room fell silent. I surprised myself by shouting that. I glared into Raiden's animalistic eyes; they squinted and showed more hatred I have even seen.

His hand immediately wrapped around again, "WHAT!" He spat, making me flinch again. Misty and Lucine were terrified, scared of what he would do.

'Hey? You think your the only badass here?' I asked Clyde.

'Yeah. Of course.' He snickered.

I mentally laughed through the link before swinging my foot. It collided with his groin, leading me to be dropped to the ground on my hands and knees. I sucked in a deep breath before looking up at him.

'Control yourself, Ylva.' My Gran whispered through our link.

"Don't ever pin me by my neck, again!" I shouted at Raiden. Everyone in the room gasped. What? No one seen a mate shouting at an Alpha?

"Don't shout at me!" He growled, getting up and coming closer.

"I'm learning about my vampire side! It can benefit you, as well as me." I snarled, shoving him away.

Raiden growled again and grabbed my wrists.

"Alpha Ryker or Raiden, whomever is in control at the moment." Gran politely spoke.

"What?" He hissed, still glaring at me. My heart beat increased again as his orbs flickered from black to red to black again.

"Ylva's brother here needs to go back with you and Ylva. Without him, Ylva could kill you. He can help her control her anger."

'What the fuck Gran! You can't just say that to the Alpha!' I hissed.

'I just did!'

Raiden was fuming by now, "That's my job!"

"I'm afraid only siblings can do this. There is a specific technique to doing it!" She sighed, crossing her arms.

"And why should I listen to you, you old bitch." Raiden snarled, clearly pissed. I let out a growl.

Clyde ran up to Raiden, snapping away from his men's grip, "Don't ever talk to my family like that AGAIN." he hissed.

Raiden's hands were already clawing at his neck. Clyde was choking against the wall as Raiden's anger was unleashed on my brother. My breathing hitched as everyone tried to get the Alpha off him.

My eyes were glued to the scene in front, afraid of what could happen, 'Ylva! You're the only one that can stop him!' Reece yelled, straining against Ryker.

I balled up my fists, "RAIDEN, STOP!"

Everyone froze, the angry Alpha included. They dropped their heads in submission but Raiden's head snapped towards me as he dropped Clyde to the floor. A low growl left him as he back me up to the wall again.

His hands planted next to my head, preventing escape as I glared up at him, a look of defiance across my face, "You don't command me anything."

"Alpha, if you want your skin on your body and to still be alive, Clyde must go with you." My Gran interrupted. She was standing on thin ice with Raiden.

He gripped my arms and tugged me out the room, "Reece! Take Clyde back home. Put him in one of the holding cells." Raiden growled.

Reece went to grab Clyde but I stopped him, "Reece. Don't."

His eyes worriedly shot towards me, frozen in the position of listening to me or his Alpha.

"Reece." Raiden warned, his grip on my arm tightening.

"I'm sorry, Ylva. I don't want Raiden to hurt you further." he answered meekly, picking up Clyde and dragging him away.

Raiden's head snapped towards me, "I'm the one who gives orders! Not you!" He gripped my waist and hauled me over his shoulder, "Burn this place to the ground." he snarled.

'Okay, too far.' Lucine hissed.

"You touch them, I'll reject you." I snapped, dragging my claws across his back.

He threw me into a wall, my head whacking against the floor. I groaned out in agony. Misty and Lucine were whimpering, telling me to obey his orders and submit but no way was he hurting the only part of my mother I had left.

"That, or you never come here again!" Raiden gave me an option.

I sat up dizzily, trying to find my feet. I hissed out when I put weight on my arm - whether it was broken or just bruised was debatable. Raiden snarled and stepped closer, warningly.

"F-Fine! I won't come here again!" I cried out in submission. Tears were streaming down my face at this point, desperate to just run.

He flipped me over his shoulder again and walked out. We were in the forest and it was dark but the only thing I was worried about was how mad Misty was. She was angry that he threatened her, angry that he hurt her, angry that he was being so cruel as to never seeing my family again.

'I'm not having this!' She screeched.

'Misty?' Lucine uncertainly asked.

'No, Misty!' I shouted but it was too late.

I was soon taken over by her, already shifting into my wolf. I leapt off Raiden's shoulder, scratching him in the process. I ran through the forest, away from Raiden and the patrollers.

But I came to a halt when the silver beast shot in front of me. His teeth sharper than ever, 'Stop disobeying me, you little runt!' Raiden growled.

'Oh, so I'm a runt now? Not your baby girl? Well good!' Misty yelled, reaching forward and slashing her foot over his face. His cheek was bleeding the thick dark blood that we have.

'You're still my baby girl. You ran away without telling me!'

'Shut your snout! I told you where I was going and you yelled at me that I couldn't go! I could kill you if I don't get my anger under control?! Is that what you want? Your pack left with no Alpha so they can be taken over by rouges!?' The courage Misty had at the moment was surprising. She usually agreed with everything Ryker or Raiden said.

'I could have come with you!' He shouted.

'Gran didn't want to see you! You would be acted just like you did! You're a fucking asshole. I wish you never marked me!'

Lucine and I gasped, tensing when those words left her lips. That's something I never thought I'd hear from Misty. Raiden's head snapped up towards us, glaring terrifyingly. Misty immediately regretted what she said and whined out, taking a step back as the patrollers surrounded us. There was no escape.

Raiden stalked towards us angrily. 'No, wait, Raiden please, I didn't-'

'Shut up!'

Misty whined. 'Ryker... I'm sorry.' I whimpered before Raiden clamped on our neck and darkness took over.

Twenty Six • Possession or Obsession

C hapter Twenty Six———

Ryker

Raiden had Ylva's scruff in his mouth as we were walking back through the forest, away from Ylva's Gran. I growled in annoyance, 'She's going to be so pissed at you when she wakes up!' I said.

'Well, I'm so pissed at her at the moment. How dare she run away like that!'

'Sometimes I think you are too possessive.' I sighed and stared at her apparent brother. Raiden gave me the control and we shifted back, carrying Ylva's wolf in our arms, "Are you her real brother?"

"Yes." he mumbled, staring at Ylva almost apologetically.

"How do you know this?"

"We have the same parents." He said in a 'duh' tone, causing me to send a warning growl. He sighed, "We are twins. But I have more vampire whereas

Ylva has more wolf, like our Dad." He sighed, stumbling weakly over tree roots as Reece kept his hold on him.

"But why have you never come to find her?" I asked. I saw his eyes flash guilt and sadness.

"It was to protect her."

My full attention was now on Clyde. His body features slumped when he talked about having to protect Ylva and I noticed his eyes fill with water, as if he was remembering something he didn't want to know, "Protect her from what?" I asked, craddling Ylva as she shifted back to human form. She made Raiden so mad. I thought at one point he was going to kill her!

'I would never dare!' He hissed.

'Yeah but now you've probably frightened the life out of her!' Her slight shiver told me that Lucine and Misty were afraid too. I never wanted my mate to be afraid of me. Where has 'us' gone?

'Misty isn't speaking to me.' he whimpered.

'Yeah because you hurt her, threatened her family and almost killed her!' I yelled.

"From the men." Clyde eventually answered.

"What men?"

He sighed. I saw his muscles tense as he glared at me. If Clyde wasn't Ylva's brother he would be dead, "The men that abused her!" He yelled. "Men that killed our parents in front of her, the ones who basically ruined her childhood!" He snapped.

I froze and stared down at my mate. She's been through more than shes told. Ylva kept something that big from me?

'She was afraid.' Raiden said.

'And you know this... how?' I snarled.

'One, it's obvious and two, Lucine's talking to me.' he sighed, 'A bit.'

"I couldn't protect her. I know I was younger but..." Clyde sniffed. He suddenly shifted. He has a wolf? I thought he was mostly vampire.

"How do you have a wolf?" I stared down at a smaller version of Ylva's wolf, at least half the size. But he had more black in his fur.

'I don't know.' Clyde sighed through the link, 'Forgive me for shifting. Sometimes I can't control it.'

I looked towards the pack house, where we were running towards. It was quiet when we arrived, most likely everyone was asleep. I knew Ylva would hate me even more if I made her brother sleep in the cells, "You can sleep in a guest room across from your cousin." I sighed.

'Cousin?'

"Yes, Aden. 8Faith left the other day."

'Faith?'

"Yeah. Well she's not your proper cousin. Your aunt found her and adopted her."

'Wow. You know more about my own family than I do.' He sighed.

"Reece, take Clyde the room opposite Aden." My Beta nodded and beckoned Clyde forward to follow him.

'Someone's coming to get her and someone in this pack knows who.' was the last thing Clyde spoke. He blocked the link, leaving me confused, angry and unanswered.

I knew who. I could tell who knew. But that's for another day. Sometime soon that bitch will pay.

'I don't want Ylva escaping again.' Raiden muttered, ignoring Clyde's words.

'No! I am not doing that!' I growled, already knowing what he was planning.

'Do it or I will. And I'm not very gentle!' He snarled.

'Fine! Only for the night though! I don't want Ylva to hate me more than she does.' I sighed. Most people follow their inner wolf. I do within reason.

'This isn't to make Ylva hate us! This is to make her understand!' Raiden huffed before hiding at the back of my mind.

I trudged up to my room and set Ylva on the bed. Pulling off her clothes, I dressed her in one of my shirts before going to my walk-in closets and opening a draw, 'I really don't want to do this.' I sighed, running my hand through my hair.

'Do it or I do.' Raiden warned. I growled lowly at him. If I didn't do it, at any opportunity he would. And he wouldn't be very kind.

'Fine! But you can deal with a pissy she-wolf!' I hissed. I took out the chain and brought them out, 'And I'm only doing one!'

'Fine.' Raiden snarled before blocking me completely. I connected a cuff to Ylva's wrist and wrapped the chain around the leg of the bed, making sure it was long enough so she could get to the on suite. She's never going to forgive me, I sighed before locking it all. I don't think she can get out of this.

I stared at Ylva. She was sleeping so peacefully yet so restlessly. She was so beautiful. She would hate me for going this, not even my dad would. What kind of man have I become? No, what kind of mate have I become?

I sighed, leaning down and placed a longing kiss on her cheek, "Please forgive me, baby girl." she stirred but didn't wake up.

I walked out my room and into Maisy's. Wow, I should have knocked. I saw Aden and Maisy making out, Aden laying between my sister legs. Now, usually I may have gone all 'big brother' on them but I was not in the mood to deal with that. I quickly shot out the door before they could notice and shivered.

Ugh, someone remind me to knock next time! But I really wish that would be me and Ylva sometime soon.

Maisy(One hour before Ryker walked in)

I sighed and slumped next to my mate. Everything about him I loved. His eyes, his personality, his muscles. He was always there for me, hugging and kissing me when I needed it.

Ylva had been brought back just now and Ryker didn't look happy. She rested tensely in his arms but she was asleep. I guess things didn't go to well. I knew that my brother wanted to keep her safe but Ylva still needed some form of freedom - Raiden was just going to have to deal with that.

I kissed Aden, trying to ignore the world. He groaned against my lips, his hands making their way down to my waist and pulling me closer. I clambered over him, my hands on each of his cheeks. Forcefully, but passionately, kissing his lips, I moaning slightly. He gripped my waist and hauled me over his shoulder, leaving me to gasp and squeal.

"Aden! Put me down, you big bully." I shouted, playfully punching his shoulder. He chuckled and made his way upstairs. I loved his laugh, it made him seem so carefree. Aden kicked open a door and threw me on my bed.

He clambered between my legs and kissed me again, "Aden." I moaned.

"Maisy?" I loved the way my name rolled from his mouth.

I hummed in response, kissing his face and running my hands through his short hair. Aden's lips made his way towards my ear, nibbling on it softly, "Can I make you mine?" he asked, whispering softly.

My breathing hitched. Hetty went crazy, running around like a mad old lady, 'Let him do it! Let him do it!' She cried.

"G-Go ahead Aden... I'm all yours." I smiled.

My mate flashed me a grin before nibbling down to my neck, pulling back slightly. My eyes widened a little when his incisors extended, "Relax, baby. I won't let anything hurt you." he mumbled before a sharp pain shot through my neck. I whimpered, digging my nails into his shoulder, pulling him closer to me with my legs wrapped around his torso.

Aden retracted his teeth and licked the mark. I moaned against his shoulder, my hands trailed across his tense back, massaging gently, "Thank you, baby. I love you." he smirked at me, kissing my lips.

"I love you too." I answered as he wrapped himself around me and we drifted off to sleep.

Twenty Seven • I'm Taking My Mother's Ghost's Advice

C hapter Twenty Seven———

Ylva

'Ylva...' I heard someone say.

I had just woken up, tugging against the retrainments as I looked around wildly for whoever said my name. That fucker locked me up! All I wanted to do is see my family, understand why I had really bad anger issues and this is how he reacts. Okay, that guy seriously needs some help.

'Ylva...' The voice said again.

"Okay. Whoever you are, stop messing with my head!" I snapped, letting out a low growl.

'Sh, now... my young Ylva.' the voice whispered. I felt something across my cheek, almost like a hand. Ryker's room was dark because of the blackout curtains. No one else was in the room except me. I was alone. Again.

"Whatever you just did is really cringey, by the way!" I yelled, freaking out a little. For someone outside the bedroom, they probably thought I was crazy talking to myself.

'Sh, now, Ylva. There's no need to be afraid.' The voice was gentle, calming. It was angelic and soft. Could it be...? No. Impossible, she's dead. But it sounded so familiar and so alike...

"M-Mum?" I asked, swallowing thickly.

'Yes, Ylva. Happy birthday, honey!'

My birthday?

"Oh, I'm having a great day. I've been locked up by my mate and now I'm talking to a ghost version of my mother." I said in a bored tone, note the sarcasm in my words.

'I know, but you disobeyed your Alpha, your mate.' She reminded me.

"Why are you taking his side? If I didn't see my Gran, I could've killed him!" I growled, "Everyone's all about rules and following the dominant wolf - not me!"

'I know it seems bad Ylva, but Ryker loves you. He's only doing it to protect you.' She whispered, 'And I know you would never be one to follow. You just need to understand why he's doing it.'

"How come I can talk to you? Have I gone crazy?" I asked. Knowing me, I probably went crazy years ago when I fought teenage boys when I was younger than them. Death wish much.

My mother laughed. Her laugh was cheery, just like I remembered, 'No, Ylva. You're eighteen and a Lycus, it's a special power you have.'

So that's what Nathaniel was talking about. I felt her pull me into a hug, which I gladly accepted, "How come I can't see you?"

'You can. Just close your eyes and you'll see me.' So I did. I saw her emerald green eyes again and her brown curly hair. Her soft skin touched mine as she embraced me in yet another hug.

'I will see you soon!' Another voice echoed through my head. I scowled at the same dark snarl. It's freaking me out and I don't know who it is!

"Ylva?" I opened my eyes and saw Ryker standing in front of me.

"What?" I gritted my teeth, clearly not in the mood for bullshit.

"I want to say sorry about Raiden yesterday." He whispered, but I still heard it. I knew that Alpha's hardly ever apologised, mate or not, but that didn't mean I was just going to forgive with a flick of my fingers.

"If he was a real man, he would say sorry himself." I spat.

"Please don't make him angry. He's already pissed."

"What and you think I'm not?" I shouted. "All I did was see my Gran, if I didn't, I could have killed you! Then, you put me to sleep again and I wake up in chains! What the hell are you thinking?!"

Ralph's body tensed, "It was either me or Raiden."

I felt myself flinch when he mentioned Raiden. My heart beat increased and Misty and Lucine already bowed their heads. I wasn't submitting. Hell no, "How nice of you." I snarled.

"Why are you so angry?"

"Because I wake up, in chains, on my eighteenth birthday! Great! I'm enjoying this day already! Thank you, mate! Love you too." I turned my head and ignored him.

"Please forgive me."

"I can't." I whispered.

"Please, baby girl. Give me a second chance." he pleads, and it's rare for an Alpha to plead.

"I already gave you a second chance and you took it. You hurt me with it. You're lucky I don't beat your ass." I snapped.

"Please! I promise nothing like that will happen again!" I could hear the beg in his voice.

Could I trust him again? He was my mate, I was supposed to put all my trust in him. I had enough to deal with already, and I know he did too, but I didn't fancy being broken again. My life was already a mess. I didn't know if I could snap and kill the ones I loved. I didn't know who's voice was continuously pestering the back of my mind. I gave him a chance already. Could I risk it again?

'Please, one more chance, Ylva.' Misty begged.

'All you care about is the mate bond Misty,' I sighed, 'You don't know how I feel bout this.'

'And weren't you the one who told Raiden you wish he never marked us?' Lucine asked and my wolf fell quiet. Misty understood how it felt to be rejected but she didn't understand how it felt to be in my position. All she wanted was her mate and nothing else. If Misty had it her way, no one would be here except her and Raiden, God knows what they'd get up to!

'Ylva, listen to me.' I heard Lucine continue, 'I know you're hurt but you need Ryker. We do. I know it may not seem like it, but you do. Later in life, something is going to come up, and you need him there with you, to support and protect you. Please.'

'What are you saying?' I asked.

She was quiet for a moment before answering, 'Give him another chance.'

I looked back up to Ryker, whose eyes were covered in desperation. I knew that he knew I was negotiating with my other forms, but I was the one who would have the final say, "Please, Ylva. I can make it up to you!" He pleads, "I need you - I need you more than anyone will ever understand."

I put a sigh and slowly nod my head, "Okay, Ryker. One more chance." I muttered. My lips were suddenly captured by his mouth. I hesitated at first before leaning closer, kissing him back. Ryker's arms wrapped around my back as he hovered over me, still kissing my lips. I tugged at the retrainments before it was released from my wrist, allowing my hands to explore through my mate's hair.

"Ylva Endrin," I looked into his forest eyes as he pulled away, "Will you go on a date with me today?"

I smiled at him, "I would love to go on a date with you." and kissed him again, pulling him in deeper.

"Take all the time you need, I'll be waiting for you, down by my Alfa." He winked, smirking before leaving the room.

Maybe this could work.

Twenty Eight • You Can Be the Fifth Wheeler

C hapter Twenty Eight———

Ylva

I had showered, dried and styled my hair, brushed my teeth and got changed all within the next half hour. Misty and Lucine where oddly excited, which left me with the nerves - I'd never been on a date before. Dressing in a light blue t-shirt and shorts, I rushed downstairs and to meet my mate.

Ryker looked hot. I know, I should be mad at him but the mate bond only pulled me closer to him - Misty and Lucine were not helping in the matter. He was dressed in a blue check-shirt and black genes. When he saw me, his typical smirk drew on his lips and he pulled me into a deep kiss. It felt right.

"So... what are we doing today?" I asked, looking at his forest green orbs.

"Well, during the day, we are going to an amusement park." He answered.

"And the evening?"

Ralph grinned, tapping his nose, "That's a secret."

He kissed my lips again, pulling me impossibly closer, "Guys! Get a room!" Someone interrupted.

I looked to see Maisy, Aden, Gracie, Reece and Clyde by the door. Maisy was wearing a crop top with skinny jeans and sandles, Gracie was wearing a long sleeve top that reached her thighs with leggings, and all the guys were wearing something similar to Ralph, only with red and green shirts and denim jeans.

"I could say the same to you." replied Ryker, with a smirk on his face. I saw Maisy blush deeply and Aden grinned back, pulling Maisy closer. As Aden reached down and pecked her on the lips, some of her hair flew back. There was a red mark on her neck. He marked her?

"Hey, look. Maisy got a wolf hickey!" I chuckled. Maisy looked at me weirdly before I gestured to my neck.

"OH, right, yeah." she replied awkwardly.

"So, what are you guys doing here?" I asked.

"It's your birthday, duh, we are coming with you!" Gracie laughed.

"Oh, okay, cool!" I smiled, before turning to my brother, "Happy birthday, bro!"

Clyde chuckled before glancing around, "I've just realised I'm the only one here without a mate." He coughed.

"That's alright," Aden snickered, "You can be the fifth wheeler."

Everyone laughed lightly before I asked, "So, if we are all going, what car are we taking?"

"We're taking the van." answered Ryker.

Clyde's orbs widened, "You guys have a van as well?" We walked to the other side of the garage. On the end was a shiny, black van, pretty much like-

"You have a car like Mr T?" Clyde exclaimed. He ran over to it, gliding his hand over the paintwork.

"You watched that movie too?" Reece grinned.

"Mr T?" Asked Maisy.

"Oh my God! You've never watched the A Team?" I replied, shocked.

"OH, yeah! That one. Of course I have! I guess it does kind of look like it, huh?" We all slipped into the 7-seater; me in the passenger seat, Gracie and Reece in the middle, Clyde, Maisy and Aden in the back and Ryker driving.

It didn't take long to get there, when we did, it was buzzing with people. There were multiple roller coasters high above all the rides, along with a log flume, mini games and a whole load of others.

"Oh my God! How cool!" Maisy cheered, being the first to run out the van.

We hopped out the van after her, Ryker coming to my side. He kissed the mark on my neck, making me bite my lip, before covering it up with my hair, "Not here, Mister." I grinned.

He rolled his eyes, "What do you want to do first, kitten?"

"Ah. They even have nicknames for each other - true love!" Gracie smirked.

I shook my head, "Hardly. How is 'Mister' a nickname?"

"He called you kitten." Gracie chuckled.

"And he called you 'baby girl' - I've heard that one." Maisy snickered.

"Dude, that's my cousin!" Aden complained, wrapping his arms around Maisy from behind to stop her from running off.

"Yeah, and my sister." Clyde muttered before looking around, "Oh, Wait I have no one."

We chuckled and I looked up to the fair. There were rollercoasters, water slides and, did I mention, rollercoasters? Glad I put shorts on - sucks to be the boys.

"How about a rollercoaster? There's seems to be plenty of them!" I laughed.

"Shall we just work our way around?" Clyde suggested.

"Yeah, that sounds good." I smiled.

We walked up to the pay point to get in. "Seven adults." Ralph spoke to the cashier.

"Okay. That's forty five pounds, sweetie. Would you like a park map? Although, you seem like someone who would know their way around the table." She flirted. I swear she even winked.

"Yes, thanks." Ryker answered. She leaned down to take get a map, giving us a very unpleasant sight. Misty huffed in anger. I looked to Ryker and saw him looking towards the park. Good.

"Ah! Here you go!" She smiled. But that smiled disappeared when she saw Ryker wasn't looking.

"Thanks." I huffed, snatching the map, "By the way, can I make a complaint?" I glared at her, "No one likes to see other people's thongs, so next time, I suggest you bend over a little less." I spat and walked away with Ryker's arm around my waist.

The others laughed behind me and Maisy spoke up, "Oh God, you missed the look on her face!"

"No need to get jealous baby girl, I only have eyes for you." Ryker whispered in my ear, kissing my head.

"Let's go have fun!" Maisy yelled. We all laughed and ran with her like little kids towards the closest ride.

"Log flume? This is my favourite!" I exclaimed, happily, dragging my mate behind me as I ran to the logs. I sat in one and Ryker slipped in behind me, wrapping his hands around my waist. I tensed when he pulled me in closer to him.

"Hold on, baby girl." he smirked as it started.

The log slowly went up, and up, and up. We got to the top. It went round the corner before racing down the slope. I put my hands in the air, cheering while Ryker laughed at me. We got to the bottom were water splashed at us, making us soaked. I could heard the screams of Maisy and other people behind us. When we got out, all of our tops were sticking to us.

"That was so awesome!" Yelled Clyde, leaning his arm over me in a brotherly way.

"I know right. But better get off before someone has your head!" I laughed, pointing to Ryker who's fists were balled.

"Yeah, okay, sis." Clyde answered, detaching his arm, "Get back to your possessive mate." He snickered.

"It's okay, weirdo. He's my brother." I placed a hand on his arm, his body immediately relaxed.

"Come on! Let's go do another ride!" Maisy yelled.

"Oh, I can think of another ride." Aden answered, and all the boys, except Clyde, pulled their mates in close.

"What?" Gracie asked confused.

"Ew, Aden! You're so disgusting!" I ran over and play punched his arm.

"What, me? Never!" He said, pointing to himself.

"Very funny, mate, but that ain't happening yet!" Maisy said, leading to another water slide.

"Water-Lanch?" Gracie asked. I saw the boys look at each other before I realised what they were up to.

"Run!" I yelled, as they went to grab us. But we were too slow. We were gripped by our waists and pulled under the bucket, just as a huge load of water came down.

"You assholes!" Gracie yelled, punching Reece.

"Love you too." Reece answered, kissing her on the lips.

"And you tell me to get a room?" I asked Maisy.

"Yeah... well you got an Alpha as a mate. Sometimes they can't be controlled!" She answered with a smirk. I looked at her with wide eyes.

"You're gross, you know that!" I exclaimed, wrinkling my nose and shoving her with my shoulder, "God, you and Aden are perfect for each other."

"Yeah, but you know what I mean!" She laughed, dragging Aden and I to another ride.

Twenty Nine • I Got Distracted

- -

C hapter Twenty Nine———

Ylva

"Again! Let's do it again!" Maisy yelled, she's such a kid at heart.

We've been here for hours - it was now four in the afternoon. We lost track of time and now we were all starving!

"Nah, I'm hungry." I complained, leaning on Ryker.

"Oh yeah, there's this cafe over in the corner." said Reece.

"Let's go!" I literally begged, weakly trying to pull Ryker along with me.

"Okay, we're coming, grumpy pants!" Clyde laughed.

The boys started to pull off their tops and I paused, "Wait, what are you doing?" I asked, letting go of Ryker's hand.

"Well, we just wanted our mates to check us out." smirked Aden as Ryker pulled me into his naked chest. I froze when his body moulded perfectly with mine.

"Yeah, that and our clothes are soaking!" Reece added.

"So, you can take your tips off but we can't?" I asked with a small frown.

"You're a girl." Reece muttered.

"Sexist!" Gracie accused.

"Well, you don't really see women walking around without tops on-" Aden was cut off by Maisy.

"Yeah because people think it's wrong." She rolled her eyes, "It annoys me that people think that."

Ryker looked over to me when I started moving about and his eyes widened slightly, "Ylva, what are you doing?"

"I'm-" I struggled slightly before pulling my soaked t-shirt off, leaving me in my sports bra, "Taking my top off."

"That's not very family friendly." Reece told me.

"I'm wearing a sports bra." I exclaimed, "This is the exact same thing as I wear when I'm training!"

Ryker growled lowly and wrapped his arms around my waist as a few guys walked past and wolf whistled, "And that's why." He muttered.

"Yep, okay. Let's go now! I'm starved!" I said, trying to pull from Ryker's strong grip.

We arrived at the cafe and sat in a booth, "Oh, Ylva, this is for you. It's from Gran." Clyde answered, taking a book from the backpack he brought. It was a smaller version of the book about vampires Gran had read from, "She said you might need it." he added.

"Thanks." I smiled, placing it on the table.

"Oh, and this is from Aden and I." Maisy smiled, giving me a small box. I opened it to find a Pandora bracelet inside. I gasped and pulled it out. On the chain there was a wolf, a heart and a star. I slipped it on and it dangled around my arm.

"Thanks! I love it!" I smiled, pulling Maisy into a hug, who happened to be sat beside me.

"And this is from Gracie and I. Gracie picked it out!" Reece laughed awkwardly, before handing me a small package. I ripped it open and saw a blue, lacey dress. This time, I swallowed and lifted it up. I would say it went about mid thigh length and had long sleeves.

"Thank you?" I smiled politely, "At least I didn't have to go out and shop this time."

"It's for you to wear tonight!" Gracie told me and I froze.

"Wait, what?" I asked, blinking.

"You and Ryker are going on a date tonight, right? This is what you're wearing!" Maisy answered.

"Uh, okay." I laughed. I put it in the back pack Clyde had bought and zipped it up.

"Hey! Welcome to the Water Side Cafe, can I get you anything?" asked the male waiter.

"Yeah, we'd like our food to go please." Gracie answered.

"Sure, what would you like?"

"Uh, two burgers and two strawberry milkshakes, for him and I." she answered, pointing go Reece.

"And we'll have two chicken nuggets and chips please, with two cokes." Aden answered.

"I'll have a bacon bagget and a Sprite." Clyde responded.

"And we'll have two chicken burgers, chips for everyone and two extra milkshakes." Ryker replied, pulling me closer by my waist, protectively.

"Okay, I'll be back with your orders in about ten minutes." And he walked off.

"Going all protective mode are we?" I laughed, patting Ryker's pectorals.

'God, they are so strong.' Misty growled and Lucine nodded in agreement.

'Oh my God, you guys have issues.' I rolled my eyes.

"He was giving you lovey-dovey eyes." he hissed, kissing my head.

"And you don't? Ryker, I'm all yours. No ones going to take me away from you." I smiled, kissing his chin, before whispering, "I mean, they could try but they could never compare."

Clyde made a sick sound, "God, go mate each other already!"

My eyes flew open as I glared at my brother. Ralph growled and pulled my closer, throwing daggers at Clyde.

"Okay, chill out, man." Reece said.

Maisy turned to Clyde and frowned, "Aren't you supposed to be the protective older brother?"

He turned and chuckled, "Nope. Because I know Ylva can take care of herself."

"That's dangerous." Aden muttered before yelping as I kicked him under the table, "What was that for?!"

"Just proving I could take care of myself."

Our food finally came and we all walked back to the car. Slipping in and belting up, Ryker pulled off, turning home.

"Thanks for a great day, guys." I thanked them.

"No problem, its what friends and mates do!" Maisy answered.

"And brothers." Clyde added.

"And cousins!" Aden yelled. Maisy rolled her eyes and kissed her mate.

"OH MY GOD! I LOVE THIS SONG. TURN IT UP!" Gracie shouted, causing Reece to jump in surprise at his mate.

I turned up the song, Rihanna's Umbrella was playing, not one of my favourite but it was always a classic, "I haven't heard this song in ages!"

"Come on girls! Sing with me!" She laughed.

"You had my heart. And we'll never be worlds apart. Maybe in magazines but you'll still be my star." Gracie started, smiling at Reece, who looked at her as she sang.

"Baby cause in the dark, you can't see shiny cars. And that's when I need you there. With you I'll always share." Maisy sang. Aden grinned as he watched his mate let lose. She had a difficult past, but now with Aden it was like it was al forgotten. He made her life worth living again.

We all sang the chorus as it came, "Because, when the sun shines, we'll shine together. Told you I'll be here forever. Said I'll always be your friend. Took an oath, I'm a stick it out till the end."

"Now that it's raining more than ever, know that we'll still have each other. You can stand under my umbrella. You can stand under my umbrella! Ella, ella, eh, eh, eh-"

I notice Ryker grinning as we continued but his grip on the steering wheel was tight, as if he was holding something back.

The girls laughed, and I continued to sing, "You can run into my arms. It's okay, don't be alarmed. Come here to me. There's no distance between our love. So, go on, let the rain pour. I'll be all you need and more!"

The drive home seemed to take a lot longer than it did to get here, and I'm pretty sure Ryker went to wrong way.

"Dude, you were supposed to go that way." Reece told him, pointing towards the exit he missed on the roundabout.

"I got distracted." He mumbled, sending me a glare.

"Maybe we should keep distracting him and keep singing!" Maisy cheered, grinning to her mate.

"I pray you don't." Clyde muttered.

Despite my brother not wanting to be in the car longer than he had to, the drive still took even longer with traffic. We were five songs in, singing out hearts out to annoy the boys. And the music kept getting worse...

"Don't tell your mother. Kiss one another. Die for each other. We're cool for the summer! Ha!" Maisy sang.

"Take me down into your paradise!" I sang.

"Don't be scared cause I'm your body type!" Maisy joined.

"Just something we wanna try!" Gracie yelled, rhythmically.

"Cause you and I," I sang the call and response.

"You and I," Maisy and Gracie responded.

"We're cool for the summer!" I sang to Ryker. This song was dangerous, and I could see it in my mate's eyes what it was doing to him.

"We're cool for the summer!" Maisy sang to Aden.

"We cool for the summer!" Gracie left a kiss on Reece's cheek.

"Sh... Don't tell your mother" I whispered into Ryker's ear. He tensed and looked at me through black eyes.

"Woo! Go, Ylva! Go, Ylva!" Maisy chanted.

We moved our body slowly from side to side as we sang, "Got my mind on your body. And your body on my mind. Got a taste for the cherry, I just need to take a bite..."

"TAKE ME DOWN!" I yelled in tune and time, startling my brother who had zoned out completely.

"Take me down into your paradise. (DON'T BE SCARED) Don't be scared, I'm your body type! Just something that we wanna try (WANNA TRY). Cause you and I! We're cool for the summer!" Maisy and Gracie sang the course.

"Summer!"

"Take me down!" I sang the off cuts while Maisy and Gracie sang 'We're cool for the summer' repeatedly.

"We're cool for the summer!"

"Don't be scared!"

"Because I'm your body type!"

"Just something that we wanna try. Cause you and I!"

"We're cool for the summer. Ooh!"

"We're cool for the summer!" I finished.

The van jolted as we parked at the pack house and before I could do anything, lips were on mine. So much passion... maybe that last song was a step too far!

Thirty • He's Going to Kidnap You

C hapter Thirty------

Ylva

Staring at the reflection looking back at me, I swallowed thickly. I was dressed up in the navy blue dress that Gracie and Reece given me today, feeling highly exposed even though it was mainly my legs that were showing. I had slipped on the Pandora bracelet and Maisy curled my dark blonde hair.

"Oh my God! You're looking sexy!" My Amista playfully winked.

"Shut up." I mumbled. Even though this dress was definitely pulled tight around my body, showing every single curve I owned, I still hated compliments.

"I don't see why you don't like compliments? You're a really beautiful person Ylva, inside and out."

I shook my head, ignoring her, "Do you know where he's taking me?" I asked, trying to change the subject.

"Oh yeah, he's going to kidnap you and take you to a secluded island to keep you away from other males forever!" Maisy laughed as I stared at her with an 'are you serious' look, "Yes I do, but I'm not telling you. Ryker will have my head!"

"Yeah, I think he's already planning on getting mine after the car ride home."

"You getting all close to him?" she smirked.

"What? No!" I yelled, smacking her, "We were playing a dangerous game though! Those songs just got worse and worse."

"Yeah, all their eyes were black." Maisy snickered.

"I felt sorry for Clyde. He hasn't found his mate yet." I sighed, running a hand through my hair. I applied some nail varnish before slipping on some Converse. Yeah, I know, Converse with a dress - classy, right?"

"Aw, poor baby." Maisy pouted.

'My God. You couldn't wear something other than Converse?' Asked Misty.

'Nope!' I laughed as she blocked me.

I went into the bathroom to brush my teeth and wash my face. I leaned against the sink and sighed. I had never been on a date before. It wasn't necessarily on my bucket list. My heart seemed to beat quicker every second.

'It's okay Ylva...' My mother's voice filled my mind.

I flinched. 'You really need to work on when you come to speak to me. You almost gave me a heart attack!' I muttered, annoyed.

'Sorry , sweetie.' She apologised but I could tell she was humoured.

"Ylva?" I heard Maisy's voice echo through my ears.

"Uh, yeah?" I shook my head and looked to Maisy.

"Are you okay?" She came over and pulled me in the room.

"I, uh, yeah. I'm fine." I rubbed my eyes with my palms and sighed. Luckily, I didn't wear any makeup, so nothing was ruined, smudged or had to be reapplied.

"No, you're not. I can tell - it's an Amista thing." She looked at me seriously.

"Okay, fine! I've never been in a date before!" I said, like it was nothing, throwing my arms up in the air.

"You've never been on a date before?"

"No."

"You've never been on a date before!"

"No."

"You've never-"

"No Maisy, I haven't!" I snapped, causing her to flinch.

"Sorry," she apologised, "It's just hard to imagine with a girl of your looks, skill and personality that you've never been on a date!"

Wow, okay! That was something I wasn't expecting! Just because I look okay, not that I'm saying I do, and that I have skills or a good personality, doesn't mean that I have loads of guys swarming around me! I probably scared them away! Ha!

'Nah, we're just hot.' Lucine snickered.

"Okay...?"

Maisy shook her head, "Come on, your mate is waiting!" She laughed and dragged me downstairs.

We walked through the kitchen where various pack members smiled and waved. The same little girl who put the flower in my fur came up to me again. This time she had an azure iris held delicately between her fingers.

"Hello, Luna. You look very pretty!" She smiled. She was wearing a denim skirt with different shades of green on it and a top with a snow leopard print.

I knelt down to her level, "Thank you. I love your top!" I smiled back at her.

"Thank you, my Daddy bought it for me. Please can I put this flower in your hair?" She asked, her brown eyes beaming.

"Yes, you may." I put my head lower and tiny hands ran through my curly hair before a flower was carefully placed under a clip on the side of my head. I leaned back, "Thank you. You should be a hairstylist when you're older."

She clapped, "That's what I've always wanted to be!"

"Just don't grow up too fast!" I chuckled and the young one ran off to find her father.

I stood back up and saw Ryker in the doorway, smiling at me. I walked over to him, forgetting about the pack members watching. Hands held my waist and lips met mine. Closing my eyes, I grinned against his lips before kissing back, wrapping my arms around his neck.

"Hello, gorgeous." Ryker growled lowly, biting his lower lip.

'Man, that was HOT!' Lucine purred, leaving me to roll my eyes at her.

"Ready for our date?" He asked, placing a gentle kiss on my forehead.

"Yep!" I grinned, "But Maisy said you'd kidnap me."

"Only in the best way." Ryker chuckled, grabbing my hand and pulling me away from the crowd. We came to his metallic red Alfa Romeo that always seemed to take my breath away.

"I still love this car!" I breathed, Ryker opening the passenger door for me.

"Is it weird to be jealous of a car?" Ryker chuckled before running over to his side.

"What's there jealous to be of?" I asked.

"Oh, there's a lot that I'm looking at to be jealous of. I'm just glad it's mine." he smirked. I turned away and looked out the window, "You shouldn't be afraid of compliments, Ylva."

I looked at him, "I'm not afraid, it's just that most of the compliments I get aren't true!"

Ralph's finger lifted up my chin, forcing me to look at him, "I assure you, every compliment I give you is one hundred percent true!" He leaned in and pecked my lips. But Misty and Lucine had other ideas. They quickly took control of my actions and my arms wrap themselves around Ryker's neck, pulling him in closer.

'Seriously, you two?'

'Sorry, Ryker's just so cute and irresistible!' Misty mumbled, enjoying the kiss.

'And we love him..so much.' Lucine hinted.

'What! Ew, no! Not happening!' I snarled as they whimpered. Not yet anyway.

'It will soon..I can feel it!' Misty said.

'That and Raiden said he can't hold much longer, especially after what you did in the car on the way home' Lucine sighed, a love sick sigh if I might add!

"Sorry." I whispered, but he just laughed and placed a hand on my waist, trailing it over my hip. Ryker bit my bottom lip asking for entrance but I was quick to deny him of that luxury, "I apologised because my actions were of Misty and Lucine's."

"So, you didn't enjoy the kiss?" Ryker asked, pouting.

I smirked and sent him a wink, "Nope, I didn't say that."

The Alpha beside me let out a small growl before turning back to the steering wheel, "Let's go, shall we?" He asked with a husky voice, starting the ignition.

"We shall." I laughed and he pulled off from the garage.

Thirty One • I Can Feed Myself, You Know

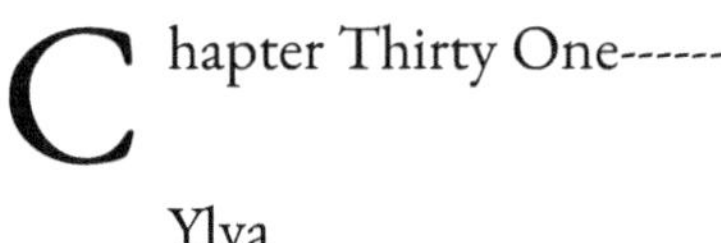

C hapter Thirty One------

Ylva

It wasn't long before Ryker parked by a forest and got out. He came over to my side and opened the door, holding his hand out for me to take, "What a gentleman." I joked, accepting the gesture.

"Manners make a man." He grinned, leaving me to stare wide-eyed at him.

"You've watched Kingsmen?"

"Who hasn't?"

"People who haven't live yet." I chuckled before looking around. Currently, we were walking through the dark forest, but with our wolf sight, it was easy to see, "Considering my surroundings, I'm starting to believe Maisy was right about you kidnapping me."

Ryker chuckled before pressing a kiss onto my temple, "You look beautiful tonight, by the way!" He spoke, wrapping his arm around my waist.

"Oh, uh, thanks." I answered, scratching my arm nervously. We continued walking further into the woods before my mate came to a halt.

"Shift."

I quickly morphed into my blue wolf, standing taller than I remember. Ryker shifted and I was an inch or two lower than him, his powerful form creating a seal of protection around me, 'How have I grown?' I asked, following Ryker onwards.

'I don't know. Maybe because you have me as a mate?' I could hear the smirk under his words.

'Of course.' I rolled my eyes. The moon was out and the stars above were bright and gleaming lighting our path. The forest seemed to glow from the moonlight and the leaves sparkled from the rain water on them.

'Where are we going?' I asked as we wandered deeper and deeper into the forest.

'You'll find out in a minute, be patient.' Ryker laughed through the link. His laugh was so amazing. When he laughed he seemed so carefree and innocent. When he laughed, properly laughed, it was like all of his Alpha duties, all his problems disintegrated into thin air.

Like today. He wasn't the strict, mean Alpha he's normally in. Ryker was more relaxed and he seemed to have a good time. He didn't seem tense like he normally did. Misty, Lucine and I liked this side of Ryker. He wasn't dangerous or scary; he was warm and calming. He didn't have to worry about anyone for a few hours.

Misty and Lucine just wanted their mate to be happy and safe. They didn't want him to get hurt in any shape or form, even if him being an Alpha made him prone to attacks. They wanted to spend the rest of their life with Ryker and Raiden.

'We're here.'

Looking up, I saw a clearing through the trees. In the middle, under the moon, were a couple of thick blankets, surrounded by candles, flowers and pebbles. Food was scattered out on one of the blankets; crisps, biscuits, cake, pizza and loads of other junk food. I gasped and shifted back to human form, following Ryker to sit.

He pulled me into him and rose a piece of pizza to my mouth, feeding me like a baby. I groaned. The BBQ chicken pizza taste filled my mouth, "This is my favourite flavour of pizza!" I smiled, leaning back on my mate.

"How did I know?" He laughed.

I sat up and studied his face, "Faith told you didn't she?" I smirked.

"How do you know that?" His eyes widened as he spun me around to face me.

I shrugged, "It's a Lycus thing, I guess." I answered before laughing, "That and only Faith knows that this exact pizza is my favourite - it's homemade." He laughed at me before feeding me a prawn cocktail crisp, "You know I can feed myself?" I chuckled, swallowing the food.

"Yeah, but I want to do it."

I smiled at how romantic he can be. Who knew an Alpha could be like this? All those people who said he killed people who entered his territory and here he was now - sitting on a blanket and feeding me food. Alpha's do have a soft side.

"What's wrong?" He sighed, resting back on his arms.

"Huh?"

"What's wrong. Your face looks confused or almost angry?" He answered.

"Just thinking,"

"About?"

I sighed before sitting to face him, "Can I ask you a question?"

"Shoot." He raised an eyebrow of curiosity.

"And can you answer truthfully?" I crossed my arms.

"Ok, I will for you."

I took a deep breath, "Do you really kill people who come in to your territory?"

Ryker's body was immediately tense as he stared at me worriedly, as if he didn't want to tell me. That was something I didn't like. His fists clenched and I looked into his eyes, "Ryke?"

Ryker's eyes met mine, "I only kill them if their a threat, or if I know they didn't kill her."

The way he said 'her' made Misty and Lucine's instinct jealous. What if he had another girlfriend that got killed and he loved her more than me? No, wait, no jumping to conclusions. You don't know the full story, do you? He must have noticed my jealous face because he was quick to add, "She was my sister, Ylva."

"Oh." I mentally sighed in relief. "What happened?"

I saw Ryker's eyes go glassy as if it had a real effect on him. I moved closer to him and wrapped my arms around his torso, trying to support him. I heard Ryker swallow before he pulled me into a tight hug. Was he crying? I didn't know what to do. How do you help someone who's crying but you don't know what for?

"She was attacked by rouges. They ripped her to nothing." He whispered, as if he was trying to hold everything back in front of me.

"It's okay, Rykes. Cry. Get all the pain out - I won't think differently of you." I whispered back, pulling him closer to me. I knew he was crying now. His shoulders shook but he still refused to make any sound. He sniffed into my chest, his arms limply around my waist. I knew what it felt like to lose someone you love. To see them ripped to shreds. To nothing.

"She looked exactly like our mother. Long, bright ginger hair and forest green eyes. She loved Maisy and always made time to spend with us." Ralph continued, a small smile painting on his features, "Her name was Randi. She was a hybrid, like you. Our Dad had just begun to train her in becoming an Alpha. She was so kind-hearted and loved everyone in the pack and everyone loved her. She was the perfect Alpha."

Ryker's soft smile soon turned to a menacing glare, "Until those rouges fucked everything up. It was late at night when she was kidnapped. Our pack was still recovering from a battle that had recently occurred and we were vulnerable. I went to find her against my father's orders. I was determined to bring her back because I knew that the pack needed her - we needed her."

He swallowed again, "I was eight at the time. So young and naive. I was trapped in the easiest way possible. My leg was strung up and yanked up on to a tree branch, leaving me hanging to watch as they killed her and took her body with them. It's like they knew I was coming. They laughed at my pathetic yells and told me that I would never be a good Alpha. And I believed them. My parents found me after a while."

I stroked his hair, trying to calm him, "I know how it feels." I whispered, remembering how I saw my mother and father die.

Ralph pulled back and I saw his eyes. So much pain and hatred, "That's why I kill rouges and people who could threaten my family, my pack. They changed me. Ever since that day, I vowed myself to kill anyone who could put people through the same thing. I don't want anyone to feel what I went felt when my sister got killed." He wiped his tear stains and looked at me, "I know it's not what an Alpha should do, but I-I'm not my sister - I'm not her."

"It's okay, Ryker. You're the perfect Alpha despite what you've been through. Maybe some people don't understand why you do what you do but you do it to protect those you care about. Everyone goes through something in their life." I looked at the mossy grass, "Trust me, I know. And I also know that you are the best Alpha you can be. That's what makes you so important to your pack."

"Thank you," I heard my mate whisper before I was pulled into arms and placed on Ryker's lap, "Tell me." he whispered, kissing my ear.

I looked at him and frowned, "Tell you what?" he gave me a pointed looked and I shook my head, "No, I can't. It's not a happy story." I sighed, trying to pull away.

Ryker used his Alaric wolf strength and kept me on his lap, "Please, Ylva. You've helped me, you've helped everyone... Let someone help you."

I drew a breath, trying to control my heart rate. No one has said anything like that to me, not even Faith. I shook my head again and whispered, "I'm supposed to be the one that can be there for everyone."

'Just tell him, Ylva. Let your pain go.' Lucine mumbled, hiding back in my mind. I don't want to be an attention seeker though. That's why I never told anyone in the first place.

Thirty Two • The Pros and Cons

C hapter Thirty Two------

Ylva

Staring at the mossy ground, Ryker's arms draped around me tightened, "Please, tell me, baby. I want to help you." Ralph whispered, kissing my mark. I twitched at the contact but made no other movement. I was considering the pros and cons of telling him this.

Pro: I would have someone close who would know my story. Someone who I can trust. I knew that this would stay between Ryker and I, possibly Maisy if I told her.

Con: Ryker was very possessive. What if he went on a rampage trying to find those guys? They could already be dead and Ryker who be on the hunt for the wrong guy.

"I can't." I told him, more firmly. Tears were welling up but I refused to let them go - why start crying about something that happened years ago?

"Clyde told me a bit. But it's bugging me not knowing everything like I should." he clasps his hands tightly around my hips, pulling me in closer in a protective mannar.

I breathed deeply, fiddling with my fingers. Pro: I wouldn't have to tell him the full story if Clyde had told him some. But that left the question - how did Clyde know?

'Just tell him, Ylva. He means it when he says he'll be there for us.' Misty whimpered, 'Stop pro-coning everything and just tell him. At least he would be someone we could go to.'

"Wha-," I cleared my throat, trying not to make it sound like I was about go cry, "What did Clyde say?"

Ryker tensed and wrapped his body closer to mine, as if he was afraid to lose me, "He said these men came. They killed your mother and father when you were watching. Then he said they-" he took a heaving breath, "They abused you. He said he couldn't protect you, even though he was the same age as you. He says that someone is after you."

I stiffened. So, it was all true. The dreams, the visions, the words in my mind? All of it was true? Someone was out to get me?

That though made my heart hammer against my chest. Ryker must have heard it because he pulled me closer to him. I gripped onto his shirt as my body began to shake violently.I've never felt so useless in my life. Why was I just sat here when someone was out there after me? I should be looking for them, demanding an answer to why they were practically stalking me!

'Lucine? Do you know anything about this?' I asked, as Ryker's chin rested against my head as he stroked my hair gently.

'No I never-' then she paused. I closed my eyes to see my ampire looking scared. I saw her eyes. Dark brown, as if she was talking to someone inside.

'Lucine?'

'Lucine!' She stayed frozen, as if she wasn't alive until she suddenly gasped for air and stared at me wide eyed.

'What Lucine!?' I practically yelled.

'I-It's true' she stumbled before falling down, 'Someone's coming for you. His name is... it's...' She panicked but shook her head, 'He was the man that killed your parent and abused you!'

'Ylva! You need to tell Ryker!' Misty whined, comforting her other side.

'Blake.' Lucine whispered, 'His name... it's Blake.'

"I, uh... R-Ryker?" I swallowed, looking up at his deep forest green eyes.

"Yes, kitten?"

"There's something you should... you should know." I kept my eyes trained to the ground as I felt myself being spun around. I was surrounded by my mate's body in a protective manner, his eyes burning holes into my skull, wordlessly saying I needed to tell him.

'Tell him Ylva! Now, before I do!" Misty screeched, giving me a headache.

"It is true." I sighed, twiddling my fingers together, "People-" I took in a breath of air, suddenly feeling very claustrophobic despite being outside in the cool air, "People did kill my parents, and abused me on that fateful day." I shivered, pushing back my tears. I've cried too many times because of that night and now it's time to be strong.

I felt arms wrap tightly around my body, pulling me close to a warm and comforting chest. Burying my face, I continued, "T-The man that hurt me said then he'd see me later in life. But recently, I've been hearing his voice in my mind and I-I don't know why." I whispered, "Maybe it's PTSD, but it was so long ago and the voice seems too real for anything else."

"But Clyde said someone here knew of what's coming." Ryker mumbled. I could hear the anger laced in his voice and he was breathing heavily, high chest rising up and down.

"I-I don't know." I mumbled into his shirt.

Someone here knew that I was in danger. They knew my fate and they could've been reporting everything to this guy and I could've been in even more danger. But how would they know to come here? No one could possibly know that I was Ryker Dawson's mate.

"His name is Blake." I whispered, finally able to stop my body shivering.

A low growl rumbled from Ryker's throat. I swallowed, thinking I should have never said his name. Ryker's eyes had turned pitch black when I looked and his grip on my wrists tightened, his claws digging into my skin. I winced, whimpering, "R-Rykes." He looked down and saw his death grip, quickly retracting his claws.

"Sorry." he whispered, crossing his legs around me and hugging me close.

"Do you know Blake?"

"No." was his quick response and I decided to drop to conversation. Con: Ryker would still lie about things. I could tell he knew something, but right now, I really didn't want to push it. I wasn't in the mood to try.

Why would someone come after me? I mean, yeah, I am a Lycus and it's a rare species, but anyone could take DNA or skills and turn someone into one. It wasn't that diffult.

Maybe it was because I was a Luna. Or, going to be. Maybe it was because I was Alpha Ryker's mate. He has killed many and destroyed many, he would have a lot of enemies because of this. This is what made me fear about being any Alpha's mate. You were used as bait to bring in the kill! Yay! Please note my un-humorous sarcasm.

I sighed. This was my birthday. I wasn't meant to be upset or angry or scared. I didn't want to talk about my past because now was time to live for my future. I was meant to be having a good time, laughing, smiling, having fun.

I knew what I wanted to do. And it wasn't just because of the mate bond. Though that pull was becoming ever stronger and difficult to control. Misty and Lucine lightened up to the idea of this and pranced around like crazy inside my head. They would have no regrets.

Biting my lip, I looked up and saw Ryker's black eyes. No wolf. Just anger. I took a shaky breath before leaning towards him, pressing my lips against his. He froze, staring at me wide eyed before kissing back. Through the passion and force, I pushed his back to the ground as to not fall over myself.

I laid against his body, and continued to kiss his now, strangely, irresistible lips. Curse Misty and Lucine for there was no going back now. His hands gently gripped the back of my neck, pulling me in even closer to him, his other hand rested against the curve of my hip.

"Please, Ryker." I mumbled against his lips, opening my eyes to be greeted with his usual cocky smirk. Oh yeah, no going back now.

Pro: I loved my mate.

Thirty Three • In Which I Caught a Dark Guy's Voice

C hapter Thirty Three------

Ylva

I woke up to icy, cold wind itching at my skin. I grinned, remembering last night's events. It was unbelievable, I couldn't ask for a better first time. Misty and Lucine were so wrapped up in love at the moment, they were still sleeping. I blushed slightly when the arm around my waist tightened and clutched my hip. I removed my arm from above my head and wrapped it around Ryker's torso.

He stirred a little before waking up, peeping down at me. When he saw I was awake, he smirked, and pulled my naked body closer to him, "I had a wonderful night. I couldn't have shared it with anyone better." he smiled, gently kissing my mark.

Now that Ryker and I had mated, we had completed the mating bond. This made me his Luna, and my wolf was now stronger, especially as Ryker was an Alpha. But a Luna ceremony was still needed to officially claim me as the pack's Luna, even though they recognised me as that already.

"Thank you, so did I." I replied, pecking at his lips, before looking up, frowning at our current location, "How did we end up in your room?" Ryker's smirk was the only thing I needed to tell me and I flushed darkly, letting out a small, "Oh."

"I will always protect you Ylva, I hope you know that." he whispered, wrapping his arm securely around me and kissing my forehead.

"I know." I smiled.

A few hours later and we were up and dressed. I slipped on some shorts and a vest top, along with one of Ralph's jumper and tried to pull my hair up into a lazy, side bun- most of my hair fell down after I let it go. I sighed before ripping out the band and letting my wavy hair flow down my back, unruly from last night's curls.

"Don't worry, baby, you look beautiful no matter how you have your hair." Ralph smiled, nuzzling his head into the crook of my neck.

"What are you doing today?" I asked as we walked down the stairs.

"Well, I have a lot of paperwork to do today and I need to sort out a few people in the cells." The scowl on Ryker's face made it clear he didn't want to talk about it nor even do it.

"Well, have fun. I'll just be here, bored out of my mind!" I shrugged, slumping down on the sofa.

"I would much rather spend the day with my beautiful mate." he leaned down and kissed my lips.

"No Ryker, you have Alpha duties. Now go do them, my big bad Alpha!" I ordered, jokingly. He growled playfully before leaving me. I sighed and flicked through the TV channels. No one was downstairs yet, which was weird because it was way past eleven. Maybe it was training day.

'Hello, sweetie! Ready to see me?' A rough voice asked. I jumped out my skin, my heartbeat racing wildly.

'Ylva... it's him... it's Blake.' Lucine trembled.

'What the fuck do you want!?' I yelled at him. Incredibly, I caught the link and was able to stop him before he blocked me again.

'Oh my dear, that's no way to respond to your future Alpha!' He tutted.

'You will never be my Alpha.' I snapped, growing angry with him already. I didn't even know who he was, except for the idea of him being the man who hurt me years ago.

'Whatever helps you sleep at night.' he chuckled. His laugh was deep and dark. Nothing like Ryker's carefree laugh or Aden's cheerful chuckle. It was rough, I could almost smell the hatred from the way he spoke, 'But my dear, I need you to come with me.'

I laughed hysterically, 'Me? Come with you! I don't even know who you are, I will never leave here just to see you somewhere!' I growled, clearly annoyed with him.

'You either come the easy way, or the hard way!' He shouted back. Blake's voice was now more serious and angry. I immediately stopped laughing and my heart rate picked up again, 'You come to me, otherwise your precious Alpha will never see tomorrow.'

'You wouldn't dare threaten Ryker.' I snarled, hissing at him through the link, 'He could tear you limb from limb.'

'Your choice. You coming to see me is the difference between your Alpha being dead or alive.' Blake threatened, honesty laced in his words.

I swallowed, Misty growled and Lucine hissed, 'You touch my mate and you're dead.' Misty manages to say, before giving the control back.

'Well then, you better come and see me!' Blake snarled back, clearly enjoying this.

'Where?'

'No! Ylva don't! It's a trap!' Lucine yelled, desperate for me to not make plans.

'I know, Lucine, but he's going to hurt Ralph if I don't!' I reminded her.

'No, Ylva! He's gonna do it either way! Please, just listen to me!' She begged.

'I know!' I repeated, 'But we need to find out what he wants. It's the only way to stop all this.'

'No! You and Ryker will get hurt! Please, just think about this carefully! You are dealing with a senior vampire, the cleverest of them all. You listen to him, then you're a goner!' Lucine whimpers.

'Lucine stop! I'm going to see him! I have to. To save the pack, our pack!' I hissed before closing the link.

'Where Blake?' I insist.

'Oh, I don't know whether to tell you. You might tell Alpha Ryker.' He taunted.

'No, I won't. Now tell me.' I hear Lucine whimper, trying one last time to make me stop. No! I needed to keep Ryker and the pack away from danger, even if it means putting myself in a worse situation. It's what Luna's do.

'Hmm, okay. Meet me tomorrow, down by your grandmother's home.' He chuckled darkly.

'You touch my Gran, your dead.' Misty snarled, taking control again.

'Don't worry. I'll take very good care of her! After all, she is my age! And she so beautiful!' Blake pestered.

'You sick bastard. You even think about touching her or hurting her in any way, the deal is off!' Misty snapped.

'Don't worry darling. Nothing will happen to precious granny. But come quickly! Before I change my mind!' He dropped the link, and I was left there shaking in anger.

If he touches my Gran, my mate, any of my family or pack mates, I will personally end his existence. I will fucking murder him, even if its the last thing I do!

Thirty Four • Important Information: He's Not Happy

- -

C hapter Thirty Four———

Ryker

I slammed my fist on the desk, growling in annoyance and the pen that was brutally murdered under my hand pinged across the room. Anger boiled in me with the fact that Blake was after Ylva.

Blake was the shit bag that killed my sister. He watched me weaken and plead as he ripped her to shreds. To nothing. I have been looking for him all my life and every time I come close to him, he always manages to slip away.

"What's up with you?" Reece asked, knowing he was on thin ice with my anger. He stepped into the room and leaned against the furtherest wall, watching me as I threw quick punches at the wall beside me.

"Blake." I snarled, smashing a large hole in the wall.

Reece was suddenly up and walking over to me, sitting in the guest chair. I saw a piece of paper that was scrunched up in his hand but before I could ask what it was, Reece beat me with another question.

"What has he done now?" His eyes flickered black, nearly as angry as me. He knew everything after all - he was my closest friend.

"He's after Ylva!" I snapped, throwing another fist at the dented wall.

Reece was silent.

Nothing's going to happen to Ylva. I meant what I said when I told her I would protect her. She was important to not only me, but our pack as well; she was their Luna. Anyone who hurts he will perish, even if I have to sacrifice myself.

There was a harsh knock on the door, before Clyde stumbled in, growling and gasping, grabbing his head as if he was in pain. He looked up to me and he growled again before falling into his knees.

"A-Alpha!" He choked. I heard pain laced in his voice. Tears were coming from his eyes and he struggled to speak, "It's Y-Ylva!"

"What about Ylva?" I questioned, my wolf at bay. When it comes to my wolf, anyone who hurts Ylva was going to get a death wish. No one dared hurt her when we were around.

Clyde clawed at his chest, blood bleaching his white t-shirt. His eyes were growing blacker and blacker by the second, "B-Blake... Ylva she... kidnapped-" but he fainted on the floor, as if all the air had come out of him.

"Clyde? Clyde!" I yelled. I saw Reece tense, clutching the piece of paper. Then I realised what had happened; it's the same for my dad. Visions can sometimes take up too much of his energy, especially if they are powerful, and he can fall into unconsciousness or faint. My eyes widened at this finding.

"He's had a vision."

Reece looked at me, his eyes full of horror, "But... but how?" He asked, carefully picking up Clyde to place him more comfortably on the sofa to the side.

"Clyde's a Lycus vampire. Vampires are often prone visions. It's similar to my Dad. When he has strong visions, it can take up a lot of their energy and cause them to pas out." I ran my hand through my hair and over my face, rubbing the stubble.

'The only person who will know anything is that BITCH!' My wolf snarled, aching to rip her to shreds.

'How do you know?'

'I've traced and read her mind link. She's been contacting an unknown personnel for over two months.' Raiden snapped, his words laced with fear and anger, 'And they aren't from the pack or any close by.'

I balled my fists and the desk came crashing to the ground. I growled angrily, boiling rage filling my body, "Uh...Ryker?" Reece mumbled. I could see the dread and fear in his eyes. He wanted to leave the room and not be here. He knew that when I became angry, almost anything in sight was demolished or killed. But no - I wouldn't kill my Beta or my Luna's brother.

"What?" I snapped making him flinch.

"Uh...um, Ylva told me to give this to you." he swallowed, handing over the piece of paper that was folded in his hand.

"What is it?" I asked, snatching it from his grasp.

"Read it, I'll take Clyde to the doctor." He answered, hauling Clyde's arm over one of his shoulders and dragging him out the room. Anything to get out of the current situation.

The way Reece spoke made me not want to read the letter. I sensed something powerful about this paper and something was stopping me from wanting to read it. But no. It's from Ylva. I have to read it no matter what it is. I opened it.

'Ryker,

I'm sorry. I know you're going to hate me for doing this, but Blake has spoken to me again. He told me to meet him. It was either that or war. I know you don't like him, I don't either, but if it prevents war between werewolves and vampires, I will protect our pack.

Please don't worry, I will be fine. I have had plenty of training. I'm sorry again, but I will be back. I will promise you that much. Thank you for a wonderful night.

Love, Ylva'

I snarled. Why would she meet him? The pack would go to war because Ylva is their Luna. And she told me not to worry? Well, hell! Of course I'm going to fucking worry! I know, she thinks she's doing a good thing, protecting her pack, but Blake is dangerous! She needs to stay away from him.

'Ylva!' I hissed through the link. But Ylva had blocked me. Typical. I could only feel what she felt and if she got hurt I would feel that too.

'No! My mate!' Raiden whimpered, 'You have to go after her! Now!'

'What if she needs to see him, like she said. Maybe we need to trust our mate. She's been trained to the highest of standards - we've seen that much.'

'No! Blake will hurt her! He will steal her from me! From us! Go get our mate!' He snapped

'Ylva, Misty and Lucine need time. Maybe she's right this time?' I suggested.

'Fine! But if it's over a day, I swear I'm going to take control and find her myself!' He threatened.

'Deal. If it's over a day, I will go looking for her. But she shouldn't be that long!' I ran my hands through my dark spiky hair.

'Good... Now we have a bitch to deal with!' He snarled, pushing me to go down to the cells.

'Yeah and I'm gonna rip her to shreds!' I growled lowly.

I burst through the office door and sprinted to the dungeons. Katie would tell me, otherwise she's going to regret ever coming near this pack.

Thirty Five • You Can Never Say No to an Alpha

C hapter Thirty Five———

Ryker

I stormed through the pack house straight into the cells. That bitch has done enough damage and she was going to die. She harmed my sister in the worse way and she made my mate unhappy. She knows something we don't and I'm going to find out what!

I shoved past some guards before making my way to her cell. Shaggy brown hair was matted around her face and her eyes were surrounded with dark circles. She stared up at me, smirking. But that gesture soon disappeared when she saw my pitch black orbs, "Well, well,well. She left?" The pathetic smirk reappeared on her scrawny face. But this time it wasn't lustful; it was evil.

"What do you know?" I snapped, leading her to flinching.

"Know about what?" She asked, trying to play coy. Katie was far from innocent. She was the only outsider and she does have something to do with it. Alaric's can sense when people are lying.

"You're the only outsider in this pack! Where the fuck is YLVA!" I shouted, using my Alpha tone. Katie is still a member of this pack. She signed to the terms, I can still yell and make her submit.

"Oh, the joys." She sarcastically replied, slumping against the wall behind her, "It was all a trap, you know."

I growled, Raiden coming full out. He stalked towards her, making her crawl back into the corner. Perfect for me. Bad move for her.

"TELL ME WERE MY MATE IS!" Raiden snarled.

"It was my job. I have always been a rouge. It was a trap. One of our elders had a vision of your mate, telling us that she came here." She smirked again, looking up at me.

"What are you talking about?" I asked. My fists were tightly balled and my chest rose rapidly due to my anger.

"Our elders had a vision. When Blake heard about it, he thought it was a great time to get back at you!" She snarled.

"Where's. My. Mate?" Raiden demanded.

"I don't know."

Liar. I can tell. Her heart beat increased and she avoided eye contact, "Katie," I spat her name, "Tell me where she is. NOW!"

"No!"

Raiden snarled and gripped her neck, "TELL ME THE FUCK WHERE YLVA IS!" he yelled at her pathetic face.

"N-No! You can't make me!" She choked out, gripping my top, trying to make me stop.

"Oh, really?" Raiden smirked and I looked away as soon as he slashed her with his claws. She cried out and gripped her stomach.

"I-Is that the best you've g-got?" She wheezed.

I tightened the grip, "Tell me. You've got five seconds."

"I-I will never-"

"Five."

"You c-can't-"

"Four."

"Never will I-"

"Three."

"But-"

"Two."

"N-No, wait I-!"

"One." I clutched her neck tighter.

"O-Okay, okay!" She cried in defeat.

I dropped her to the ground, making her shiver in fear, "SPEAK." Katie flinched at my Alpha tone, making her crawl back.

"B-Blake's going to kill her!" She whimpered, tears streaming down her face as she rubbed her red neck.

"WHAT?!"

"H-He wanted to make you break down and fall. S-So then he could take over." She clutched her chest.

"Why did you do it?"

"B-Because he's my mate. I-I found him when I was roaming alone and he took me in. He promised me that he'd look after me and protect me but he made me do his dirty work. I had no choice. He made me!" She cried, curling in a ball.

"Your pathetic trash, you know that?" I snarled. She sobbed and slumped onto the floor. I knelt down and gripped her hair, pulling her closer to me.

"Where is my mate?" I seethed.

"S-She's going to meet him now." She whispered through tears.

"Where?!"

"A-At her G-Grans."

I growled before chucking her away from me. I don't want to be near that piece of shit. I stormed out the cell in attempts to leave but someone called, "Wait! Alpha!"

I spun round to see Karen leaning out of one of the bars, "What? I'm not in the best of moods so don't waste my time!" I snarled. She jumped back a bit before moving forward again.

"No, this is important!" She pleads.

"What is it?" I sighed, running my hand through my hair.

"It's about your mate." She mumbled.

My head snapped up and ran over to her cell. Slamming open the cell door, I roughly gripped her arms, "What about her?" I hissed, ready to kill her if she has done anything to my baby.

"No, don't worry Alpha. I haven't hurt her in any way." she swallowed. I listen for a nervous breath or a increase in heart rate. Nope. Nothing! Dropping her, I leaned against the wall, running a hand over my face with a sigh. Ylva's been gone less than a day and I'm already a mess.

"Alpha. Your mate could be in serious danger." Karen's mate spoke.

"What?" Hmm, seems like a word I'm using a lot lately.

"Blake, you know him, right?" He sighed.

"Yes, he killed my sister." I growled lowly.

"Well, you kill his dad, didn't you?" he cautiously asked, knowing he was close to thin ice.

"Yes." I sighed.

"And his brother?"

"YES! Okay? Please cut to the freaking chase!" I snapped. My anger was so close to blaring and killing everyone and everything in sight.

"Sorry, Alpha." He bowed his head.

"Continue." I growled.

"Well, Blake wants revenge. Ever since he heard about Luna Ylva, he's been desperate to get her, use her, weaken her." He told me. "When he meets you again, he will kill her. Unless you have backup and a good plan, she and you will die and your pack will be Alpha-less."

I growled angrily and punched the wall next to me. A brick crumbled and cracks trailed up the wall.

"Alpha." I turned my attention back to Andrew, "I know you have no reason to trust me, but I would like to help."

Andrew was right. I didn't have a reason to trust him.

He was a rouge. He was born one and will die one, even if he is in a pack. He was an ally of Blake's and stole another pack's Luna. She was special abilitied, like Ylva. Andrew, Blake and a few others used her hidden abilities to try and kill her own pack. They mostly succeeded, until they reached the Alpha. Luna April recognised him and felt awful. She wanted to end Blake herself and tried to kill him, but Alpha Jensen stopped her because he knew that wasn't who she was. Physically and mentally she was damaged, but now Luna April rules with a big heart, promising her life to her pack. They're happy with their three children.

"Why should I trust you?" I asked, glaring at him, "Why should I even think to believe you?"

He sighed at me, "Blake's goal is power, he doesn't care about anything else, not even Katie," he pointed to a passed out wolf on the cell floor opposite, "He needs to be stopped. It's gone to far now."

"And how can we use you?" I asked him the same questions I always ask someone who wants to help. I need to get every detail I can out of him and continuously check for a stuttered sentence or skip of a heart beat.

"I know Blake's territory inside and out. I can be of great assistance." He smiled, holding his hand out.

I hesitated. I didn't know whether I could trust him. After what he did, he could use this as an escape. But he did have a point. Andrew was a good tracker, he knows Blake and his team, and he knows their territory well. I gingerly reached out and shook his hand.

"If you fail, or are against us,I will kill Karen and you slowly after" I snarled, giving him a promise.

I saw him swallow, "Please, if that is the case, just don't hurt my mate."

"I won't, only if you rebel or are using this as an escape." I growled.

"I'm not. I want Blake to stop. And I know the other allies they have."

I nodded my head and unclipped his cuffs, "You are staying in a guest room, I will kill you if you cause trouble or hurt anyone!" I snarled, still not completely trusting him.

"Thank you, Alpha."

I nodded again before instructing a guard to take them to a spare room, thanking me again as they left. I inhaled the air around me but could catch no scent of Ylva. I growled and looked towards the woods.

Ylva, you're coming home.

Thirty Six • Why Did I Do This?

C hapter Thirty Six———

Ylva

I was in wolf form, slowly padding my way towards my Gran's home. Every scent, every tree became familiar. Nothing seemed out of the ordinary, and they only thing that was bothering me was Lucine's constant whining.

'Please, Ylva! Please turn back!' Lucine pleaded.

Lucine has been non-stop begging. She's been pleading me to turn back and go home. But I can't. I have to do this. For Ryker and for the pack. Blake was threatening me and threatening everyone I loved and cared about. Even if I couldn't kill him and his gang myself, I would still protect the pack. I would use my Lycus wolf to be the Luna that everyone wants me to be - but a Luna that doesn't constantly need an Alpha.

I know Ryker's going to be so mad when he reads the letter. Yes, I know, it was probably the most stupidest idea ever of writing a note, telling him where I've gone, but Misty wouldn't stop whining and speaking to him face to face wouldn't accomplish anything. I just hope Raiden doesn't kill me.

'No Lucine, I've told you. We are doing this for Ryker and our pack!' I hissed.

'No, Ylva! This is a trap. You're getting everyone in more danger because your following Blake's orders!' She cried.

'Lucine! Why don't you understand my reasons?'

'Because you're making a bad decision! Please, just listen to me!' Lucine whimpered.

'No, Lucine!' I yelled, and blocked her out, 'If I meet him, I can put an end to his plans - the least I can do is attempt to stop him.'

'Ylva, honey, you should listen to your vampire!' My mother's voice echoed through my mind so suddenly that I almost jumped out of my fur.

'Seriously, Mum? Please, let me handle this!'

'But, Ylva-'

'No, Mum.' I blocked her out as well and continued on.

It was gradually growing darker and daker. I had been out all day and Misty and Lucine were becoming more on edge, still begging me to go back. The hair on the back of my neck stood up, and everywhere felt eerie. I spun around whilst walking forward, looking up at the stars. Everything looked so beautiful and peaceful yet so creepy.

Nothing felt right.

What if this really was a trap? What if I was bait to bring in the kill? What if Blake wanted to use my Luna position and abuse it to trap Ryker? Blake did say he wanted to be an Alpha...

'P-Please Ylva. Turn back. Now!' Lucine screamed.

I froze in my position and sniffed the air, before turning to look my surroundings. Blood and fire swarmed around me. Misty whined lowly, slowly pushing forward to back up. We looked around wildly; the stench of fear and death surrounding us. People were killed, scattered randomly around. I saw their lifeless eyes, glaring at me and something in those dead eyes told me to run, go home.

I took off sprinting, running back. Bones snapping cause my attention and I glanced around to see five other wolves chasing me. My eyes widened slightly and I picked up the paced, using my hybrid speed. Three more wolves came to the sides of me, blocking my exit. Great! Eight wolves! I came to a halt as they surrounded my form and I let out a warning growl, telling them to back off as they stalked forward.

A grey wolf snapped at me before lunging forward. I growled again and ducked before swinging my hind legs around, slamming him to the ground. He whimpered, laying down, holding his paws over his snout.

They're Psoriasis wolves? Wow, thank you - that makes it so much easier for me! Psoriasis wolves take damage more painfully. Unlike normal wolves, they can only heal using the power of the full moon - tonight was a new moon. Blake must've found them as rouges. Psoriasis wolves aren't uncommon but are often kicked out of packs for being too weak - it's awful. I know for a fact that most of the Psoriasis wolves in the Golden Raven pack are maids/cleaners, and even though it's not the best job, at least they don't get kicked out to fend for themselves.

Two other wolves leapt for me in my realisation. I snarled before moving aside, so they collided before harshly smacking my paw against them, blood gushing from the open wound. I gave a wolfy grin, my eyes adjusting.

'Ylva. Calm down!' Misty hissed.

Red was slowly overcoming my orbs, darkness taking over. I tried to clenched my eyes shut, trying to break from the need to kill. But nothing could stop me.

'Clyde?' I cried through the link, hoping to catch him. I may be to far away.

A ginger wolf growled in front of me. I hissed back, using Lucine as a back up. The wolf looked surprised but whacked his paw against my chest. I yelped out before sinking my teeth into the flesh of his neck. I tore the skin off, blood dripping from the tear. He fell limply to the ground, his body lifeless. The five remaining wolves snarled angrily.

'Ylva?' I heard Clyde's voice rumble through my skull.

'Clyde! Please help!'

'Ylva! Where the fuck are you! Ryker's going crazy and searching for you! The whole pack's worried and you've gone to see Blake! He's dangerous! He's gonna kill you get home n-'

'I'M SEEING RED!' I snapped.

I could feel him freeze before his heart rate picked up.

'Ylva...what are you doing? I've just had a vision. Are you...' He swallowed, 'Killing... rouges?'

'Yes. They're Psoriasis wolves.' Lucine hissed again at another wolf when he came too close. She took control, gripping his front paw and slamming him into a tree, a loud snap ringing from his small body. He cried out before his body went limp.

'Oh my fucking God! Ylva, breath!' Clyde begged. I could hear the pain, panic and fear in his voice. Nothing could compare to how guilty I felt. I had ignored Lucine, Misty, Ryker and Clyde. I've put my pack in danger. Blake wants to kill me, not talk.

'C-Clyde. I'm sorry!' I cried, ripping another piece of flesh from a brown wolf. His light red blood mixed and stained his coat. He whimpered and backed away.

'Ylva! No time to be sorry! Fucking breath. Take large breaths!' Clyde panicked, 'I can't stop you from here!' He was silent as I continued fighting, eyes slowly blurring to a blackout, 'Okay, draw blood from your leg.'

'What? No! The rouges would think-'

'They're Psoriasis wolves right? Just do it!' Clyde yelled.

I growled at him before slicing my through coat. The remaining three wolves turned their heads slightly, confused. I suddenly realised what Clyde meant. Psoriasis wolves are highly sensitive to the fresh blood of their prey. This often leads them to a disadvantage in battles which is why they hardly fight with warriors. I snarled before attacking a golden blonde one. She locked her jaw to my paw, making me howl in pain. Slashing her neck with my teeth, my jaw snapped down on the scrawny thing. I ripped my teeth out, allowing her to fall limp and let me go.

'Ylva... Ylva! Look out, he's coming!' Clyde shouted before my connection was cut off. A sharp needle was shot into my shoulder, making me cry out and tumble to the floor.

"Well, well, well! That's not anyway to treat your future Alpha's guards!" I sly voice filled my ears. I growled, looking up to see a brown haired man with piercing yellow eyes. His scent told me he was a vampire, an senior one. Immediately, his sharp nails dug into my flesh, slowly and agonisingly dragging them across my back before throwing me directly into a tree. I whimpered and looked at him.

"I am Blake, She-Wolf!" He spat the word She-Wolf as if it poisoned him.

"So, you're the bastard whose been messing with my mind?" I snarled, having to shift back to human form due to my weakening wolf, ""Bad idea to have Psoriasis wolves as guards, don't you think?" My head snapped to one said as a slap came across my face. I glued my mouth shut,not letting out any sobs. If I did, he would hurt me more, right?

"DO NOT SPEAK TO ME LIKE THAT!" Blake snapped, gripping my chin.

"What do you want?!" I shouted, pushing away from his rough hold.

"Why, my dear, you!" He smirked, showing his disgusting yellow teeth, incisors bleached read with blood.

"Why?"

"You have many powers that I want. I can use you. You would be of great assistance in taking down your big bad Alpha." Blake spoke, walking around me. I could feel his eyes on me and I spun round to growl at him.

"I'm not doing anything to hurt my mate." I snarled, balling my fists.

"Well, we'll just have to change that, won't we?" his smirked returned, filling me with caution and dread. My body suddenly felt even weaker, and pain shot through my limbs causing me to stumble into a nearby tree, "I must say, I thought you would be harder to catch!"

I hissed out, gripping my arms from the seering pain. "Asshole, what did you inject me with?" Another slap came across, but it didn't hurt, not with the other pain I felt.

My eyes dropped as I struggled to keep them open and I dropped to my knees, "Goodnight, She-Wolf!" And that was it.

Pitch black.

Thirty Seven • It's Not That Easy When You're Being Tortured

Chapter Thirty Seven————

Ryker

I sat at my new desk, tapping my foot angrily. I needed Ylva back. She's been gone for over two days and her scent has completely vanished from the house. None of my warriors, nor my best tracker, could locate my mate. Raiden had been over edge and pissing me off - if anyone pushed him to far, he would snap, mostly likely kill them.

I whimpered involuntarily for the tenth time today. Soaring pain flew from my legs, gradually moving upwards to my stomach. Growling angrily, I tried to ignore the pain resonating from my mate.

I know Ylva's been kidnapped. Everyday I can feel her pain and emotions. She's opened the link, probably not on purpose but I can't even reach her. Ylva's either too far away or she is in too much pain that she can't connect to me.

"Ryker!" My mother flew into the room suddenly. My parents came around yesterday after hearing about the disappearance of Ylva and my dad has been getting visions. I had cried over the phone to them, something I never do. Or haven't done since...

I clutched my stomach and groaned. "I-I'm okay." I choked, gripping to my mother's arm.

"No! You're not! We have to get you to a doctor!" My mum panicked.

"Mum, I'm fine!" I protested.

"No, Ryker Alexander Dawson!" She only used my full name when I was in trouble or if she was certain she would do something - that I had no choice in. She gripped my wrist, pulling me out of my office, and down to the pack hospice.

"Dr Kai, Ryker has been experiencing pains because of-"

"Luna Ylva." Kai finished before sighing lightly, "I cannot do anything for it."

Dr Kai came over to me and placed a hand forcefully on my stomach. I growled in pain and fear, shoving harshly him away. His eyes went wide and he looked at me worriedly.

"Kai?"

"L-Luna, she's...been beaten." Kai stuttered, slowly backed away. My fist connected to the wall as I snarled in anger.

'How dare he hurt my mate! I'm gonna fucking murder him! And his bitch!' Raiden snarled, my eyes blackening.

"REECE!" I shouted, storming back up to my office, leaving my mother and Dr Kai alone.

"Yes, Alpha!" Reece called, running through the door.

"Prepare our best warriors, trackers, scouts and bring the Gamma." I ordered.

"Yes, Ryker. Might I ask why?"

"We are getting Ylva."

Ylva

I tugged against the chains, screaming out as the hot silver blade retraced it's steps across my thigh. I let the tears slip, biting on my lower lip, trying to hold back the cries as I prepared for the third round.

After Blake knocked me out, he dragged me to an old, rundown building. It had two secret basements, and guess what - I was on the lowest! He's never yet told me why I was here, only that he would use me to get what he wanted. And from all that I know, I can only guess it was to bring Ryker down.

It's been two days. Blake has been none stop. He and two other guys, Cameron and Drake, come into this cell, using silver whatever's to inflict wounds onto my skin. They are not wolves. Wolves are extremely sensitive to silver.

I tensed, as another short, sharp blade was suddenly stabbed into my thigh. I groaned a scream in the back of my throat, fresh tears pouring from my eyes.

I whimpered, "Why are you doing this?!"

I received a slap for my troubles, my head hitting the concrete wall behind me, causing my vision to go blurry. The metal, not to mention silver, door creaked open and I shivered, crawling back further into the wall.

A chuckle rumbled from the beast in front, "Why, my dear, you look better than yesterday!" He replied, too cheerfully.

"What kind of sick person are you!" I yelled. A fist came hurtling towards me and I barely dodged it, the attack slamming into the wall beside my head. My body felt like it was on fire with my sudden movement and my eyes were yellow, a deadly yellow. It only meant that my wolf was coming through my human form.

"STOP BEING A BITCH!" Blake shouted. I growled back.

"I'M BEING THE BITCH?" I laughed sarcastically, "If I remembered correctly, I'm not the the one whose stole someone, I'm not the one who beats girls, I'm not the-"

I screamed in pain as a sharp claws dig their way across my face as I was slapped again. Blake slowly stepped back and I fell over, slamming my head against the cool tiles. I coughed and choked up blood, leading me to I freeze. I stared down at the small pile of thick, red blood and didn't even twitch.

I saw hunger glisten in Blake's horrid yellow eyes, before his vampire teeth grew larger. I shrunk back as he stalked forward, "You know, you should really keep you blood in you!" He snarled,

"It's not that easy when you're being tortured." I spat, yelping as he gripped my hair.

He un-cuffed me and threw me back down, "GET UP!" I wobbled to my knees and eventually my feet, gripping to the rocks of the worn walls, "You are very useful." Blake sickening smirk applied his face. "For more reasons than one."

"T-Tell me why I'm here! What the hell do you need me for?" I snarled. Misty and Lucine were absent. I couldn't speak to them, probably the wolfsbane in the cuffs, and that scared me. I relied on them.

"One, you can help me complete my mission. Two, you're very strong. Three, you can help me take down Ryker." he spat my mate's name with venom.

I clenched my fists, my eyes growing darker, I glared at him, "I will NEVER hurt my mate."

"Oh, I think you will!" Blake came and gripped my arms, "Do you think he cares about you?"

"Yes!" I snarl.

"So, you think he loves you?"

"Yes!"

"Well, do you see him looking for you? Because for two days you've been here!" Blake laughed evilly.

"He is coming!" I hissed, "Anything you say won't stop me from believing that!"

"He doesn't care about you." Blake spoke, "If he did, he would have found you by now."

"No! H-He's just figuring out a plan!" I protested.

"He never loved you. He never wanted you. You're nothing to him." Blake smirked when I growled at him. I suddenly heard Lucine and Misty snarl within me.

'Where the fuck have you been?!'

'Wolfsbane's a bitch, but with your anger, it's been removed.' Lucine answered.

'I'm gonna kill this fucker!' Misty screeched.

"You're a fucking dickhead. My mate loves me but that's something you could never understand because you're a cold hearted monster!" Misty managed to shout.

She cried out when he slapped her, "No one loves you. You need to kill them all."

My eyes turned black and shade of red pierced my eyes, 'Ylva! Please calm down!' Lucine pleaded, trying to gain control.

"Ah! There's the big bad wolf!" Drake smirked, or maybe Cameron. They were twins - identical twins.

"I told you that stuff works!" Cameron laughed darkly, or possibly Drake.

"What stuff! What the fuck did you inject in me?!" I snapped, stalking over to them.

"Not to worry young vampire, all will be...deadly - very soon." Blake hissed, supporting his comment with a sinister grin.

"Leave me the hell alone!" I growled as he placed his hand around my wrist and dragged me closer to the chains in the corner of the room.

"No! Why do you struggled? No one loves you. No one would care that your gone!" He showed his yellow teeth.

"That's a lie!"

"You're useless to them - not much of a Luna. No one could want you. What kind of pathetic person are you?" Blake smacked the chains around my wrists, "Your mate only wants you to bare him a heir, then you're gone."

"No! Leave me, get out my head!" I screamed, covering my ears.

'Not even your parents would care. It was so beautiful watching them suffer, She-Wolf!' His voice hissed through my mind.

My head shot up. "YOU KILLED THEM?!"

"Yes and how lovely it was too. Their cries were pitiful!" He laughed. I ran forwards, only to be yanked back by the restraints, "Ah, ah, ah!"

I ignored everything and pushed forward. Every doubt, every piece of anger, every growl of hatred pushed me forward. I heard a crack before the chains flew across the walls. Drake and Cameron gasped, ducking quickly as I swung the chains around, smacking them against the twins. They fell, knocked out, on the floor. Blake snarled before sprinting at me, a injection in his fist.

I growled, aiming the shackles for his legs but he leapt, missing them by a few inches. I was gripped by the hair and thrown onto the floor. I screamed at the pain that shot through my arm.

"You're going to be perfect soon." was all I heard before a jab was piercing my arm.

"Y-You're... a... m-m-monster!" was all I could whimper before my body went limp and my eyes shut.

Thirty Eight • The Disadvantages of Having a Mate

C hapter Thirty Eight———

Ylva

Running.

Don't stop. Keep running.

The thud of shoes echoed behind me and his voice was crackling in my head. 'There's nowhere you can't go without me finding you!'

I was knocked down, my hind left leg shattering on impact. I howled in pain and sharp nails dug into my flesh, drawing blood, 'No one loves you. You should be like me! Ruthless, free, no one to control you!' He hissed, tightening his grip, claws digging into my flesh.

"Wake up!"

'No! No, no! Please stop! It hurts!' I whimpered, submitting.

'No. You're a bitch, a dog that needs to be put down. No one would care if you were gone. Things like you don't deserve happiness!' He snarled. I screamed in pain and fear whilst he continued to draw blood with his claws.

"Hey? Wake up!"

'No one loves you.' he punched my weak and lifeless body.

I kept crying, begging him to stop. 'PLEASE!'

"WAKE UP!"

I screamed again and jolted up. My heavy breathing was all that could be heard in the silent room.

"Are you okay?" I flinched as a voice spoke to me. My eyes met some honey coloured ones. Her brown hair was matted and dirty, her body was thin and scrawny and she had black and blue bruises scattered over her body - much like me.

"Hey. It's okay, I won't hurt you." she whispered, holding a promise as she crawling closer. Her thin arms wrapped gently around me and pulled me into her, in a calming way. I sobbed against her, letting all my stress out.

"W-Who are you?" I asked, whipping away my tears.

"Oh, sorry!" She smiled brightly even though the situation was bad, "I'm Rialy, spelt R-I-A-L-Y. I'm a Lycus, like you and have no mate!" Rialy sighed at the last part, "I mean, I haven't been out of this prison to get one." She chuckled grimly.

"Hi..." I didn't know what to say to her. Rialy seemed like she had been here a while. Her thin stomach told me she hadn't eaten for a while and her baggy eyes told me she hasn't been sleeping well.

"What's your name?" Rialy asked.

"Ylva. My wolf is called Misty and my Vampire is called Lucine." I smiled, knowing that she'd understand.

"Oh, cool! My wolf is called River and my vampire is Suri, it means private and doesn't like to share feelings." Rialy told me before laughing, "Kind of accurate."

I sighed and looked at my hands. I was missing Ryker, and even Raiden. He was my mate, my other have, my equal. The disadvantages of having a mate. 1) Part of me was missing and nothing felt right without being around Ryker.

I glanced around the cell. It had multiple holding cuffs, some whips, a punch bag, and other stuff. A shiver crawled up my spine, looking at the whips, 'Lucine, I'm so sorry. I should have listened, I should have-'

'No, Ylva. You were right' Lucine interrupted.

'What?'

'You were right. You needed to come here. You need to destroy Blake.' She told me, but she continued to watch Rialy.

'How the hell am I supposed to do that?' I asked.

'Blake's only concern is power. You can use that against him.' Misty snarled, a small grin plastered her face.

'Yeah! You should tell him you'll help, then he'll take you to the pack to destroy them. You can give Ryker a heads up.' Lucine smirked.

'Great idea. I'm taking Rialy with me!' I joined the smirking.

'And hurry up about it. Raiden's driving me up the wall.' Misty breathed heavily.

2) Mates are very annoying and highly over protective.

"Hey... Rialy?"

"Yeah?"

"How long have you been here?" I watched her eyes flicker sadness and anger, before quickly changing back to normal.

"Five years." she whispered.

"WHAT!" I screeched.

"Shh! If they hear you, you'll be hurt!" She quickly snapped.

"Why have you been here for five fucking years?" I whisper yelled. Rialy looked away and I stared at her, inhaling the scent of salt.

Tears.

I pulled Rialy's face towards me, and saw the water rolling down her checks, "Rialy?" I asked, alarmed and worriedly that I caused this.

"M-My family... They d-didn't love me. They gave me to Blake." she whimpered, "They chose the money." I gasped angrily and hugged her tight.

"What kind if sick parents would do that?" I snarled. Rialy sniffed.

"My mother was wolf and my father was a hunter. She was able to keep it a secret from him for fifteen years. She had me three years into their relationship. But he when he found out she was a wolf, he killed her and I was shipped off to Blake for a large sum of money. He told me no one would love me." She choked, clenching her fists around my clothing.

"Well, he's said the most stupidest thing I've ever heard. I may not have known you long, but you seem amazing, beautiful and cheerful!" I smiled. She looked at me. Rialy's honey eyes lightened.

"Really?" She sniffed.

"Yes. I'll tell you what. We are going to get out of here and you are coming to stay in my pack!" I told her.

"I don't think your Alpha would want a rouge in his pack." She sighed.

"If the Alpha wants his mate happy, I think he will!" I smirked at her shocked face.

"You're the Alpha's mate? The Luna?" Rialy gasped, bowing slightly.

"Yes, and no need to bow. We are in a different situation entirely. I have a plan!" I grinned a playfully evil smirk.

"Should I be worried about how you're grinning?" She raised an eyebrow.

"Nope! Now, here's the plan!"

Ryker

I snarled and gripped her hair.

"WHY THE FUCK DID YOU DO THIS? YOU'RE NO LONGER PART IF THIS PACK. I'M TAKING YOU WITH ME WHEN I GO AND SLICE BLAKE'S NECK!" I snapped at Katie. Her eyes blackened in fear and anger.

"You wouldn't dare hurt my mate! I'll kill you!" She yelled. I threw her across the room.

"You can try. It'll end up with your head on a stick." I hissed and walked out. I've disconnected any ties with Blake to her so Katie cannot tell her mate anything. I smirked.

"Ryker!" I heard Reece call.

"Yes, Reece?"

"We may have found a trial." He grinned.

"Who found it?"

"Kai and Clyde."

"The doctor?" I stared at him.

"Yes. He located her scent and wishes to speak to you immediately."

"Where is he?"

"Your office, Ryker."

I sprinted up the stairs and into my office. Kai was busy looking at a map whilst Clyde was pacing the floor. When he saw me, he sighed in relief and ran up to me.

"Alpha! We've located Ylva's scent. She's on the far east corner, where most rouges stay." Kai spoke. Clyde dragged another map out that was written all over.

"Where is my mate being held?" I asked, leaning against the table.

"We believe she is being held in an old broken house. There are two basements, and unfortunately, she's on the bottom." Clyde growled angrily. I knew how it felt, not knowing were someone you care about was. It was the same for me.

"There are guards around the perimeter at all times, but after staying there for a night, their shifts are at twelve-noon and eleven-evening. The guards are all Psoriasis wolves." Kai replied.

"We need a good strong team, and a great plan. Blake's not going to let us in that easily. From my opinion that's just a distraction." Clyde continued.

"I agree." I answered, "Blake is a criminal and a highly sneaky vampire m. The Psoriasis wolves are a distraction for him to get victims out. A team will hold off the wolves while myself and a few others will head in."

"I shall come in with you. Ylva may be your mate but siblings are closer than any wolves. I can pick up her scent in a few seconds." Clyde sighed, looking at me, "It will be faster if two of us can locate her at once."

I nodded my head, "Very well. I will bring you, Reece, my Gamma and another person, Kai?"

Kai looked thoughtful for a minute, "Of course, Alpha. But if anything happens to me, please promise me my mate to be safe."

"Your mate will be safe anyway." I growled. Clyde and Kai bowed their heads in respect. "Right! Let's gather the warriors and bring this plan together!"

Ylva... I won't ever stop till I find you. I promise.

Thirty Nine • Blake, Blake, Cut Off His Head and Put it On a Cake

C hapter Thirty Nine------

Ylva

"Okay, got it?" I asked, pointing at the dust on the floor scuffed up with trashy plans. Rialy nodded and grinned. We've been here for what seems like months and it's only been five days. Little food and harsh treatment meant that we were weak and scrawny. Blake and the twins come and mess with us mostly every day, but today they've yet to come... I wonder what's up.

Misty has been dying inside. Being away from her mate is killing her. Lucine can't reach Ryker or Raiden to help her; we are either too far away or that shit they've been injecting in us is blocking them.

Rialy told me more about herself. No one gave a fuck about her. Apparently she was blamed for the death of her mother when her father held the gun. I promised her I'd be there for her, I'm not leaving here without Rialy.

Misty and Lucine have already taken an interest in her, and whether it's just instincts or the I'm a Luna, I feel protective of her.

Pain suddenly shot up my legs and I cried out. Whimpering, I looked to see a massive bruise forming on my thigh. My breathing hitched; is it Ryker? Lucine tried again and again, trying to connect to him. But... nothing.

"Ylva?!" Rialy called, crawling over weakly.

"I-I'm fine." I whispered hoarsely, biting my bottom lip from screaming. Rialy gasped and removed my hand from the black bruise.

"Ylva. Misty... she's dying." Rialy whispered as her eyes widened in horror.

'Misty... MISTY?!' I yelled.

'I-I'm h-here.' she choked, wobbling to her paws.

'No, Misty. Lay back down. Sleep. It will help!' Lucine ordered. Misty flopped down tiredly and I stared at my vampire. Her eyes were dark, a sign if sadness as she stroked Misty's fur.

'Please, Mist. Hold on.' I begged, leaving her to sleep.

"S-She's fine... for the minute." I reassured Rialy. She exhaled her breath and kept her eyes trained to the ground.

I wobbled to my knees and stumbled over to the dented wall where I had been getting my anger out. Every time I saw Rialy hurt, I almost had a blackout. But I need to try and stay calm, especially in these dire situations. So, I've taken to punching a concrete wall. I know, sounds childish, but it helps. I've lost count the amount of times I've either broken a bone or sprained my wrist, Lucine trying to fix me. I've apologized countless times, but the vampire understands.

Clenching my fists, I growled. I saw Blake's face appear on the wall, laughing at us, showing his yellow sharp teeth. I snarled before punching the brick wall, hitting his pathetic face. I continued relentlessly, tears streaming down my face at the pain in my hands. But I didn't stop. I only paused when my arm when straight into the wall, a crack crawling it's way up the cement. I glanced back at Rialy, whose eyes widened in surprise. She pointed to the wall and I nodded.

I thought of my parents. I thought about my brother who had to stay away from me just to protect me. I thought of my mate, my Amista, Reece and Gracie. Those who have to put their life in danger for me. Because that fuck head took me, stole me from them and my home.

I vowed to do anything to kill him. I'll rip his flesh out and crush his heart in my own hands. After that thought, Lucine began begging me to calm down but I couldn't. I wanted his blood. I wanted to kill everyone who hurt the people I love, who put them through so much pain. I growled at him again, digging my class through the fabric. I felt my orbs turn black, and anger flood through me.

"I hate you!" I screamed, tears forming in my eyes.

I continued hit the concrete, dark black and purple bruises printing on my knuckles. But nothing could compare to what I felt. Misty was dying inside me, a piece of me forcefully being ripped away. All I wanted was to be happy. I want Rialy to be happy and find her mate.

"IS THAT SO MUCH TO ASK?" I cried angrily, dropping to my knees. I sobbed on the floor, covering my face from everyone. Rialy remained quiet and we heard shuffling in the corridor of the cells. I didn't move, only listened.

"I think it's working."

"It better be."

"Do you think Blake will be happy?"

"Probably, he wants her to be this."

"Yeah, to turn her. Change her."

"Let's go tell him."

And then the footsteps descended. I looked to Rialy who nodded, telling me she heard in to. What did they mean, change me? No one could, or would, change me. I am who I am, and will always be.

'Cause I'm only human,' I whispered, leaning back against the wall, 'and I bleed when I fall down, I'm only human. And I crash and I break down.'

'Your words in my head, knives in my heart. You build me up and then I fall apart, cause I'm only human.'

'I can turn it on. Be a good machine. I can hold of world's if that's what you need. Be your everything.'

When everything seems to go wrong, I turn to singing. It's the only way I can express how I feel without verbally saying it. I felt a few more tears flow before I was knocked out of my trance. Clapping was heard and a snarled laugh laced in our ears. I growled and shot up at the scent, my fists clenched.

"Blake." I hissed his name like it was poison. It was to me. I couldn't take much more of being nice to him. His pathetic words and scratchy voice sounded like dragging chalk across a blackboard.

"Why on earth are you singing such a song? You're not even human, she-wolf." he laughed until he couldn't breathe.

Oh, how lovely it would feel if I was the one not making him draw breathe, I smirked at that thought before coming back to reality when a whip echoed around me.

"I would advise against that. You've no idea who you're messing with." The senior vampire snarled, throwing the whip to the side.

"Maybe not, but I know what I'd do to you." I snapped, walking over to stand in front of Rialy, mumbling, "Blake, Blake, cut off his head and put it on a cake."

"Disgusting cake." Rialy muttered.

At once, Blake was in front of me, glaring down at me with his piercing yellow eyes, "You call me Alpha Blake, mutt!" he snarled, making his point very clear.

"Yes, sir!" I say sarcastically, in which, I received punch around the jaw. I groaned in agony, stumbling backwards.

"Pain is for weaklings!" Blake hissed.

"No, pain is for people who have been strong for too long!" I snapped back. I glared at his eyes. They suddenly shifted red and stared back at me. No matter what I do, I couldn't take my eyes away, like I was in some sort of uncontrollable trance.

"Pain is for weaklings." Blake repeated, but got my full attention this time. I swallowed thickly as something deep inside snapped. No pain. No fear. No...

Nothing...

Forty • I Volunteer As Tribute

C hapter Forty------

Ryker

Something's wrong.

Ylva's connection with me has faded. I can hardly hear her thoughts, feel her emotions or join her in her pain. The guilt, pride and partial happiness I felt just now coming from Ylva, is gone. I can feel Lucine or Misty trying to connect with me, but something is preventing them from doing so, like there's a forced blockade between us.

"Ryker!" I heard Reece call. I growled at him and he put his hands up in surrender, "You're spacing out again."

"Something's happened. My connection with Ylva has suddenly been blocked." I mumbled subconsciously, glaring into space.

"What?" Clyde hissed. I glanced at him to see his orbs turning a bright bronze colour. He suddenly groaned out, looking up as if he was being strangled by a ghost. I was frozen in my spot when I realized what was happening - vision.

Clyde started gasping for air, clawing at his chest, "Y-Ylva." He gasped, "Don't l-listen... D-Don't go!" He choked.

Don't go? What the hell does that mean?! Where would Ylva go? She's trapped, kidnapped, stolen. A victim of Blake with nowhere to run, "Clyde?" I speak as he rested his hands in the floor, panting heavily to regain air.

"R-Ryker. W-We need to get to Ylva soon!" He stuttered.

"What's happened, Clyde?" I raised my voice, ignoring the fact that he called me by my name. But right now, not even Raiden cared as he tried to take over.

"B-Blake's t-trying to change her to evil. He's going to make her against us, and everyone she loves. He's going to make sure she doesn't feel emotion." Clyde hoarse voice mumbles, looking like he's about to collapse.

Reece's eyes are wide and shocked as he quickly runs over to stable my mate's brother. I glanced over to everyone else in the kitchen. Various mumbles and gasps could be heard before the room buzzed with anger.

-"Let's save our Luna!"

-"I volunteer as tribute!"

-"Luna?"

-"I want to come!"

-"I will not rest until our Luna is safe!"

I growled out, making everyone silent. They stared at me, waiting for my response, "I know you want your Luna back, I do too," I started, "But we need a good plan. Blake is a skilled, senior vampire who will stop at nothing to get what he wants. I need strong warriors and patrollers. But those of you who come, I cannot guarantee your survival." I walked out and into the woods, shifting into my wolf.

'I want my Ylva back, my Misty and Lucine back. I want my mate back!' Raiden snarled, taking off into east direction.

'I know you do, so do I. Let's go to the planning station.' I suggested. Raiden took this option and rerouted his tracks, heading south.

'Reece, grab the five top warriors, the Gamma, the top three trackers, Clyde and Aden and meet me in the planning station. NOW.' I ordered my Beta.

'Yes, Alpha.'

Five minutes later, I arrived at the station before shifting back into my clothes. I stormed through the door and growled loudly. I saw everybody I had called for, "We need a plan. Ylva's getting taken over by her evil vampire and Misty is dying. I need to get my mate back - your Luna." I snarled, grabbing their full attention.

"Alpha!" One of my trackers called, I believe his name was Owen, "Where around the territory is Luna Ylva?"

"The east corner, where the rouges mostly are." I replied, pointing at the map of the area. "I'm going to send Theo, Diego and Eden to scout the area immediately." I ordered, pointing at three warriors. They responded a 'Yes Alpha' before shifting and taking off, "BE BACK WITHIN TWO DAYS!" I yelled after them.

"Ryker, what about the Psoriasis wolves?" Reece asked.

"I want Leo to take fifteen warriors to keep them busy. You, me, Clyde and Kai will go into the building, along with Owen, to find Ylva. When Blake finds out we've got her, all hell's going to break loose!" I clenched my fist, banging it on the table.

"Alpha. I can take twenty other warriors as back up and follow behind. When called, we can be used as a secret attack." My gamma, Logen suggested.

I though for a minute, taking on board the idea. I nodded, "That could work, Blake would not expect it. Well done."

"Thank you, Alpha." Logen smiled, walking out to gather troops.

"I want women that aren't warriors and children to stay here. I want twenty-four hour protection over them while I'm gone. Every male that's left I expect to be on territory patrol or house patrol or border control at all times. Zack, you're in charge of this." I pointed to my second strongest warrior. He nodded, crossing his arms.

"No one will get passed so long as I get these men trained. I will do this immediately, Alpha!" He signaled before walking away, leaving me with Reece, Clyde, Aden and the trackers.

"Owen, Josh and Abby, I want two of you to be scouting around as well. As soon as you pick up Ylva's scent, contact me and follow it. If you get into danger, keep running towards the pack house and the warriors will be on hand. The remaining of you will be staying beside the pack house, as soon as you smell danger, signal everyone and get the women and children into the safe house."

They nodded before walking out, squabbling over who's doing what job - after all, what do you expect from triplets? I mentally laughed and focused on Reece and Clyde.

"Ryker. Once we get in, what are we going to go? We don't know the area, outside or inside." Reece contributed, giving me an already known fact.

"I know. I was going to ask Alpha Franklin for his help." I ran my hand through my spiky hair.

Usually this made girls go crazy, but Ylva was different. She hated me at first, I thought she was going to reject me. Ylva was so complicated and difficult to understand. But that's what I love about her, she's different, unique and all mine. I growled remembering how that bitch made everything wrong. Katie's going to die in front of her mate. Not for him, because of him. Let's see him weakened.

"Ryker." I flinched up to see Clyde looking at me, worriedly.

"What?"

"Ylva... she can't feel emotions."

I growled furiously. I will get my Ylva back, my baby girl. I will not stop until I find her and I will never stop looking. She's mine and always will be, no one can change that. Blake... you're gonna die.

Forty One • Her Blood Smells Good

Chapter Forty One------

Ylva

Nothing...

Emptiness...

Emotionless... I can't feel anything. What am I becoming?

"Ylva? Ylva, listen to me-"

"Shut the fuck up. Nobody cares about what you have to say!" I shouted at Rialy. Her eyes went glassy and she stared at me. A look of horror flashed through her orbs before she turned and glared at Blake.

"It's working." Blake grinned darkly.

I growled at him, "Pride is a luxury you don't have!" I hissed, smacking Blake across the face. He looked shocked, holding his pale cheek before he smirked at me.

"Do you remember, nobody loved you. Not even your uncle, the person you thought saved you. You were just a burden to them." Blake spoke, walking closer. I stared that the man in front of me with a blank face - did they truly not care about me?

'Yes, they did care! Ylva, you're in a trap. Ignore him!' Lucine hissed.

I whimpered and clutched my stomach. Pain shot through my legs and arms and through my body. I felt a flash through my eyes before the original violent returned,'W-What's happening to me?' I asked, groaning in agony.

'Blake's trying to manipulate you. Don't let him. He will make you kill your family, friends and even your mate!' Misty cried, forcing the pain away as best as she could.

"Y-You're lying." I whimpered, stumbling over to Rialy. She gave me a knowing look, smiling tightly.

"Hm, seems as though we need a few more tries at this one." Blake muttered before walking away.

"R-Rialy, I'm so sorry. I didn't-I didn't mean to yell at you. I'm sorry!" I said, hugging her tightly as my body began to shiver.

"Don't worry. Blake tried it with me before, but..." She sucked in a breath, biting on her bottom lip, "He made me kill my cell partner."

I gasped, "No, no, no. I don't want to hurt you!" I cried, moving away from her and wrapping my arms around myself. Rialy got up and walked to me, "No, don't come closer, I don't want to hurt you. I'm supposed to protect you."

"Ylva. I don't care. I know that whatever you do, it won't be you who did it. It was that monster upstairs who drinks champagne and sleeps on his own money." Rialy whispered, embracing me in a tight hug.

"Whatever I say to you or do to you in that form, I promise I will never mean it. I will never try to hurt the people I love!" I insisted.

"We have a plan; stick to it. Don't let Blake take this chance away from you. You need to destroy what destroys you. My mother always said that to me." Rialy smiled a bit, remembering her mother.

"I will not leave you here. You will come with me no matter what!" I told her, leaving no room for debate.

"You don't have to." Rialy said, looking away.

I pulled her to stare at me, "I will." I confirmed and she sighed, nodding her head, "Let's get some sleep. We will try tomorrow, no matter the punishment." I mumbled the last part.

I walked over to the corner and snuggled up into a ball, no longer able to shift into my wolf. Rialy shifted closer to me, both trying to keep warm in this freezing cell.

'You can never get away!' His evil voice snarled through my mind.

'I can try!' I hissed, pelting my way through thick trees and bushes. My paws were thudding against the damp mud, making branches crumble and shake to the ground.

'Give me your power and I will leave you alone!' He suggested.

'No! My power is special, I can kill you with this and one day I will!' I snapped, smacking my paws against the filthy vampire behind. He stumbled over, knocking his head against a tree.

'I doubt that sweetheart.'

'You shouldn't doubt someone you don't know.' I told him, 'Do you really believe that you will succeed?'

'Yes, because all I have to do is catch you.'

I cried loudly in wolf form when a man jumped in front of me, his teeth baring, claws lengthening, face angry, 'Gotcha!'

I gasped awake, panting heavily. I whined in pain at the restrainments that were slowly tightening around my wrists, waist and ankles each time I moved.

Wait... Restrainments?

I glanced down to see thick metal cuffs, attached to a large chain, connected to me. I looked around for Rialy but couldn't see her. What if Blake's got her? Misty growled at the thought of someone she loves being hurt.

"Looking for this?" I heard a vile voice echo around the cell. I looked to see Blake holding Rialy, with his teeth close to her neck. Rialy's orbs looked so scared and full of fear. I growled lowly, my eyes seeing strips of red. I shook my head, erasing thoughts of how nice it would be to see Blake in pain and begging for his life.

"Put. Her. Down." I snarled, struggling against the chains.

"Hm, no. Her blood smells good." Blake teased, trailing his tougne along a shivering Rialy.

"Don't you dare!" I shouted. He looked at me expectantly and laughed. I growled again and Blake glared at me.

"You won't do what I want, I'll have to do it a different way." he smirked. He forced an incisor into her delicate skin, blood pouring from the broken skin. Rialy screamed out before biting her lips, closing her eyes tightly and whimpering out. Blake groaned and closed his eyes, sucking her blood.

I snapped. Something inside me was changing, wanting to rip his head off for hurting someone I loved. I tried ripping the chains from the wall but they were securely locked in. Looking back, I saw Rialy's pale body somehow go paler. When she looked up, her eyes were brimming with tears, and seeing someone I cared about being hurt was all that Misty, Lucine and I needed.

I saw Drake and Cameron gasp before fiddling with items on a table. I had gripped my waist chain, using all my strength, and crushed it under my palms, breaking it in two. I was quick to my feet before clutching the other cuff on my wrist and yanking it from the wall. I launched it across the room, smacking Blake across the head, making his canines leave Rialy. She fell helpless to the floor, blacking out. Whilst everyone was recovering, I used my Lycus speed to pull my friend away from danger.

I growled at Blake who hissed at me. I watched his eyes. I saw them glance at my stomach. His fist came hurtling towards me, so I shifted my hand forward, blocking his attack. Blake's right foot was forward, so I ducked at his second punch and kicked his feet from under him. Blake fell to the ground with a thud. Cameron hissed before leaping towards me. I landed on my back with his body laying over me, sending hit after hit.

I snapped at his face, my wolf surfacing. Fur erupted from my skin.

"Sustain her!" Blake yelled. Cameron gripped my wrists and pinned them while Drake gripped a needle, walking over to us. No, no, no, not the fucking needles again. I squirmed, forcing my shift to happen faster. But Drake was quicker and lodged the needle into my neck. My wolf whimpered, and my shift was failing, forcing me back to human. My skin returned and my canines were gone.

I felt weak and helpless. A sudden sharp impact attacked my thigh and I smelt blood - my blood. I glanced down and saw a blade lodged into my leg, reopening wounds that had healed. I whimpered and cried out at the pain. The blade was silver, making the agony a hundred times worse. A silver collar was strapped around mine and Rialy's neck, forcing us against the concrete wall, by chain.

"They're coming, sir. They'll be here by tomorrow." a guy spoke through some speakers.

"Excellent. Let's see how Ryker reacts against his injured mate." Blake laughed like venom before exiting. Darkness was flooding over me and the pain increased. I cried out one more time before plunging into utter darkness.

Ryker, please hurry....

Forty Two • She Knocked Me Out!

- -

C hapter Forty Two------

Ryker

"Okay! Does everyone understand?" I yelled, looking at over fifty faces. They all replied with a confident, 'Yes Alpha', "I will quickly go over the main parts" I walked over to a map.

"Team Psoriasis, you will first go in, distracting the wolves. Kill them. Even if they beg, remember, they work for Blake." A few members growled, "Myself and a few others will go in. Team Guard, you will be standing watch and if I need you, I will call you. If you see Blake or anyone else, contact me that very second."

"Team Back-Up, you will stay in the trees. Do not draw attention to yourselves. Alpha Franklin will arrive with us on scene with a group of his troops. Each team he has will be split up, tell them what they must do then continue. Protect every pack member you can. If you are to die, you die fighting. You die making me and your families proud."

'We are leaving now.' I got an announce from Franklin.

'On the way, please split up your troop into three or four teams. One team is guard, one Back-Up and another fighting Psoriasis wolves.' I ordered.

'Very well. I'll meet you halfway. Permission to enter your territory?'

'Permission granted, see you soon.' I closed the link and focused on my main leaders. I saw three wolves come out from the trees, Theo, Deco, Eden. I ran over to them with Alaric speed.

"What do you have?" They shifted back into human form, panting before they spoke to me. They looked angry, upset almost. My stomach clenched.

"They must have an elder who can see the future because yesterday their patrollers went up by twice as much." Diego stated.

"More guards are around the main area of entrance" Eden sighed, running a hand through her brown hair.

"Well what do you suggest we do? That's the only way Franklin and I knows in." I growled.

Eden bowed her head, "We have found a back entrance - where they bring in food because only Blake and his men stay in the building, not the whole tribe."

"Good. How many people guard?" I asked, crossing my arms.

"We have pinpointed around five. On lunch break, at twelve forty, they break off and don't guard for ten minutes. That's the best time to go in. But not to attack fully." Theo massaged his head, as if it gave him a headache.

"What do you mean?"

"We may have to be there for a day at the least. If you and whomever is going in with you, go in at their lunch and hide out, the rest should stay in the trees. The guards outside slowly descend from nine o'clock onwards so around ten pm should be good to start attacking." Theo explained.

I growled again and punched the nearest tree. I can't wait that long to get my mate! I felt a sharp pain lodged into my thigh. I groaned in agony, knowing Ylva was getting hurt again.

"They're hurting her again!" I yelled, "I can't fucking wait that long!"

"I'm sorry, Alpha. It's the way Blake has laid everything out. He knows our next move before we do." Eden bowed, sighing.

"We know you want Luna back, we do to. It's hurting us when it hurts you." Diego added.

I needed my Luna back, my mate back, my baby girl back. Nothing's going to stop me from getting what I want. I nodded at them, "Get some rest, see your mates. You need it, you deserve it. Thank you." I told them.

"Our pleasure, Alpha. It's our job and thank you!" Theo said before racing away, probably to see his mate for heading out again.

I walked into the pack house; everyone was weary and quiet. Nobody seemed to be having as much fun with their Luna gone. I walked up to my room. The scent of Ylva has completely disappeared from the room, the house. Nothing to calm me down, nothing to get me through. There was a small knock on the door before Maisy appeared.

Her stance was small and she had red, puffy eyes and messy hair - she had not been great. Maisy had obviously felt some of Ylva's pain too because of the Amista connection, but she felt lost and alone, even with Aden there. Maisy's eyes pooled again and tears dribbled when she looked at the empty spot next to me.

I sighed and walked over to her, pulling my sister into a hug, "I will bring her back." I promised, my own eyes stinging. Maisy sobs filled the silent room, sending Aden over. He sighed, looking down when he saw his mate crying.

'She's not taking this well.' Aden said through the link, swallowing. I knew that he was trying to make sure Maisy was okay, but I knew it affected him a lot as well. He and Ylva were like siblings.

'I know. I will bring Ylva back, I mean it.' I said, looking a Aden.

'I know you will, that's why your perfect for her.'

'What do you mean?' I asked, tilting my head.

Aden sighed again lightly, 'She's never really had anyone around to protect like you. Sure, she had us but she usually did everything herself.'

I tilted my head more, showing him I understood a little but not the last part. Aden rolled his eyes and chuckled to himself, 'She used to fight boys when she was younger, myself included. I told her that she was a tomboy and never really a girl. She knocked me out!'

I laughed out loud, causing Maisy to look at me strangely, "What where you two mind linking about?" She asked, pulling away and hugging Aden instead.

"Aden told me that Ylva once knocked him out" I laughed so more. My baby girl knocking out him? Could be true. I smiled but that was short lived and replaced with more pain. I gasped loudly, dropping to my knees and clutching my stomach.

"Y-Ylva!" Maisy whimpered, gripping to Aden's arm so tightly that blood seeped through his white shirt.

"Ylva!" I hissed weakly, inhaling a deep breath to calm the sudden ache. It felt like someone had clawed four lines across my stomach, slowly and painfully.

"W-We need to get her quick!" Maisy cried, leaning heavily in Aden's arms.

The pain slowly subsided and I stood weakly. I glared into Aden's eyes, "I'm getting Ylva back. NOW!" I stormed through the house, meeting everyone outside.

"WE LEAVE NOW!" I shouted, immediately shifting into my large silver wolf. Everyone followed, their small brown, grey, black, ginger, blonde, chocolate, orban, white wolves bowing in front before following behind me.

'Ylva, if you can hear me. I'm coming to get you.' I tried the link. I knew she would never be able to answer me; she was in pain. Someone was blocking her from speaking or connecting me. Then Raiden jumped for joy and howled happily. But that was immediately replaced with fear and anger at the sound and tone if her voice.

'R-Ryker...'

Forty Three • I Forgot Being Locked in a Cell is Nice

C hapter Forty Three------

Ylva

I gasped when I could here Ryker's sweet voice fill my mind. Oh the joy I could've been in, the sweet sound of music to my ears. Could've. Blake was repeatedly trying to attack me, yelling things that I barely paid attention to as I barely dodged. Rialy was in hundreds of chains, unable to move, begging him to stop. Blake just laughed and hit me harder. A silver blade was lodged into my side and a pull of the silver collar had me screaming in pain.

'R-Ryker...' I whimpered back, trying to hide my fear and pain but failed. I heard Raiden's growl through my head, making me sob more.

'I'm coming, Ylva. Blake will pay for what he's done to you!' Ryker snarled. I could feel his intense heartbeat and his achy legs. He was coming for me. My Alpha, my mate had been searching for me. For over a week, I'd been here, in pain, guilt and losing hope, and now I finally hear the wonderful huskiness of his voice and the fact that he's coming for me!

Misty and Lucine were sobbing and whimpering loudly, but after hearing our mate's voice, it somehow became more bearable. Nothing could be compared to how much pain I felt but hearing Ryker's voice after so long made everything better.

Almost.

Blake laughed. "I heard your Alpha is coming here." He retorted, "Good luck to him!"

"R-Ryker will come. And he will kill you." I hissed, receiving an extra hard punch across the face. I glared at Blake through fuzzy eyes and spun on the floor, hitting his legs so he tripped. Blake landed face first on the floor, groaning in pain. I smirked at how good this felt. Seeing him in pain, seeing him suffer.

'N-No Ylva. D-Don't think t-that!' Lucine stuttered, pleading me to think positive.

"Bitch." Blake snarled, stabbing my ankle with a blade, then clutching it. I whimpered as the crack of bones echoed through ears, causing Misty to whine out. Blake let go and I gripped my ankle, tears rapidly falling.

"LEAVE HER ALONE!" Rialy snapped, making herself known. Blake hissed at her before slapping her across the face. She cried out, her head whipped to the side before being roughly pulled to look at Blake.

"I've been nice to you in the five years you've been here. I can change that right now." he threatened.

Rialy spat in his face, "Oh yeah, I forgot, being locked in a cell is nice. Right, sorry!" She spoke sarcastically. Even though it was a bad situation, I had to hold back the urge to splutter with laughter. A punch collided with her stomach, making her wheeze and cough.

I limped to my feet, holding my bleeding nose. None of my wounds seem to be healing, making it more painful to me. Ignoring all the pain, I leapt onto Blake's back, covering his face with my hands. I wrapped my legs around his torso, 'accidentally' colliding my feet with his crotch, making him ball over and groan. I landed over him and smacked his head against the concrete floor, knocking him out cold. I winced as I got up and walked over to Rialy.

"Oh my God! Are you okay? I'm so sorry, I could helped y-"

"No, you couldn't have. You were tied up. Don't worry, I'm fine." I told her, sniffing harshly as I snapped the cuffs.

"Don't be ridiculous, of course your not fine! You're covered in scars, bruises, cuts, fucking hell, he snapped your ankle!" Rialy pointed at my swollen foot that had already turned black. It was slowly healing due to hearing Ryker, and Lucine was making sure to try and numb it, but that didn't stop the ache.

"It's nothing." I insisted, hulling her up to her feet.

"Ylva-"

"RIALY, IT'S NOTHING!" I snapped. She flinched back, stepping away. I put my hand over my mouth and gasped, "Rialy, I-I'm so sorry!" I stutter, staring at her.

"It's fine." she said meekly, grabbing the keys from Blake's pocket with her steady hands - it was a power she had.

"No, it's not. I shouldn't have-! I'm sorry, I'm -"

"Ylva, stop. It's not your fault. Blake is injecting you with shit. When you get to your mate, it will get better for you! I promise!" Rialy replied with a small sigh. I knew that sigh.

"It's going to get better for you, Rialy. You're joining the pack and living with us. Your life will get better!" I told her, pulling her into a hug.

"Okay... if you say so" Rialy muttered as if she didn't believe me. She's been given up hundred of times before, of course, she wouldn't believe me.

"I know so." I smirked, before springing into action, "Come on before he wakes!" Rialy nodded.

We rushed out the cell, locking it behind us. Throwing the keys in a corner, we sprinted up the concrete steps. We froze as two shadows came closer to us, "Do you think Blake's changed her yet?"

"No, but he's doing it today."

"Hey, she's so hot."

"Yeah, sometimes I wanna strip her down and-"

I growled loudly. How dare they talk about me like that! Their heads snapped our way and their eyes widened. My orbs turned a menacing black before I leapt at them. Misty took control, not allowing them to scream before she ripped out their throats. She laughed at them as they fell, enjoying the smell of blood that scented the room. Rialy smirked as well, enjoying being free and killing the people who hurt her.

We continued our trail up the stairs until we came to a large hallway. The wooden floor boards, eerie, mouldy walls. We used our Lycus speed and sprinted to a door. We locked ourselves inside, trying to catch our breath, "Ylva. This is not the ground floor. We need to cover another floor. This one had guards everywhere." Rialy sighed, pulling on the ends of her hair.

"We can shift." I suggested.

"You can't. Your wolf is too weak because she is not with her mate." Rialy responded, factually.

"Yes I can!" I said, determined to prove her wrong. I felt blood rushing through my body. Fur erupted and my snout appeared. But Misty howled in pain, giving up and giving control back. My bones replaced, blood slowed and snout disappeared.

"I told you!" Rialy hissed.

My head felt dizzy and my mind went blank. I dropped to my knees as pain hits my back. Ryker! What are you doing? I slowly spin round, landing in a heap on the floor.

"Ylva? Ylva!" I hear Rialy call, but it's so faint and hard to answer back.

"R-Rialy. I'm s-so tired..." I whisper before darkness encloses me and sleep takes over.

"YLVA!"

Forty Four • You Should Always Think Before You Speak

C hapter Forty Four------

Ryker

My paws pounded along the ground. I could hear the whimpers and howls of my angry pack warriors behind me. The anger burned off them, trying to intimidate one another, 'Warriors, calm down!' I ordered them. 'Intimidating each other is making you weak. Man up!'

'Sorry, Alpha.' they replied in sync.

I growled at them before concentrating on my previous mate. More anger rose, more pain spread and more punches were felt. Ylva was fighting someone, the feeling made her happy. No, Ylva. Calm! I thought, knowing I wouldn't be able to connect to her at this point. I could feel determination travelling through my bones, a sign that Ylva was making up plans. I could feel her determination to run, escape. I would save my mate. She belonged with me and nobody dared take her away from the Alpha of one of the biggest packs in the world.

I have killed. I was forced into it at Alpha School. They taught you not to care for anyone, always kill and never be threatened. Once my father heard about this, he killed them. He said and I quote, "No Alpha should be evil. A good Alpha is strong and respectable to his pack and his mate. An evil or nasty Alpha comes down easily when weakened."

I'm glad he did. I may have been the strongest to-be-Alpha but I missed my pack and my family. That may sound babyish of me, but it's true. Just like I miss Ylva. She was my rock, my other half, my Luna. Ylva was mine and no one took her from me. Blake was going to die. I can't wait to watch him bleed and suffer. I glanced over to see his pathetic mate, surrounded by a large group of strong warriors. Katie was staring at the ground. Her tense body looked up to me, guilt and apologetic looks flashed through her eyes before she looked away. I growled at her, focusing on Ylva to calm me.

'I want my mate back!' Raiden snarled, pushing me faster.

'What the fuck do you think I'm doing?' I snapped. Raiden's mood has been pissy lately and it was annoying me. I want my mate back as well, but it doesn't come fast, not with someone like Blake. We needed a good plan, good troops, and the help of others. Franklin's voice tapped into my mind.

'We're at the meeting point.' he huffed.

'Okay. We're about five minutes away. Get your troops into groups.' I replied. Franklin answered with a quick 'okay' before cutting the link.

Within a few minutes, we arrived at the meeting point. Franklin stood up to attention and bowed slightly, showing respect, "Alpha Ryker. Good to see you again, but on terrible terms. How have you been?" He asked.

I shifted back and stuffed my hands in my pocket, walking forward. "You know how." I sighed, running a hand through my hair.

"Indeed, I do. Blake is a creature of darkness, he'll do anything and use anyone to get what he wants, even if it means his mate." Franklin growled Katie's way. She flinched back and bowed, pleading in her body structure. I snickered, glaring Katie's way.

Franklin and I walked around our warriors, watching them as they set up, preparing.

"Keep those arms steady. Even if you are a wolf, you may still need to used daggers." I looked to see Owen training Team Guard, setting them up with knives and daggers as a second fighting option.

"When you go to attack, never allowed them to wrap their arms around you. They will tighten their grip and break your bones, killing you that way." I heard my Gamma, Logen, tell his team, the Back-Up squad.

"And you know this, how?" Snarled someone from Franklin's pack. Franklin stiffened, ready to shout but I stopped him, pointing at Logen. My Gamma stalked towards him. The blonde haired male gulped and took a step back.

"How do I know?" Logen hissed.

"Y-Yes!" The guy said, standing up to try and show he wasn't scared - but of course, we all know he was.

Logen ripped off his top, showing the large scars that were implanted in his skin, "THIS IS HOW I KNOW!" He snapped before shooting away from the crowd and into the forest. The hatred and anger burning in his eyes was clear.

Those scars happened about two years ago. He was protecting his injured mate. She was being attacked by a senior vampire. Logen got caught around his neck and the vampire tightened his grip with the intent to kill him. I went to save him, but his mate got there first, gripping the vampire away and snapping him to nothing and burning the pieces. Unfortunately it took too much out of her and she died saving him. Logen wanted to die, kill himself, but he found out just then, she was pregnant, six and a half months. Logen named her Shelly, after her mum. He would never leave her side until his mum stepped in and helped take care. It was a miracle that she survived.

And that senior vampire was Blake.

I looked to Franklin who was yelling at his warrior before sighing and walking over. I put a hand on Franklin's shoulder, "He's telling you this because it's happened to him before. He was protecting his mate and she saved him just before the vampire got to kill him, even though she was badly injured herself. She didn't make it." I lowered my head in respect to Logen and Shelly.

Franklin's warrior stared in horror and looked ashamed of himself, "A-Alpha Ryker, I'm terribly sorry!" He gasped.

"It's okay. It was over two years ago. He now concentrates on his baby girl." I replied, smirking at his fear. Good.

"He has a child?"

"Yes. We found out his mate was six and a half months pregnant that day. His daughter was old enough to come out, she just lay in a coma though." I answered.

"I'm so, so sorry." he whispered, bowing his head.

"It's fine." I said in a stern voice, reclaiming my posture. "Just be careful what you say in future and think of others!" I walked away to find Logen. I saw him sat on a tree stump with Owen in front of him.

"I just miss her so much." he whimpered.

"It's okay. She would be proud." Owen smiled, trying to comfort his older brother. Logen is the older child and likes to exploit that - it really pisses Owen off but it's a laugh for the surrounding people!

"I just wish she could see our beautiful daughter." Logen sniffed, running his hands over his face.

"She can see Shelly Jr. The Moon Goddess wouldn't want her to miss seeing her daughter." Owen said.

"If we didn't have that argument, she would have still been here! It's all my fault!" Logen cried.

"It's not your fault!" I insisted, joining the conversation between them.

"It is." Logen looked at me. "I can never remember what it was about."

"Don't worry. Shelly would have still loved you and she does now. She doesn't care what you said. Shelly's proud of you for raising and protecting her daughter." I told him.

Logen looked down and nodded, whispering, "Thanks, guys."

Everything went silent as we listened to the rustle of leaves and chirps of birds. The silence was soon disturbed with the sound of pounding paws. I looked up to see Abby and Josh shifting to human form. They were gasping from running fast and stumbled over to me.

"Alpha!" Josh wheezed.

"What?" I asked, concerned about the tone of his voice.

"B-Blake.... knows your coming...he got... got..." Abby stuttered over her words, figuring a way of telling me something.

"What, Abby?" I asked using my Alpha tone.

"He got witches!" She gasped. I felt my shoulders drop and my stomach flipped. Witches... The power of everything... "No!" I yelled.

"One of his elders...saw in vision...t-told Blake...witches came....but only... p-purple witches... weakest ones!" Josh wheezed out before fainting from exhaustion, Abby barely able to stop her brother's head from smacking into the ground.

Witches had the power. Black witches were good, the strongest and the most courageous. White witches where the most evil. They have power that they can use whenever they want. Purple witches are weak but their power is still as deadly.

Everything was perfect until now. The plan, the route, the warriors. Now that bastard had to go and get witches, making it a hundred time harder, meaning we had to be quieter and more stelf. I growled at the top of my lungs.

"FUCK!"

'Maisy!' I growled through the link.

'Yeah?'

'Bring her.' I spoke, emphasising the word 'her' so my sister knew who I was talking about.

Maisy gasped through the link,'You want her. As in HER?'

'Yes her!'

'Are you sure?'

I took in a final breath and said one word I would either regret or praise,
'Yes.'

Forty Five • It's A Bloodbath

C hapter Forty Five------

Ylva

'Ylva...' I heard my name being whispered over and over. Pain was soaring through my body and my chest felt like it was being pressed down on. All I saw was darkness. No light. No freedom. Nothing...

'Ylva...' I heard the same sweet voice again. It was soft and delicate. Nothing could compare to it... so why did she leave me?

'Mum!' I responded, desperately needing help from this dream I was in.

Then Blake appeared in my mind. He was going to kill Ryker. NO! NOT BEFORE I KILL HIM! Blake was going to die, seeing his blood on my hands felt very satisfying. I could feel the shift in my orbs. Black.

'Ylva, honey, calm down.' Mum's voice was heard again.

'Mum... MUM! You have to help me! What do I do? Where can I go! Please Mum. Please-' I was cut off from my ramble with warm familiar arms wrapping around me and pulling me against her warm, embracing chest.

'Hush, baby girl. Everything will be okay!' I looked at her. Her green emerald eyes, brown wavy hair. Everything that I remembered about her, was here. Her soft skin, always happy smile, eyes that showed truth and honesty.

'W-Why didn't you tell me about Clyde?' I whispered, feeling her body tense.

'Clyde was born mostly vampire. It was unusual to have hybrids between vampires and werewolves, usually it would be between werewolves and humans. Both you and Clyde were in danger and your Gran was the only person who Clyde would be safe with.' She ran her hand through my hair, sighing heavily, 'I'm sorry, honey. I would've told you if we... if we didn't...'

I felt her tremble as if she was crying and hugged her tighter, 'Mum... what do I do?' I asked quietly, pulling her closer to me. I felt weak. Nothing felt like this before. My world has been nothing but pain since being with Blake. Oh, how I miss everyone. Ryker, Maisy, Aden, Clyde, Reece Gracie. I want to be near them and hug them until I die, they are the ones I truly love.

'I'm afraid you can't do anything.' My mother whispered, 'Blake will try to change you. The only thing you can do is be brave and fight against the demon inside you.'

'Demon? What?' I asked, my breathing hitched.

'Don't worry, sweetie. You fight against it, you fight and kill Blake.' My mothers stern voice told me.

'Why does Ryker hate Blake? Why is Blake after me?' I asked, pulling away from the hug.

Mum sighed. 'Ryker killed Blake's father and brother in a rouge attack. Blake killed Ryker's sister, making him watch. He has an elderly that sees the future. He knew that you were Ryker's mate, that's why Blake came after us and you. Clyde had to leave so his scent wouldn't follow us, leading Blake to you. For you not to know about Clyde was a big thing. I'm sorry.'

'It's fine Mum. I understand' I answered.

'Blake's going to use you to kill Ryker then claim you as his own. He doesn't care for his own mate.' my mother continued, 'It's a bloodbath between Blake and your mate - you need to be the one to end it.'

'Who is his mate?' I asked.

'Katie.' I gasped and growled lowly. 'Blake will place a demon in you to kill him, do not look into his eyes. Lycus' can capture these easily. If he does somehow do this, you must fight the want to kill. Your mate needs to bite your mark again, only then will the demon disappear, but Ryker needs to be smart enough to know that.' My mother was slowly backing away from me. The light above me was glistening brighter every second until nothing was there.

'Mum?' She had gone...no goodbye. No last kiss. No last hug. 'Mum!' I called louder. I wandered around the dark and empty blackness. 'MUM!' I cried out, tears falling from my eyes. No, she can't leave me again!

I felt a sudden shake on my body and soon my orbs opened...

"YLVA!" I heard someone scream. I looked around to see Rialy glaring at me.

"Y-Yes?" I asked, rubbing my head and getting off the floor.

"It's eight o'clock! You've been asleep for five hours when we could have escaped!" She hissed. Then everything came back. The hitting, the running, the killing. I gasped and nodded to her. Grabbing Rialy's hand, I paced over to the door, opening it slightly. I peeked around, my eyes landing on Blake and a few men.

"WHERE IS SHE?!" I heard Blake's rough voice yell, sending chills up my spine.

"We do not know, sir?" Someone answered, his response more like a question than an answer. Blake snarled, running his hand through his head.

"We can't let her escape, we need her to kill Ryker!" Blake snapped, glaring down the hall. I moved swiftly, closing the door. I steadied my breath, calming my nerves.

Silence engulfed the halls but steps moved closer to us. The pound they made seemed to shake the room before they walked past and down the hall. I drew a sigh of relief before nodding to Rialy. I opened the door and tip toed out, cautious to not make any sound.

"Well, well, well," I froze at the sound of his voice. I spun around to see him right behind me, Rialy in the hands of a bulky guard, mouth covered from screaming out, "Look who's trying to run away! Didn't get very far did we?" Blake laughed. His other group of dipshits crackled along, their laughs echoing through me. I glared at them.

A hand flew, connecting to my jaw and I didn't react quick enough, my body was sent tumbling to the ground. A cry left my parted lips as my head crashed into the wall. I rose forward on my hands, coughing and spilling tears. No, I will not show this fucktard weakness. He does not deserve my tears!

I got up and growled at him. Blake glared - if only looks could kill, I'd be six feet under. Quicker than I could move, hands latched around my waist and arms, pinning me to the wall. I growled louder, snapping my growing teeth at them, "FUCK. OFF!" I screamed, thrashing around. But their grips tightened, vampire claws digging into my flesh. I whimpered out, still trying to get away from their clasp.

"I have a very important job for you!" Blake smirked.

"Piss off. Get your mate to do it, she seems to do a lot for you but doesn't get was she deserves!" I snapped. Blake's fist connected with my stomach, making me ball forward and cough harshly.

"I hate her!" Blake yelled, causing me and Rialy to flinch, "You WILL do as I say, and you WILL kill your MATE!" I growled at the mention of him, my ache for Ryker to hold me only growing stronger.

"Never will I do such a thing! Go fuck yourself!" I said, raising my hand as much as it could go and gestured to him with my middle finger.

Another slap came to my face, "Look at me." Blake hissed.

"No!"

"Look at me!" Blake's voice rose. Two men came forward and lifted my head higher, angling my face towards Blake. I shut my eyes tightly. My eyelids were forcefully opened with an unknown force and I looked around to see... a witch in the corner, her eyes glowing purple.

"Get off me, you freak!" I shouted. I rose my mouth and snapped my teeth at one of the guard's hand. The satisfying sound of bones breaking filled my ears as I gripped onto his hand. The man cried in pain, snatching his hand away and cradling it. I smirked.

"LOOK AT ME!" Blake shouted.

"NO!" I yelled. A hand clamped around my mouth and my eyes were glued open. I couldn't shut them, or snap at the fuck heads. Blake came forward, his red eyes piercing into my soul. His eyes. Those eyes. He spoke a few

Latin words and then I felt nothing. No thoughts, no feelings, no pain, no hurt. NOTHING! Something snapped inside as I looked at Blake.

"Ready to comply."

Rialy whimpered, "No! Ylva!"

"Shut it, she-wolf!" I snapped. Only, it wasn't me. Something inside had taken control, something Misty, Lucine nor I could kill.

'Don't look into his eyes.'

'Fight against the demon!'

I heard my mother's voice repeating. I had to destroy this demon!

Forty Six • Do Vampires Sleep in Coffins?

C hapter Forty Six------

Ryker

I stood waiting. Nothing has bothered me more than that. I could wait for hours for Ylva to get ready but waiting for something that could help me save Ylva? Na ah, no way.

"OH, HURRY UP!" I growled, alarming the warriors.

"Be patient, Ryker." my Beta spoke, "You know she doesn't like you as much as you don't like her."

"I'm well aware but I can't fucking be patient when Ylva's in danger!" I hissed.

I winced in pain at a sting to the cheek. I stared at a tree in horror as I placed my hand on my face. Blood drew from the area. I snarled loudly. He's fucking beating her up again! I'm going to murder him! I plunged my fist into the tree- it crumbled on impact.

'I'm going to rip his heart out!' I snapped to Raiden. My wolf has been going crazy, wanting to be let out so he can stroll in to Blake's house and rip him bone from bone. I've had to hold him back and it's straining on me.

'No, no, no. First we're going to destroy his mate, then we'll kill him.' Raiden paused for effect, 'Slowly.'

'But Blake doesn't love or even like Katie.' I imputed.

'Doesn't matter. The mate bond will cause him pain.' Raiden snarled, masking a wolfy grin. A blow to my mate's stomach impacted me, making me grunt. I leaned against the tree, coughing.

"What are they doing to you, Ylva?" I whispered. I could feel tears prick at my eyes. But I didn't let them fall. I can't be weak in front of the pack, I'm all they've got.

"Ryker?" I barely hear Reece call out. I glanced at him, "She's here."

I stood up and walked over. A sixty odd woman stood before me. A senior vampire. The familiar, plain look was on her face, unamused - which is not surprising considering on our last visit to her, Raiden threatened to kill her.

"Ah! Alpha Ryker! It hasn't been so long!" She replied sarcastically - a little like someone else I know.

"Hello, Agatha Endrin."

Yes, you read right. Agatha Endrin. The person standing in front of me, is Ylva's grandmother. The one who I threatened to kill, the one I strangled Ylva in front of - that person was the one I needed to help me.

"Lady Agatha. How pleasant to see you again. Please forgive me for our last," my Beta sent a small glare towards me, "Encounter." Reece said, bowing. Yes, Ylva's grandmother is a Lady. I guess Clyde was right when he said I know a lot about his family. However, I had never heard of him. Granted, Agatha and I barely met to talk - we weren't the best of friends.

"Hello, dear." Agatha said, pulling Reece into a hug. She may be old, but she has some strength about her. Reece was always a favourite when she visited the pack house on my Dad's orders. That's why she and her clan lived in part of our territory.

"Agatha, we need your help." I told her, directing her over to the planning area. Alpha Franklin nodded to the witch, no all fond of them to begin with. She smiled at him irrespective.

"I know what you need, Alpha! You need me to mask your scent and freeze the witches that Blake has so your warriors can kill them and you can go in and get back your mate, your Luna, my granddaughter. Correct?" Agatha stared at us.

We all looked back dumbfounded. I nodded, "Yes. Can you help us?" I asked, eager to get Ylva back.

"Well," Agatha looked down at the map and covered her mouth with her hands. "It's not impossible." I sighed in relief, "But I must abide by my laws - I cannot kill those who have not explicitly done any harm to my family themself."

"But you won't, we will!" I protested. Reece gave me a pointed look, as if to say 'like that's any better'. Raiden was on edge, mentally begging her to do it no matter what. He has never acted this way before.

"I know. I'm just messing with ya!" She laughed. A few others laughed with her, but I growled in annoyance - Ylva was in danger!

"Okay, so," I pointed at a map, "This is the area. We will all travel together until we get to here-" I pointed to about a mile away, "Then Logen's squad, or Team Back-Up, will split from us and go around their border, its only small."

Logen nodded, "That's right. And ma'am, we will protect you along with Team Guard."

Agatha nodded before Logen's younger brother spoke up, "Do vampires sleep in coffins?"

"Owen!" Logen exclaimed, looking at him in shock, "This is serious and you're here asking ridiculous questions!"

"Hey, I'm only curious!" he looked at Agatha expectantly.

The elder chuckled lightly, "That's a big stereotype from dracula stories. Do I turn into a bat? No. Do I burn in the sunlight? No. Do I sleep in coffins? No."

Owen looked amazed, "Wow, you just answered all the questions I ever had." Agatha grinned at him before gesturing for me to continue.

"Anyway." I sent a confused look towards whatever just happened before continuing, "At quarter to ten, we will move as close to their borders as we can. You will do your vampire thingy-"

"It lasts half an hour only," the vampire interrupted, "You must be quick. As soon as you kill them, burn them."

"Yes, Theo, Diego and Eden will carry matches and other fire equipment to burn them with. But before, Owen's squad, Team Guard, will check that no one is around. When you do freeze them, Team Psoriasis will attack the witches, killing them off. Reece, Clyde, Kai and I will go in the back entrance."

Ylva's Gran nodded, "But do you know your way around?"

"No, but Alpha Franklin will be there with us. He's been here before." I told her. Gran's eyes found Franklin. His eyes looked glassy, as if he was remembering the day Emerald was taken. He put his whole pack in danger that day, not a plan in sight. His wolf took over and found his Luna. He snatched her back, killing anyone in his way.

"Is this true?" She asked.

"Indeed, ma'am. My Luna, was taken. I put my pack in danger that day. But Blake wasn't as prepared as he is now. More guards, less prisoners. He has only taken people with great skill." Franklin answered.

"What kind of powers does your Luna have?" Agatha questioned.

"Healing. She can heal people of our pack. She has saved the lives of many." Franklin spoke proudly.

"Good. I'd love to meet her one day. I can put you under my protection, you are doing so much for my grandchild." Gran smiled at Franklin. The Alpha smiled back, less tense around her than he was before.

"I'm sure Emerald will love that. Thank you, Lady Agatha." Franklin shook her hand.

"Okay!" I clapped, grabbing everyone's attention, "Does everyone know the plan?" They all nodded.

I ran outside and shifted into my silver wolf. "Ylva said that your wolf reminded her of snow. She was right." Agatha laughed lightly, clambering up. Werewolves can run faster than vampires, it's a known fact. I snorted, before standing to my full height.

I howled and started to sprint towards my mate. With Franklin to my right, Reece to my left and my warriors behind me, we took off into the night.

Ylva, you're coming home. No one's going to stop me from taking what's rightfully mine!

Forty Seven • I Have a Pet Demon - You Know, From Hell

C hapter Forty Seven------

Ylva

I was stood on a balcony, looking up at the night sky. It was half past nine. I couldn't feel anything. No emotions, no pain. My mind was on high alert, Misty and Lucine were pacing back and forward, scared that the demon inside would hurt our mate.

'Please just stop. You don't need to do this!' I told the demon. She had been ignoring us. Nothing can stop her from killing everything except Ryker biting back down on his mark again. Which could kill us.

'NO! I must obey my master!' The demon hissed. 'Only if I am stopped, will I leave.'

I cried in the back of my mind, but in truth, I was boiling with anger. She lays one finger on my mate, I will kill her, even if it means killing myself.

Rialy was in the corner in chains, watching me. Her partially dark orbs stared at me in fear.

"They're almost here, flower" Blake spoke, wrapping his arms around my waist. It was a touch I hated and one I jerked away to but the demon inside allowed this. The arms didn't mould with my body and the touch was cold, nothing like Ryker's warm embrace.

'Give me to fucking control!' I yelled.

'No!' She screamed. The demon was like another me. A human. My hair was no longer fully blonde, but where the demon had been in control, the ends were turning brown. My eyes were no longer violet but pitch black - no white, no purple, all black.

Using Misty and Lucine's help, I shoved her to the back of my mind. We forced her back into the edge, as far as possible. I smirked at her as she hissed. I gained my control back and ripped myself from Blake's hold. He wasn't expecting it, so I flung my arm back and pummelled it forward, smashing it against his face. Blake stumbled back, gripping his jaw. I kicked up my knee, colliding it with his crotch, then elbowed him in the face. Blake groaned before falling unconscious as his body ran into the wall. I grinned darkly before running over to Rialy.

"Oh my God! Rialy, I'm so sorry!" I said, grabbing the keys and unlocking the chains.

"It's fine, the demon was in control." Rialy said, pulling me into a hug, "Where is it now?"

"Misty as Lucine have forced her back as far as she can go but it won't be for long. We need to get out of here now!" I said, checking in with my other sides.

'She's coming loose. Hurry, get out, it will hold her back for longer without Blake!' Misty shouted, I could here the struggle in her voice.

"Come on, she's breaking through!" I said, running out the room with Rialy on my tail. We sprinted through the halls.

"Hey! You two! Stop!" Someone yelled. I spun around and saw a guard running towards us. I growled at him, a look of fear and panic flashed in his eyes, but was quickly replaced with anger. He charged towards us, his dagger raised. I snarled at him, flinging my fist towards him. I whacked him in the nose, just as he caught me with the silver blade. Growling out in pain, I gripped his head and snapped his neck. I threw his lifeless body into a cupboard before grabbing Rialy's hand again.

"Alert! Alert! Look out for two teenage girls. They are escaping!" A voice echoed through the speakers. The hallway was suddenly filled with, what seemed like, millions of guards, all with their own silver blades.

"Fuck." I whispered harshly. I immediately shifted, followed closely by Rialy. Her wolf was a shimmering blonde with black and purple stripes. Wow - that's cool.

I growled at the men as they formed a circle around us, covering my territory. I lunged forward, tackling over a young boy with a crippled face. He looked no older than sixteen, but he was still the enemy. I latched onto his arm, ripping it from his body like it was nothing. He screamed in agony but still managed to drag the blade over my back. I whimpered out before slashing my claws into his chest and gripping his heart, tearing it from its archeries. The boy shrink back and fell lifelessly to the ground.

I glanced over and saw Rialy being pinned down. An older man was above her, ready to take the final kill. Hell no way was that happening! I shot over, gripping his head between my teeth and popping it off like a cork. Rialy managed to free herself from the clutches of the killers and was tackling and killing again.

I looked forward. Three or four men came closer, trying to pin me in the corner. Fuck this. I leapt in the air, pouncing on my prey. His muffled scream penetrated the air before gasping and groaning was heard. I had claws through his skin, digging deeper, all the way towards his back. A silver blade was stabbed into my thigh, making me cringe. I whined loudly, grabbing the attention of Rialy.

'Ylva!' She cried through the link.

'I'm fine.' I gritted my teeth, glaring at the guard who stabbed me. He looked fearfully into my orbs, as they transformed to black. All I saw was red. I wanted blood, their blood. I snapped forward, watching as he stumbled back until he trapped himself. Fool. He yelled out loudly on impact, before my teeth clamped down on his leg. He tried to shake me off, but I shook my head, making him fly around until his leg detached. He cried out, before his eyes became lifeless and his body went limp. I shifted back, panting heavily.

'Ylva, calm down!' I heard Rialy yell through the link. I sprinted over to her, knocking off the three bulky men that were over her. They flew across the room, and a satisfying crack was heard from each of them.

'Snap, crackle and pop!' I snickered to Rialy. I saw her eyes flicker black and darker. She could see red too. Rialy smirked at me and walked over to them. I picked up a non-silver blade that was laying on the floor and stalked closer. I stabbed one of the men in the heart, watching his orbs die slowly. I felt my eyes flicker. Nothing but evilness and revenge was running through me.

We continued this until they finished their slow painful death. Rialy and I looked at each other, grinning happily but darkly. Never had I felt so much venom run through me. What's worse, Lucine was no longer warning me of anything - she let it happen. We ran towards the back doors and barged through. I ran straight into a wall, falling down with a thud. Tingles shot through me on impact.

Wait a second.

I looked up to see the person I had been longing to see, "Ryker?"

Forty Eight • Curiosity Killed the Cat

C hapter Forty Eight------

Ryker

We ran until we got a mile out. It was around half nine, I decided to give our warriors a quick break. I shifted back to human form and looked at the panting wolves, struggling to remain standing.

"Get a quick rest guys, you need it. Team Guard, go and scout around, you can rest when you get into your positions. But be on high alert!" I instructed. Logen nodded his wolf head and howled out to his group. They all stood to attention and wandered off.

Agatha walked beside me, looking out to the empty forest. I swallowed thickly before sighing, "I-I want to apologise for my behaviour last time I saw you." I expected a rant from her, isn't that what adults usually do? But no. I was surprised to hear laughter coming from her, "What are you laughing?"

"Apologizing isn't in your nature, is it?" she snickered, reminding me a lot of Ylva.

But that wasn't the point. I frowned, "How are you so cheerful?" I asked, "You know this circumstance and you understand how bad it is. Ylva is in serious danger. Why are you laughing and making jokes?"

She turned to me and let out a genuine smile, "Because I believe in you."

I paused, stumbling on my words, "Wh... What?"

Agatha sighed, settling on a tree stump close by, "I know that this is a dire situation and I know that things could be back, but I also know that now is the only time we have. No matter the situation, you should always make the most of if. Even if Ylva is in a bad situation, I can guarantee you she is making the most of it - learning from it."

"But don't you ever just stop and realize all the bad things around you?" I asked.

"I do," she sighed, "But you learn from everything. The only thing I regret is not being able to tell Ylva things she needs to learn about herself. There's so much about her that is incredible and powerful, but I cannot tell her - I can merely guide her."

I nodded and we sat in a comfortable silence until Logen mind linked me, 'We are all ready and have had a five minute break. Ready to move when you are.'

'Good job. Be prepared for anything and be on high alert until I call you home or need your help.' I replied.

'Yes, Alpha.' I cut the link for the moment and created an open link, so I could have access to everyone's words.

"Okay, everyone!" I shouted, grabbing their attention, "Team Back-Up are ready. We leave now." They all nodded, "I have created an open mind link, so if any of you are in serious danger, you can connect to anyone in the group." They nodded.

I glared at the forest in front of me. Ylva would be coming home today, no questions asked. I shifted, digging up dirt with my claws. I growled loudly before sprinting forward. The thud of paws echoed around me, moving forward through forest together.

We came to a stop about a tenth of a mile out. I could see the rundown house in front and the purple eyes of the idiotic witches patrolling around. Agatha hopped off my back, making sure not to make a noise. I nodded to her and her eyes glistened a bright purple before Ylva's Gran focused her attention towards the witch's. Their eyes suddenly locked on ours and their body's froze. The vampire nodded my way.

"I'm going home now. I cannot be caught doing this!" She whispered, "Please make sure you bring Ylva home to us all." I licked her arm, saying both a goodbye and a promise before she used her vampire speed to sprint off. A few of the Team Guard warriors went with her, making sure she arrived safely.

'Team Psoriasis! Go! Go! Go!' I yelled through the link. A group shot towards the frozen witches and the sounds of ripping flesh and burning wood could be heard. Soon more vampires and other guards of Blake's came out. They all fought, my warriors obviously winning.

'You hold them off, we'll go find our Luna!' I hissed to my warriors, Raiden desperately trying to take control.

I cautiously and silently padded towards the back door, Clyde, Reece, Kai and Franklin on my tail. We shifted at the door, preparing to enter. Muffled screams and sounds of panic were coming from the other side. I gripped the handle. Pain shot through my thigh and along my back.

"Ylva's getting hurt again!" I snarled.

"Come on, we can save her. She needs you!" Clyde growled, anger laced in his words at his sister being hurt. The door suddenly burst open and someone ran into me. Sparks flied from the touch and a delicate, weak voice filled my ears. The voice I've been wanting to hear for ages.

"Ralph?"

I glanced down and saw Ylva. Her small, thin arms weakly holding her up. Her hair was ratty and dirty, covered in blood. I saw scars and blood across her body. The old shorts she was wearing along with an old, minging t-shirt barely covered the damage Blake had caused. I scanned her, checking for serious injuries, there weren't any seeable major ones only loads of small ones. Two huge stab marks on her thighs, her breakable arms that had red grip marks on them, her face, covered in bruises and her hips that were stained in blood. I growled loudly, and scooped her up in my arms. She whimpered at the touch, bruises taking a strong impact.

"Sh," I hushed, holding her close, "It's okay, I got you!" Ylva sobbed against my chest, gripping my shirt when she looked up suddenly, staring at me with black piercing eyes.

"Ylva..." I whispered. She flew from my touch and pushed my back, so much force and anger, I smacked against a tree a few meters behind me. I grunted on impact and stood back up. Ylva's hair was no longer blonde, but dark brown slowly crawled it's way from the bottom. Her once beautiful violet eyes were now pools of death and hatred, black.

'R-Ryker!' I heard her cry through the link, although it sounded like it took up a lot of energy to connect with me.

'Ylva! What the fuck is wrong with you?' I snapped. I could feel her flinch against my words.

'R-Ryker, please. Help me. B-Blake's brought out a demon in me. Only you can help me!' She whimpered as the demon side stalked closer.

'How?' I asked, running forward. I gripped her arms but the demon was still there. She snarled at me, before racking her sharp nails against the flesh if my stomach. I cringed on impact and fell back, clutching the wounds.

'R-Ryker. Bite me. Bite my mark!' The real Ylva cried, sounding as though she was close to blacking out.

'What! No, it could kill you!' I hissed. Remarking your mate could kill them. Too much venom would flow through their bodies, killing the nerves and muscles slowly, detaching the mate bond.

'You have to. I-It's the only way to kill the demon!' Ylva whimpered. I could hear the struggle in her voice, the sound of hurt and pain, trying to pull the demon away.

'No! I'll hurt you!'

'I'M HURTING YOU!' Ylva snapped. The demon ran forwards, gripping my head. I snarled lowly, shaking her off, pushing her to the ground. She hissed back up at me, reaching forwards. Her fist connected with my jaw, a crack made me whine in pain. I could feel Ylva's connection fading from me, and she couldn't talk anymore.

I couldn't do it. 'Give me control!'

'No, Raiden. You'll hurt our mate, possibly killing her!' I shouted, blocking a punch the demon launched at me.

'Fucking give me control!' Raiden had too much power over me and he took over. My eyes flashed black and the demon stared in wonder.

Ylva

I was yelling at him but I couldn't keep the connection anymore. He had to do it - he needed to! I could see Raiden take control and the demon stopped dead in her tracks. Curiosity took over her but was soon replaced with anger when Raiden grabbed her. Curiosity killed the cat. She clawed at his face, a deep scratch penetrated into his flesh. I whimpered in pain as it reflected back on me.

Raiden growled before slashing his hand. It swiped across my face, making me hit the ground. The demon was in control and she was taking the damage - I could only feel part of it. Although it hurt, I knew it's what he had to do. Raiden gripped us again, not wasting any time before he sunk his teeth into my neck. Pain soared through my body, making me let out a blood curdling scream. Venom was twice as strong and increased dramatically. I cried in pain, clutching my neck as the demon left me, no trace left. I dropped to the ground, just missing the impact as Raiden scooped me up again.

"I'm sorry." he whispered, his voice hoarse and deeper than normal in wolf control.

"I love you." I spoke, smashing my lips against his. He groaned out before kissing back, our lips moving in sync. We were stopped with an evil laugh that echoed through the air, giving me more than an eerie feeling.

"Well, isn't this great!" Blake snarled.

But before anything, a loud snap was heard that vibrated through our ears. Everyone's head snapped towards Franklin. My eyes widened as I saw a lifeless Katie clutched in his grasp, "Man, I wanted to do that." I heard Raiden mumble. Even in this serious situation, I couldn't help the small chuckle that left me.

Franklin's eyes were black and filled with anger as he dropped the corpse. I heard Blake whine and hiss in pain and anger, "Y-You killed my mate." he growled weakly.

"You didn't love her." Franklin snarled.

I saw Blake's eyes change and sprint towards me. His eyes, those orbs. Black, red, death, hatred, anger. He let out a loud, pain filled growl before leaping in the air. I was passed into someone's arms before Raiden shifted, tossing him away. Blake glared at him as they circled each other.

"No, Raiden..." I whispered.

Forty Nine • You Need to be Level Headed

C hapter Forty Nine-------

Ylva

Fuzz. That's all it was. A blurry vision. The quick movements of Ryker and Blake were hard to keep up with. I was in Reece's clasp, keeping me away from the fight in the middle of the field. My weak body rested tirelessly against the Beta I first attacked. All the pain, all the hate and anger, slowly entering my body. Never had I felt so weak in my life. My body was like a sack of bones. No fat, no muscle, just skin and bones.

I glanced over to Clyde. He had his arm wrapped securely around Rialy's waist. She clung to him and flinched every time a whine or hiss was heard. Were they mates? Clyde growled possessively each time someone got too close, so I take it yes. They look so perfect together.

A loud snap was heard. Everyone's eyes shifted to Franklin who had transformed into his large wolf, a pitch black one. We could all see his wolf was in control, obviously wanting to have a bite of the action. Franklin's wolf is almost uncontrollable. He doesn't think of others, only death when it comes to things like this. His sturdy figure pounced on Blake's, throwing him to the ground. He slashed his paws against Blake's chest, ripping a chunk from his frozen body. Blake gripped Franklin's snout, clawing against it, along with kicking his chest. The Alpha snapped, aiming for Blake's neck, but only caught his arm. He tried ripping it from his pathetic body, only managing to snap it before he was roughly shoved away.

This is my fight. I thought. Everyone's getting hurt because of me. I felt guilty. I've killed guards, I've hurt my own mate!

I glared at Blake. His evil eyes that stared into Franklin's soul. His claws and grip that had hurt me so much. His bulky body and thick figure that punched the shit out of Rialy. The one who hurt my mate. The one who killed Ryker's sister and caused him so much pain.

My eyes froze and all I saw was black. I wanted to kill. Kill Blake. Clyde was over to me in seconds, his claws digging into my skin. I yelped in pain as an unfamiliar impulse ran through me but my eyes slowly turned back to their original violet.

"You need to be level headed." Clyde stated, focusing back on Rialy, "I know you want to kill, but you need to do it without the darkness, otherwise you will never gain control of it."

Blake snarled suddenly and my attention was suddenly focused on them again. Blake was aiming for Franklin's legs, snapping them. Everyone's eyes widened at the sound of the wolf's howled that echoed through the forest. Franklin's figure laid wildly among the floor, his back legs sticking out in odd directions. Some of his pack members ran forward, lifting up his weak body and pulling him from the fight.

Raiden growled loudly, sprinting forward. He gripped Blake's shoulder, biting out a chunk of frozen flesh. My mate shook it from his mouth, "RYKER, LOOK OUT!" I screamed. But it was too late. Blake had swiped his fist. Everyone froze. Ryker flew across the air, twirling and tumbling until he smashed against a tree and crashed against the mossy ground. A few pack members had tried to prevent his fall, but that only resulted in more injuries, "RYKER!" I cried, leaping from Reece's grip and sprinting over to him. I flung myself down and rested my head against his hot and heaving body. His laboured breathing was the only thing that was letting me know he was still alive. I glanced at his stomach, my fingers gently tracing the deep flesh wound Blake had given him. I growled lowly, my eyes turning darker.

"You hurt him." I mumbled. I heard Blake shuffle closer, everyone around me was moving forward, prepared to attack if he hurt me.

"Yeah? So, what?" His sarcy voice spat. I growled, gently gripping Ryker's fur before standing up. I felt Blake's presence close behind me and I clenched my fists.

"YOU HURT MY MATE!" I shouted, flinging my fist around. Blake didn't anticipate the sudden movement, for a third time, and my knuckles connected with his jaw. His body flew backwards and the fimilar and satisfying sound of cracking filled my ears. Blake hissed out, leaping at me. I in-distinctively shifted into my blue wolf. I stepped to the side, allowing his body to fly past me.

As my back was turned, he whacked my back laws, my body flinging into the air. I tensed my body and landed on all fours, listening out to the gasps in the warriors. Blake glared at me. My claws and teeth grew sharper and Misty and Lucine were clawing to killing him.

We joined together, our bodies mixing and strengths at an all time high. Blake sprinted froward, shortly followed by me. We head butted each other, pushing against each others weight as we fought for dominance of the battle. I slashed my paws out, gripping his frozen stomach in my grasp.

Blake's hands gripped onto my front leg, hauling it forward. My wolf form moved with it, but the painful and unpleasant sound of my bones cracking, filling my body and my wolf let out a cry. I limped backwards, away from this beast.

'Don't help me. This is my fight!' I told everyone through the link.

'Come on! We are stronger than this monster!' Misty yelled. She forced me forward with our Lycus speed, my razor teeth latching onto his arm, ripping it from his pathetic body.

'He hurt you, he hurt us and he hurt our mate! He deserves to die!' Lucine screamed, making my gripping his l leg, and flinging him across the field. His body landed in a heap on the floor. Blake hissed at me, wobbling in his legs as he gripped his wound. As I sprinted forward, he latched onto my fur and I was unable to shake him off. He punched my snout, making my vision go blurry. I yelped in surprise before silver was drapped over my body. Heavy chains wore me down, making my weak legs weaker.

"YLVA!" I heard my mate yell. Loud thuds if paws were heard before Blake's claws were ripped from my flesh. Ryker's silver wolf was standing tall above Blake, ready for the final kill. But Blake had other plans. He kicked up his legs, making Ryker launch from him again. Blake gripped my mate's wolf from mid air and wrapped his arms around Raiden's neck.

'NO!' I screamed. I used all my strength and pushed away from the silver chains. Blood heavy on my back, I quickly stumbled forward, my weak body coming to a slow end. I heard a whine from Ryker and that's all it took.

Blake's head was in my mouth in seconds. His pathetic muffles and snaps cheered me forward. My wolf stood tall and proud as she ripped his head from his body in one swift motion.

Blake's gone...

He's... Gone

BLAKE'S GONE!

I howled at my victory, shifting back to human form. My body was even more bruised and even more weak, "Ylva!" I heard my mate's voice. I looked to see Ryker running forward, towards me.

I smiled. But my body was giving in. I was tired...so tired. I felt myself drift away, landing in strong fimilar arms. Pain shot through me as I whimpered out. Darkness was slowly taking over my body.

"YLVA!" Was the last thing I heard before the darkness consumed me.

Fifty • Don't Make deals With the Devil

C hapter Fifty———

Ryker

It's been two weeks.

Two weeks since the fight.

Two weeks since Ylva's return home.

Two weeks Ylva's been asleep.

Her weak, fragile body is simply laying on the hospital bed. She looks so lifeless. The colour had drained from her skin, the bruises and scars still showed and the heavy bags are still under her eyes even though she has been asleep.

I feel weak myself. What hurts my mate, hurts me. I haven't shaved, haven't slept, haven't done anything but sit next to Ylva, just to see hurt wake up. I've given Alpha duties to Reece for a few weeks. Of course, he still needs to ask me things, but I rarely answer other than a half heart grunt.

After the fight, Ylva became unconscious. Even if I shook her, she wouldn't wake up. Reece, Clyde, and other stronger warriors had to hold me back as Kai looked at her.

Flashback.

"No! Stop it! You hurting her!" I growled angrily, struggling against the hold of others.

I stared at Ylva. She lay there, shaking, crying out, and punching thin air. Kai was by her side, desperate to quickly calm her from whatever was happening. She was still asleep.

"There's too much silver running through her body." Kai yelled over her screams and pleas, "She's experiencing hallucinations."

It was as if she was having a nightmare, something she couldn't escape. Kai was struggling to hold her down. When he touched her, my wolf let out a painful growl and got angrier very quickly.

'They're hurting her! They're hurting my mate!' Raiden snarled, trying to shake the grip others had on him.

"Stop! Please, stop! You hurting her!" My wolf whimpered out loud. I gave him control and he started attacking the men that held him away from his injured mate.

"Kai! Hurry the fuck up!" Reece yelled, fighting back. He was a strong Beta, I know, I trained him myself. But it would only hold me off for so long.

"We need someone to hold her down! Aden! Get your ass here!" Kai yelled, taking out an injection from his pocket. He filled it with a mysterious red liquid that we stared at in horror.

Aden ran over to Kai's side, whispering words I couldn't hear. Aden nodded and moved to hold Ylva down, harder and more painfully.

"Get your filthy paws off my mate!" Raiden growled. "I'll kill you."

"Alpha! He needs to hold her down otherwise she dies!" Kai shouted. He only received a growled in response.

Aden pushed Ylva against the ground, struggling against her fighting body. He ended up laying right over her, pinning her down. Aden hissed out as Ylva's fist caught him on the jaw, a satisfying whimper left him.

"That's my girl." I whisper.

Kai looked over her arm, looking for the main vein. Once her found it, he slammed the needle into her, Ylva's body cringed on impact and she let out a cry of agony before her body relaxed and she stopped fighting. Her laboured breathing was the only thing telling me she was alive.

Kai and Aden quickly moved out the way when the sound of bones snapping and fur erupting came to hear. Ylva's beautiful blue wolf laid on the ground, whimpering from the pain. I shifted seconds after, growling at everyone. They all backed away, head bowed. I ran over to Ylva's body, whining when I still saw the cuts and bruises. I wrapped myself around her small figure and rested my head carefully on her neck.

Flashback over

I growled, balling my fists.

I looked around the hospital room. Ylva's uncle, aunt, cousins, brother, and Amista were here. Sunbrooke completely broke down when she saw Ylva's body. She cried for ages, making it more difficult for me. Clyde and the girl she came out Blake's prison with stood in the corner. Rialy had her hand on his chest, gripping it tightly and whimpering softly, saying how it was all her fault. Clyde growled at this, wrapping his arm securely around her waist and pulling her into a hug. They were mates.

Aden just sat there most of the time. Wen he first saw her in this stated, he just stared at Ylva, water running down his face. Maisy wiped it away, and kissed him, hugging him tighter. Maisy though... She just broke. Even if she always looked okay, she wasn't. Her Amista just got attacked, almost killed and now she's lying in a hospital bed for two weeks. Reece came through the door, Gracie clutching his torso, gasping when she saw Ylva's body. Reece looked at me and nodded.

A faint mumble came from Ylva's lips. Everyone's heads snapped towards her. I saw her body tense, then her fists balled. A whimper echoed around the silent room and Ylva's body shivered. I held tightly onto her hand, squeezing lightly.

"Ylva?" I whisper, smoothing down her hair.

Ylva

I was sweating, panting. Misty howled louder, gripping tightly to the wolves neck, swinging him around until his body became limp. I growled around me, wolves circling me, preparing to attack.

I lunged forward, Lucine helping with the impact. Two ginger wolves cried out when they smacked into each other. I nipped at their ears, slowly dragging my claws through their flesh.

I inhaled deeply, trying to calm myself from having a blackout. Clyde wasn't here - I needed to learn to control the darkness.

I saw his figure - someone I didn't recognise and yet he looked oddly familiar. His dark shadow cast over me, making me feel small and weak again. Pain coursed through my body was sharp teeth clamped on my neck. I growled, kicking up my hind legs, knocking off whoever was trying to kill me.

"Where is he, Ylva?" The man asked, his voice deep and heavy. The snarl that came with it told me he wasn't a happy Larry.

"Who?" I asked with a snarl, clawing at random rouge's bodies, forcing them to whine and step back.

"Your mate! Your fucking mate!" He hissed.

"He's safe and alive!" I snickered. This man wanted Ryker dead. Almost everyone I've had these dreams about wanted him gone. He wanted to kill Raiden for killing his Dad and brother or something. Everyday I've been killing his men, and I have no idea if this is real or not. I know I'm asleep, but Misty and Lucine have been telling me to keep fighting. It feels real.

"Bring him here...to me. I want to show him what happens when he messes with us!" He snarled.

"No!"

I knew very well I was in a hospital bed, in one of Ryker's t-shirts, covered in Maisy's body wash and shampoo. But this man talked as though this were real. Like I was in a different place, one much darker than a hospital room.

"Bring him!" He yelled, "He deserves to feel what I felt when he destroyed my only family!"

Wolves were surrounding me. And not good ones. A ginger one suddenly sprung towards me, latching her teeth into my paw. I hissed out, growl erupted from me as I sunk my teeth into the flesh of her neck. She whined in pain before whacking me with her paw.

"Come on, Ylva! You are weak and you know it. Bring me your mate and you can roam free - that's what you always wanted!"

"You don't know what I want at all!" I snapped, keeping an eye on the wolves that circled me, "I want to live in peace with my mate and not have to worry about bastards like you!"

"Ah, Ryker. It's been so long since I've seen him." I heard his pathetic voice snarl.

"Nigel."

I flinched when I heard a voice echo in the air. The man turned to see one of his men walking up to him and he snarled at him. I snickered, "Nigel?"

He glared at the man who submitted under his gaze before turning to me, "You should ask his mate and see if he remembers what he did." Nigel hissed, stalking closer. I growled lowly, telling him to back away.

"I don't even know who you are!"

"Of course not, your mate hasn't told you yet because he's scared. They didn't deserve what he did to them!" Nigel yelled at me, like it was my fault.

"I don't believe you!" I snapped, "Ryker wouldn't keep secrets from me."

"He took my only family away when he did what he did. I'm just waiting to return the favour." Nigel crept closer.

"You touch my family, I will fucking kill you." I growled, Misty making an appearance.

"Oh, it's not your family I'll hurt. It's your mate!" He snapped. And then all I felt was pain as I was slammed back into the real world.

Fifty One • Pretty Damn Lucky Lycus

C hapter Fifty One———

Ryker

Everyone in the room seemed to breathe in a sigh of relief when Ylva suddenly bolted up from whatever nightmare she was experiencing. Multiple cheers were floating around the room and happy tears were now pouring but Ylva's hand shook in my grasp.

"I-I... Ryker?" She whispered, turning to face me. Her violet gems were wide and fearful, unshed tears residing in them.

"Sh, Ylva. It's okay, I got you. Nothing will happen to you anymore." I whispered, wrapping an arm around her as I sat up on her bed. She curled into to my side, still shivering slightly.

"I love you, Rykes." Ylva sniffed, gripping hold of my shirt.

"I love you too, baby girl." I replied.

"I told you they had nicknames for each other!" Gracie grinned, punching Reece's arm. My Beta looked at me apologetically before dragging his mate out, not before a quick wave goodbye.

I stood up, scooping my mate into my arms before wandering through the pack house. I made my way up to our room and I pushed open the door, laying back on the bed with Ylva still in my hold. I placed her down on my lap, running my hand through her hair. Her body visibly relaxed when my scent surrounded her and I smiled slightly but frowned again when I saw her frame properly away from the covers of the hospital bed.

Abused, beaten, weak - but still my gorgeous mate. I pulled off the rags she had on, and wrapped her in the dovet. The sheets outlined each of her perfect curves, and her thin body snuggled deep under the covers, her body shivering. I sighed before I got under myself, wrapping her naked body close, inhaling her intoxicating scent.

Raiden purred at the thought of his mate back, safe and sound, 'She's mine and mine only! And bastard who touches her will die.' He hissed, pulling Ylva closer to us.

'I know. I'm never letting her out my sight again.' I spoke, watching her sleep. Ylva's eyes fluttered open and her eyes met mine. Guilt, anger and sadness flashed through them, alarming me, "What's wrong, baby girl?" I asked, pulling back a bit so I could see her properly.

Ylva ran a hand through her hair, looking at the strands in disgust when she noticed the brown curl at the bottom. Her eyes became teary as she stared up at me again.

"Baby, what's wrong?" I asked again.

Ylva inhaled a shaky breath, "I-I killed people." she whispered. Was she really that effected by it?

'Shut up and listen! Our mate is hurt!' Raiden snapped.

"You were protecting yourself." I told her.

"Yeah... but anger was running through me. My eyes were black. And then I had these dreams but they felt like nightmares about someone called Nigel." Ylva's innocent eyes looked at me again.

I must've been silent because it wasn't king before she spoke again, "Ryker, who's Nigel?"

My body tensed. Nigel. I hated the name. It sickened me every time I heard it. I'm glad he's gone - he didn't belong in this world. I felt a soft touch to my cheek, and my body instantly calmed down. Ylva's eyes were closed, as if she was straining herself against something.

"Ylva, what's wrong?" I asked.

"Y-Your grip." she whispered, hoarsely. I gasped and retracted my claws from her hips.

"Sorry, baby." I kissed her head, making her breathing hitch.

"I-Its okay, Ryker." her stutter made me nervous. Did Blake do something to her? "Who's Ryker?" She repeated, much more confident this time.

"He was... someone I had a run in with when I was young. It's not a happy story." I muttered, "I don't want to talk about it." My mate nodded in understanding but I could tell she wanted to push further. I sighed, cupping her cheek, "When the time is right, I'll tell you. Just not now."

She seemed to accept the answer and nodded before I spoke up again, "Hey, uh, Ylva... Can I ask you a question?" I asked gently, it was probably a sore topic for her.

"It's about what happened when I was gone, isn't it?" Ylva sighed, looking down. I caught her eyes staring at my abs and a small smirk pride itself onto my lips. But it was quickly washed away when I focused back on the real topic.

I nodded, "Yes. But if it's too much then-"

"No." Ylva cut me off, "It needs to be done. Just... I don't want to now."

I hugged her tightly, trying to calm her from her nerves, "You don't need to be scared about how I will react. He's gone." I whispered.

"Okay, but on one condition." Ylva hesitated. I raised an eyebrow curiously. "If I tell you what happened with Blake, you tell me who Nigel is."

My breathing hitched again, but my mate had my trust. I nodded, "Okay, deal." Ylva slipped out of bed, giving me a perfect view of her ass.

"Oi! Eyes are up here!" Ylva hissed, spinning around. I trailed my eyes up slowly, taking in everything of my mate. She still looked beautiful in every way. Ylva cleared her throat loudly, making me flinch and meet eye contact. "I'm going to take a shower first because I need to wash everything off me." I nodded and she walked into the bathroom. I sighed and rolled out of bed.